He Looked Like A Man Until He Barked

Patriece

He Looked Like A Man Until He Barked
Copyright © 2008 by Patriece
All rights reserved

Cover photographer: Frank Rhem

Cover models: Ebony Frelix
               Eve Adams
               Teela Smith
               Calvin F. Jenkins Jr.

Hair & Make-up: Shaunté

Printing by Falcon Books

San Ramon, California

ISBN 13: 978-0-9778096-1-5

Published by
Pressin On Publications
P.O. Box 2304
Oakland, CA 94614-0304

www.PressinOnPublications.com
www.myspace.com/justpatriece

Except for brief quotes used in reviews, no part of this book may be reproduced by any means without written permission of the author.

PRINTED IN THE UNITED STATES OF AMERICA

Acknowledgments

First, thank you Jesus!

I acknowledge my editor, Ms. Phyllis Jones—Thank you for supporting me in EVERYTHING I do. I love you so much.

Thank you Dr. Harold Orr.

Thank you to my family, extended and genetic. My mother Mattie, my mother-in-law Connie and my siblings, Stephanie and Tarenté.

Thank you to every book club, social group, girlfriend, cousin, play cousin, God sister…that hosted a book signing reception for me! I couldn't have done it without your support! You all are so awesome. I know y'all love me, I love y'all too!

Thank you to the bookstores that supported me on my first time out and those that support me now. Love you Bernard!

Dedication

Jamellea Deary—1952-2006

> Thank you Lady, for reading my first book, *When Somebody Loves You Back*, and making everybody you know read it too!

Robert Rogers—1950-2006

> In your memory I am careful not to complain, quick to appreciate and eager to strive! Your example is alive in me.
>
> I love you immeasurably!

Gerald Cass Bryant—1960-2007

> Your brilliance taught me to strive and push for greatness. That part of me that is tireless labors in your example of excellence. I love and miss you, for an eternity.

Chauncey Bailey—1949-2007

> Thank you for moving inside of your fear, I will stroll through mine. I will say exactly what I mean and my words will make a difference, as did yours.

To my babies, Ayanna, Ari, Jasmine, Neisha, Destiny, Taylor and Priscilla. [Lil Joe and the twins].

To my Joe.

1

Troy closed the door gently behind him, careful not to wake up Deanna or Ashley. Deanna had warned him before about waking the baby with the sound of the door slamming shut.

Deanna was awake. Ashley had been up crying a good portion of the night, but it was her husband's empty side of the bed that prevented her from sleeping. She tightened the covers around her body and curled into a ball. Instantly sleep came over her. It was as if his mere presence relieved her of the stress that was keeping her awake.

She'd vented to Carla, her best friend, earlier so there was no need to cuss him out about his whereabouts. Besides, it had been going on for over two and a half years. Even before Ashley was born Troy was staying out late, sometimes all night. For some reason she thought changing her last name would change his behavior.

Troy dropped his pants on the floor and eased into bed next to Deanna. He scooted up under her and placed his arm across her waist. He knew she loved it when he held her at night. (She was phobic about sleeping alone—a childhood scar that had yet to heal). It worked. Deanna relaxed into sleep.

Troy lay there thinking of how good the sex was with Asia. He was surprisingly impressed with her exhibitionistic spirit.

An hour later Troy was falling asleep too when Ashley cried out. Deanna didn't even hear her. She was so ex-

Patriece

hausted from worrying, crying and hurting all night. Her heart told her that Troy was with another woman again. She'd pretended not to know about the indiscretion during her pregnancy because Carla explained that most men cheat when their wives are pregnant. It was hard, but she swallowed it. Now that Ashley was almost 18 months old, she wondered what was his excuse? Every man whose path she crossed desired her—except her husband.

When Deanna woke Troy was sitting in the middle of the living room floor playing with Ashley. It comforted her heart to see them together, in spite of her decision to leave him if she could prove this was another affair. *If he has any common sense, he knows I'm not accepting another indiscretion.*

The afternoon was pleasant. Troy stayed around the house. Deanna wrote a shopping list and invited Troy to go to Walmart with her and Ashley to do the shopping. As expected he declined. Deanna knew then that her intuition was right again. She had learned his method of operation.

He is going to wait until I leave for Walmart, then he'll call his new mistress and make plans to hang out with her for the next few days. Deanna dressed, packed up Ashley, kissed Troy on his forehead and left. She went out to the attached garage and placed Ashley in her car seat. Then she darted back into the house under the guise of needing Ashley's pacifier. She really just wanted to double-check her intuition. *If he's on the phone he's making plans. By the time I get back from Walmart, he'll lie and say the hospital needs him.*

He Looked Like A Man, Until He Barked

Troy sat on the couch with a sexy grin on his face. His tone was one octave above a whisper. When Deanna walked into the room, he looked as nervous as the little boy holding the bat when the window broke. He sat up straight, stumbled over his next mouth full of words and smiled nervously. She grabbed the pacifier off the coffee table and left the room.

As she pulled away from the house she positioned her rearview mirror to see the picture window of the living room. Her pain was so great; she felt it pulsating in her throat. *I bet he's looking out the window to make sure I'm gone this time! This marriage is over! He's never going to stop, and I'm never going to learn to live with it!* Her mirror aligned with the house and there he was as predictable as morning breath, standing in the picture window of the living room.

Before she arrived at Walmart, her cell phone rang.

Deanna wiped her tears to answer Troy's call. *Now he's checking to see if I heard anything. If I have an attitude then I heard, if no attitude then I didn't hear his "I miss you" to his new trick.*

"Hello?" (no attitude)

"Hey Baby, you there yet?"

"Almost. You need something?"

"Razors."

"Ok. Will you be home when I get back?"

"Yeah, for a little bit. I gotta go to the hospital to pick up my itinerary. I'm driving up the coast tonight. Don't forget my razors."

"You're leaving tonight?"

Patriece

"Yes. Only for two days, this is a short assignment."

"Ok." Deanna knew that meant *she* was new. As time progressed so would the length of his assignments.

Deanna parked, hung up the phone and cried in the parking lot before going into Walmart. It hurt so bad that her husband looked outside of their marriage for excitement, comfort, or whatever it was that he sought from other women. She knew in her heart of hearts that her marriage was over. If not now—eventually. A strange calm came over her. She would soon be free of headaches, stress and the jitters. It wouldn't matter when his blue-tooth light was on walking up to the door and out when he walked through the door. Deanna wanted a man that was into her and made her and their family a priority. Troy was unable to do that with the exception of finances. He took good care of their financial needs, but they were emotionally bankrupt.

The thought of helping her husband groom for a date was unbearable. In the store she walked right past the razors. She knew that Troy didn't really need razors. He was simply trying to see what she'd heard. She stopped in the baby section and grab Ashley a few things. While there, her eyes landed on an Early Pregnancy Test kit. She decided to grab it too since her faithful period was a day late. That one night about a month ago when she managed to trust him, no condom was used. He was okay with it. He said he wanted kids 2-3 years apart, and he wanted 3 kids. It wasn't a bad idea at the time, but now it seemed like a death sentence. Her prayer was that she miscalculated or it was stress related—anything but a baby. She was serious about leaving her marriage. A baby would complicate those plans.

At home, she unpacked the shopping bags and took the pregnancy test while Troy changed Ashley's diaper.

He was immaculate; even had a fresh shave. It was real obvious that he was itching to leave, but was waiting on a distraction so he could leave without questions. He feared questions more than death. Finally, the phone rang. Troy immediately grabbed his bags and headed toward the door. This was his blessed opportunity to leave while Deanna was distracted.

Deanna answered the phone. It was Carla. Troy kissed her forehead and walked out the door.

Deanna broke down. "Carla, he's at it again and the test is positive."

"Oh Deanna. It's going to be okay. Whatever you decide, don't terminate your pregnancy. I'll help you in any way I can. Just keep your baby. " Carla spoke with conviction as this was a tender spot for her. She regretted terminating a pregnancy during high school. She didn't want to be an embarrassment to her mother. Carla became pro-life after that experience. She believed children had a right to live. She kept her second baby, in spite of her circumstances and just prayed for the best. Ronika was the dearest thing in her life, next to Ron.

Patriece

Ron was teased in school and didn't really have any friends with the exception of Carla. She'd been kind to him in his adolescence when other kids were cruel.

Carla was drawn to Ron's gentleness and his decency. None of the other girls noticed him, but she could see that underneath those outdated clothes and mass of hair was a good looking man. Ron needed a new wardrobe and some finesse. Carla started taking him shopping with her and having subtle conversations about style. He actually had great taste once he took an interest in his appearance.

Their friendship eased into an unspoken commitment. The day they made love for the first time was beautiful. Their feelings were genuine. Carla, however, not being a virgin herself, was a little disappointed. She married Ron anyway and hoped that his lovemaking skills would improve.

Their marriage was good, but Carla longed for good sex. Ron just didn't know how to pull it off. He handled her roughly and kissed her hard. It wasn't smooth, but chalky. In addition he suffered from premature ejaculation. After six months, Carla gave in to a burning attraction shared with a co-worker. This man dressed good, looked good, and smelled good too. She knew that he was attracted to her by his stare. It was filled with intense, blatant desire, and made her feel like an evening with him would be a bitter/sweet sin.

The meeting was planned. The sex was spontaneous. He was a good lover. He satisfied her thirst for a man that knew his way around her body and didn't require her leading. The experience was grand. Carla returned home as if nothing had happened. Ron wasn't there. She showered. She douched. She forgave herself. By nights end she resolved to stay away from him, even if it meant quitting her job.

That evening Ron walked into a bar alone and took his first drink. He knew that Carla was unsatisfied, and he was unsettled about it. The idea came to him to have a drink to "take the edge" off. He arrived home that night accompanied by rum and coke and his new friends "courage" and "confidence". He left fear, doubt and insecurity at the bar. Ron made love to his wife that night. It was uninhibited love, full of passion and his truth.

Okay, now I can do that for the rest of my life, thank you God. Carla recommitted to her soul mate and secretly willed away her day of sin. Yet, her guilt weighed on her like heavy eyelids.

After that night, Ron changed. Drinking became a big part of his life. What used to be shared information became *'his business'*. Nightclubs replaced the bars. The only place he felt completely safe was at the club. Most of the people there were worst off than him. This afforded him the feeling of self-esteem. He made new friends and developed new behaviors. Still feeling inadequate sexually with Carla, he collected partners and won the admiration of his peers. This was great. He remembered being on the outside of the "in crowd" and how bad he wanted to belong, so he took advantage of his acceptance. Ron was easy going and almost too green to pull off being in the scene; but in time, his "cool" showed up and he fitted right in. No one knew that he was overjoyed to be in the company of hustlers, lightweight pimps, players and all kinds of drama. The excitement was like a drug. He loved being in the midst of the "know." Some of the "know" included the cat fights among women over men, jealous men fighting for a woman, drunkards vomiting curbside outside the club, bouncers escorting troublemakers from the club, and the gyration of a low self-esteemed woman against him on the dance floor. It was all he thought it would be and then some. In spite of his addiction to the drama, he had every intention of getting back to the business of marriage after this little phase ran its course. Ron truly loved Carla.

2

Troy wasn't a bad man. He was an ignorant man. He was selfish and totally inconsiderate. This was not his fault when you consider his environment. In his neighborhood there were grown boys; unemployed men living off of unemployed women who had babies to capture a moment of accomplishment. They used the babies to provide an income for themselves and their mates.

He, too, was from a broken home, but his mother instilled in him qualities of manhood, which promised to bring him a grateful wife. He knew he had to take out the garbage, help with the chores, the kids, participate in family outings, maintain the yard and the cars. He even knew he was supposed to practice monogamy and that was the one thing he had the most trouble with. He just couldn't fathom the idea of just one woman for the rest of his life. He saw so many other men having a bevy of women and decided that was the one thing he would not take his mother's suggestion on. He was going to have as many women as he liked. In his mind, six hands touching him were so much better than two. He wore condoms with everyone accept his wife. Occasionally, he wore them at home too. It was habit for him because of his lifestyle. He explained to his wife that it was the best thing for her health—which drew suspicion away from his motives. He didn't mention that it also helped him maintain his habit of wearing a condom at all times.

Troy had no desire whatsoever to practice monogamy. He felt that it was his right as a man; he believed infidelity was expected of him. He figured women had also come to the realization that infidelity was a part of life. *It's just the way it is;* was his take on relationships, and he governed himself accordingly.

Troy enjoyed having multiple partners. He truly believed that a boy's rite of passage into manhood was to see how many women he could sleep with. His partners were being tallied and ranked and disclosed to his best friend Brian.

Troy would never admit that he idolized Brian, but he did. Brian had had sex with more women than "Magic". He had his wife, Gabby, trained to accept him on his terms. He even had three children outside of the marriage that he was not financially responsible for. In Troy's eyes, Brian was a real player.

Troy was looking to out rank him with Asia. Asia was so fine she made females heads turn. She was finer than Brian's best chick. That's why he picked her. Originally he had gone to Home Depot to get with the cashier, when he spotted Asia.

Asia drew him in like a teenager withdrawing a bubble blown with bubble gum. He had no choice in the matter. He picked up something off of the first shelf he came to and got in line behind her. By the time they paid for their items, he'd gotten a smile, her phone number and made a promise to call. He called her as she was driving out of the parking lot and simply said "Just checking your number before I let you get away." She laughed and they talked for 20 minutes more.

The next day he went back to Home Depot to return the $45 pipe he had no use for, while completing his mission of pursuing the cashier. Everything went smooth. The cashier gave him her number, no problem. She was real easy going. That same night he took her for a ride in his BMW, told her she was beautiful and she opened up like the automatic doors at Safeway. The chase was over—he was back to Asia.

His plans for Asia included making Brian jealous.

Brian's marriage to Gabby started as normal as any other couple. Gabby was headstrong with good direction and ambition beyond the average woman. She was not a bad looking woman but never had she been accused of being beautiful. She was cute—a smidgen less than pretty though some days she glowed just perfectly and her cute became pretty. She didn't have voluptuous curves or flowing hair or any of that. Her eyes were her best feature—not the shape, the presence. She seemed to possess a naiveté that added a girlish quality to her person. She seemed cuddly and honest, even gullible.

It's hard to say how she became introverted but the third year of their marriage changed her. Gabby went from headstrong to reclusive in a matter of months. Brian had been involved in several affairs and each time she searched her soul for shortcomings. She personalized his behavior and most of the time she blamed herself. The thought that he was just a dog never came up for her. In her mind there had to be some logic behind his madness. She spoke with counselors, elders of the church, and she prayed about it to no avail. Brian's behavior grew worst and she became a defined "people pleaser". She began catering to his needs, overlooking his indiscretions, justifying his behavior and inevitably became depressed. She remembered her mother's endurance of her father's infidelity and she fought tooth and nail against it. She started out exactly like her mother—yelling, screaming and threatening. When that didn't work, she tried the softer approach of rolling with the punches while threatening less and sharing with him that his behavior was hurting her. Still the women called reporting their encounters with her husband. Some even sent word of their unborn babies. She would confront Brian in this meek and mild manner, and he would deny it over and over again. He would take her out a couple of times, do something nice for her and as soon as she smiled at a good joke or smirked just so, he went back to his business of womanizing.

Gabby was miserable. It pained her something fierce to accept children outside of her marriage and not a single pregnancy inside of the marriage. She wanted babies so bad, but they just weren't coming. She and Brian never used birth control, yet she never conceived. It seemed as though her marriage was doomed. Her isolation grew quickly. She routinely prepared dinner and herself to receive Brian whom rarely arrived in a timely manner. For a few months she got up when he came home and they shared light conversation and an occasional exchange of affection. She smiled and cuddled as if everything was fine, but insecurity had developed in her and there were times when she felt that it would swallow her whole at any given moment.

He Looked Like A Man, Until He Barked

Gabby went to her mother after about a year and a half of suffering in this manner. Her mother ministered to her concerning marriage. Gabby listened intently as she watched the once young and vibrantly beautiful woman share her story with her. Her mother, Esther, spoke of her fathers tiptoeing (as she put it). She told her story after story about things she did to nip it in the bud. They talked for about five hours about the indiscretions of men. Gabby learned that some of her favorite uncles were a part of a pack instead of generations. Esther gingerly explained that "men are jes' like dogs. Don't b'lieve me just watch'em. Sometime when you out late at night looking for Brian, and I know you do it 'cause ain't but three kinds of folks out at night—them that ain't got no biz'ness out, them that are doing biz'ness and wives looking for stray dogs. Men and dogs flock to one another. Next time you out looking for him I bet ya' see a dog. And within five blocks you'll see a man. Mark my word. That alone ought to tell ya that's how they became best friends. Do we have a saying 'bout cat is woman's best friend? Naw, but e'rybody know dog is man's best friend. Why is dat? 'Cause dey da same. Only a dog will sleep with it's kin, will sleep with its friend, will sleep with its enemy. They protect, but rarely do they love. They will let you take good care of them and one day for no reason at all; they will bite the very hand that feeds 'em. They'll up and walk away for no reason at all. They are a strange creature. So are men." Esther was wise in her approach. By nights' end, Gabby understood that this phase of Brian's life would run its course and his life with her would begin. The painstaking reality was when?

Patriece

Brian was aware that Gabby was unhappy, but he was also aware that she was the "one". Other women were a means to fulfilling his manhood. He knew that there were times when his behavior was uncomfortable, but he thought she knew the game(s) of love. It was his understanding that wives knew that they were a notch above women, broads, tricks or chicks. He thought she knew that she was special. She was the chosen one. He'd been with some of God's finest creations, but she impressed him. In his mind her staying power should be great because her parents had been married for 32 years. Surely her mother's tenacity would sustain her. She had survived her father's manhood and watched her mother overcome it.

Brian was the product of a broken home and he recognized Gabby's pain just as he did his mothers. He purposely stayed away until she was sleep as to avoid those beautiful eyes overshadowed with pain. They spoke volumes in whispers that screamed why? He didn't really know why himself. He was a man is all he knew. He thought he was living the life of a man. He thought he was cool. He thought he was slick and accepted and respected among his peers. There were times when he wished that he could open up and just be true to her, but monogamy was misunderstood in his generation. Players were expected. If he didn't play he may be labeled a "Mark," so he played hard. He'd rather be an urban legend than a "Mark."

He Looked Like A Man, Until He Barked

When the time came for him to retire his youth and get serious about life in general, he rested assured that Gabby had what it took to make a good marriage. She was the kind of woman whose presence added prestige to the man. She looked real good on his arm. Gabby had eyes that said "trust me, I'm wholesome." It was those eyes that stopped him dead in his tracks that day at the office. Brian refused to let her get away. He stopped everything he was doing and rushed to make her acquaintance. He didn't treat her as a thing as he did most women. He didn't want a piece of her, but all of her. So, he courted her. Gabby got flowers and candy and gifts. When the time came for the move in, he proposed marriage to keep it respectful because in his heart of heart he held her in high regard. He cherished his life with her. He loved her.

He thought she loved him enough to let him be a man until he was ready to be a husband.

3

Asia buzzed around the apartment making sure the place was tidy enough. Her depression had caused things to get more out of hand than usual, but this was not the time to fix it. So, she stuffed clothes in the hamper, put the dishes in the dishwasher, and threw everything else in the baby's room and closed the door. Tonight she was having company. A man she'd met at Home Depot Home Improvement Store about two weeks ago. She'd talked to him a few times and finally decided that she'd end her four + years of celibacy—she was celibate by default, not choice.

He was nice enough. She was desperate enough. She took extra care in preparing herself for tonight's visitor and when he arrived his stare confirmed that he noticed.

"Are you married? Involved? In love? Engaged? Or in the home?"

"What? What do you mean in the home?"

"I mean are you living with your *'friend'* but sleeping on the couch because y'all don't feel the same and it's basically over?" Asia explained masking her irritation of his veiled ignorance.

Troy smiled. "No. You cover all bases huh?"

"Yes. I am not for any games. I've been single for four years, and I'm ready to be touched. This is for me not you. So you don't have to play the games men play to get laid." Asia had made up her mind. It wasn't that she was attracted to Troy especially, but she needed to be held. It was time to be in the arms of a man. She was tired of waiting and tired of the silence that filled her apartment. She needed the heat of a lover's breath on her neck and the touch of a man warming her skin.

"We play games to get laid?" Troy asked.

"Yes, basically lie."

"Lie?"

"Yes, lie. You lie and say you're not married. You say that you're sleeping on the couch, y'all ain't together, you're there for the kids. Y'all go so far as to say "I love you" if you think that's what we want to hear. That's why I asked you those questions because I don't want to hear any of that crap later on."

"Who broke your heart?"

"No one. The question is who broke my sister, friend, aunt, cousin, mother and grandmother's hearts? I have seen the pain they've endured with men, and I don't want any part of that."

"Well, I'm available to love you back—no games."

"You didn't have to say that." She tried to respond with the same controlled tone, but it was evident that she'd softened with this news.

"So that's what this is about?...heartache and pain?"

"Yes. My Daddy hurt my mother so bad, I'm sure that pain can be detected in her DNA. I'm talking the kind of pain that has scar tissue so thick you can't make another decision without reflecting back on it. It's like—"

"That's called a keloid baby." Troy laughed. He liked the way she detailed things.

Asia laughed too. "Yeah that's it. I don't want that on my heart. I got that one crack in it from losing Big Tony, but it's still in tact and I don't want it broken or decorated with a keloid." Asia replaced her laughter with seriousness. Troy noticed and his stomach gave a little shutter, but he kept on smiling. He fell for her, at that moment, with no reservations in spite of his situation.

He pulled her down onto his lap and his breath warmed her neck as he whispered "I'm not going to hurt you. I'm not going to make your beautiful heart ugly with keloids, and I'm certainly not going to break it. I am here because I like you. I like everything about you, especially your heart."

"You don't even know me. You don't know if I have a good heart or not."

"Yes I do. I could see it in your smile; it's so warm and inviting. It made me feel like I would be comfortable in your presence and I am."

"So, why are you available?"

"I'm divorced."

"Oh. Your fault or hers?"

"Both. Irreconcilable differences."

"Oh, what do you do?"

"I'm a Hospitalist. That is...in layman's a doctor that travels. I even work in different hospitals, here locally."

"You're a doctor?"

"Yes."

"That's good."

"What about you?"

"I'm a part time professional dreamer with mad writing skills. Full time, I'm an Administrative Assistant to a Public Relations firm." Asia laughed.

"No kids?"

"Yes. One. He's at my best friend's house who's also his Aunt, his Dad's sister. I don't think it's good to allow dates around your children. My motto is *mates not dates*. In light of Lil' Tony not knowing his Dad, I don't want just anybody in his life. I want someone special that can be a father figure for him, but they've got to have love for him. You know it's got to come naturally. So if you meet my son, know that you are someone special."

"So, he's your fiancés son?"

"Yes."

"How old is he?"

"He'll be three in four months. I didn't even know I was pregnant when I got the news that Big Tony had died. I was scared of single parenting, but there was no way I was going get rid of his baby after that. I just had to press on. I get a lot of support from Sheila, his aunt. She's Big Tony's only sibling and since Tony died, their mother has passed too, so she's Lil' Tony's only family." Asia smiled weakly realizing that she had accepted Troy into her life.

Troy's stomach was shaking. *This might not work after all* he thought. He shook it off realizing her kid was not his problem. "Can I kiss you?"

Asia answered by remaining still as Troy leaned into her.

Patriece

Sheila was so happy Asia had finally found someone. She hoped he was a good guy and not a deceitful lying dog. Asia was not ready for that. She'd been in a sheltered relationship with Tony since high school. She'd never been through any BS and Sheila wasn't ready for her to go through it now. Asia was tough, but she wasn't ghetto. Her threshold had never been measured. In a way that was good and in another way that made her vulnerable to reality. Sheila worried about her new mate. She knew how men could ruin a perfectly good woman. She was once a perfectly good woman.

When Sheila realized that her husband's drug use had turned into drug abuse, she had no choice but to leave. It took three years, but she grew tired of the women, the binges, the disappearing acts and the lies. She was tired of hiding money only for him to find it. Tired of debt that he racked up. Tired of being begged for money for more dope all day, all times of day and everyday. Tired of feeling ashamed and embarrassed. Sheila had hung in there for as long as she could. The day she came home and the house was nearly empty she held her tears until she opened the freezer. Every piece of meat she owned was gone. She fed her babies peanut butter and jelly sandwiches, mostly jelly because they were too young for peanut butter, according to their doctor. When her 2-year old told her that she looked like a crybaby and her 4½-year-old agreed, she packed up his things that night.

She was wiser now. No man would ever make her feel ashamed or look stupid again. She concluded that men were

He Looked Like A Man, Until He Barked

for pleasure and that's what she used them for. Promiscuity was her new reputation, but she didn't care. It was painless compared to the hurt she'd felt during the end of her marriage.

Sheila was back on her feet, repairing her credit and working hard to provide for herself and her kids. She didn't have to hide her purse at her neighbors. She had replaced her TV's, DVD's, and other trinkets. She could even buy and freeze meat again.

Sheila had taken her vows seriously. In her heart she always thought that women that divorced their husbands didn't take their vows seriously; that's why she stayed so long. Now that she was free and in absolute control of her life she no longer trusted men. Deep down in her soul she was like Asia, just longing to be loved. The keloid on her heart wouldn't allow it.

4

Asia fell harder than expected. Troy did the most romantic things. He was everything she wanted in a man. In the course of three months she felt like he loved her all of his life. One night they were chatting on the phone while he was in route to a hospital, and she mentioned that she was cramping, and wanted chocolate. The next morning while she was sitting at her desk a delivery person showed up with flowers. About thirty minutes later a young lady walked in with a gift basket. The basket contained Midol, an electric heating pad, a throw, a coffee mug, a mug warmer and herbal teas for such an occasion. Thirty minutes later while she was still digesting all of that another young lady came calling with a box of Sees Nuggets. Asia didn't know what to do or what to think. She didn't even really know how to feel. It felt good, but a flabbergasted kind of good. It was the best feeling she'd ever experienced. She called and thanked him after each delivery, but the chocolates took the cake.

"Dr. Arlington." He smiled with his voice.

"Dr. Arlington do you treat all your patients this good?"

"I try. Yes."

"Well, I have a treat for you too. In approximately one week I'm going to hold my leg up my damn self." Asia blushed. She'd thought that, but it came out of her mouth on its own.

"Well, now. I like that. I could do a whole lot more if I didn't have to hold that leg. Once I even thought about amputating 'em."

"You can, as long as you have'em back on in time to pick up my baby." She laughed.

"You crazy. How you feeling?"

"Better. I haven't had a cramp all day."

"Well, good. I hoped that if you focused on something else your cramps would be more tolerable. I hope the chocolate with nuts was fine. Black folks like nuts."

"Baby, everything was just perfect."

"Good."

Troy felt good about making Asia feel better. (He'd done the same thing for Deanna when they first got married and she simply said 'thank you' and cooked dinner as usual.) He hoped his trinkets held Asia until he got back to her. It would be about four days. Deanna and Ashley both were not feeling well. Deanna had been vomiting a lot so he supposed it was viral. Ashley was running a fever.

"Are you going to make it tonight?" Asia asked.

"Naw. You'll have to hang out with the flowers and the chocolate. It's that time of year when viruses are in the air. I have some patients to tend. It'll be real late when I leave here and I don't want to bump heads with Lil'' Man in the morning." Troy was taking off his white jacket, to leave, as he spoke. He loved her rule concerning her son. He'd used it against her often.

"Okay. But you're about to be a mate in my book." Asia sipped some more tea.

"Babe, I gotta go. I'm being paged. Love you, feel better." He hung up.

Asia held the phone, realizing that he'd hung up. If he were anyone else she would have been hurt.

"Hello." Troy answered.

"Are you able to get off? I'm really too weak to care for Ashley. I need to know; I can send her over Carla's if I need to."

"Deanna, I'm off and on my way. Do you need anything?"

"No. She needs Tylenol. I think she's teething."

"Probably. You still vomiting?"

"Yes."

"Want some chicken soup?"

"No. Bring me a cheese burger from In-N-Out burgers a large fry and a frosty from Wendy's."

"Deanna, that's not what you eat to stop throwing up."

"But it's what I want. I haven't eaten in two days."

"Alright. I'll see you in a minute."

They hung up and Deanna sighed. This pregnancy was not the breeze that she experienced while carrying Ashley. Ashley didn't cause her any morning sickness. The census was that morning sickness subsided after the first trimester. In two weeks she would be entering her fourth month of pregnancy and she was still suffering.

Walking to his car Troy noticed how round Kelly's butt was for the first time. Normally she had on a uniform—which hid what she was working with. She was in street clothes today.

He Looked Like A Man, Until He Barked

Kelly noticed him too. Immediately she began *the rolling of the hips*. Sure his attention was on her, she waved and he waved back. Since he didn't seem to notice, she stopped her performance and proceeded into the hospital.

Troy pretended not to notice her *rolling of the hips*, but he knew then that he had action at getting next to her in the near future. What he didn't know is that his wife was almost four months pregnant. His girlfriend was ready to kick it up a notch and that someone had keyed his Beemer.

Kelly looked out the window at the silver Beemer with the plates that said ALL MIN and smiled.

Troy drove off. At In-N-Out burgers he went into the trunk and put the car seat back in the car. He took it out most mornings. He replaced it in case Ashley needed to go to the ER later. He noticed the key line on the driver door. *DAMN!*

Before he went in the house he took his keys and scribbled on the driver door, further keying his car. That way it would look like juveniles instead of a scorned woman.

Deanna and Ashley lay on the couch under a blanket. They looked miserable. Troy brought the food in and went to get Ashley's high chair. Deanna started eating. Normally she waited for a plate, but her craving wouldn't allow that. Ashley wouldn't sit in the high chair. Troy had to hold her and let her eat out of his hand. She was whiny. They watched an HBO movie until the girls fell back to sleep. Troy sat there looking at them and thinking *it's good to be home tonight*.

5

Sheila decided now was a perfect time to drop in on Asia. She worked at the Telephone Company about three blocks away. Occasionally they met for lunch, but today's visit was pure nosiness. Sheila hadn't been able to talk to Asia like she wanted to because this new guy, Troy, was always there. She wanted to know about him. She entered the building and spotted Jerome. *Damn! I didn't want to see him. If Asia knew I did the Security Guard for her office lobby she'd kill me. I guess now is as good as time as any to set him straight, maybe then he won't approach me when I'm with her.*

"Hey Lady." Jerome licked his lips and let his eyes roam all over her body.

I wonder did this fool see the Ross tag under my shoe! (He starring so hard). I hate dealing with bottom feeders, they never realize there was never a future in it, just a night of fun. Well it's morning, get away. "What do you want?" Sheila asked in a firm parental tone.

"I was just speaking to you."

"Well don't. It's done. Don't harp on it, just be glad it happened, remember it and allow me to forget it." She marched passed him like she was royalty and he was a peasant.

"Bitch!" He mumbled loud enough for her to hear it as he accepted her bait. It would be a cold day in hell before he acknowledged her again.

Sheila hoped that was enough to put their rendezvous behind her. She tapped on Asia's door and then stepped in.

"Asia you look cute. You got that, I've been laid glow."

"Girl, shut up!" Asia blushed. She wasn't sure if it was good because it was good—or if it had just been so long.

"Details!" Sheila sat down.

"Sheila, we are not in the 9th grade. I'm not giving you details. We are the mother of three little people, two of which belong to you so it's not like you don't know what happened."

"Whatever, you gone want to talk when it gets old."

"And you gon' listen, so whatever." They laughed.

"Troy's leaving for a week and we want to spend sometime together. Can Tony come over, or are you entertaining?"

"Of, course my baby can come over. Even if I am entertaining. Ain't nothing going down 'til my kids, eat and are in bed, that includes Tony. If he can't wait, he can't play—that's how it is when you date a woman with kids."

"Okay, can you pick him up from daycare? I don't want him to bump heads with Troy."

"I will, but you need to rethink that, because this is the real world and if Tony meets the wrong person he'll have to meet someone else anyway."

"Don't hate me because I got mad parenting skills and you have zilch. If it weren't for my influence your girls would grow up without a Diva card. You should have had the boy. He could learn first hand how to *mis*treat a lady."

"On the real Asia. Kids are more resilient than you give them credit for. Exposing Tony to life ain't gone kill him."

"Exposing him to disrespect will cause me problems that will make me kill him, so look at it as me preserving his life. Because when I tell him no overnight guest, he will not be able to tell me 'you did it' or even feel that way, cause I don't do it either."

Sheila decided to end the conversation. Asia was stubborn and especially when she thought she was right. And she really thought she was right by keeping distance between Troy and Tony.

She recognized the glow on Asia's face.

"Are you pregnant?" Sheila asked realizing it was either real good or she was with child.

"No!" Asia shooed her away. She was doubly careful about that. He protected himself and her birth control pills protected her.

"It must be hell of good then." Sheila laughed.

"Bye, Sheila. Don't forget my baby. I'll see you tomorrow."

Sheila kissed Asia's cheek and left.

Jerome looked straight ahead as she strolled pass him, she did the same.

"Babe, I can't make it. I have to work up to time for my trip. I'll see you when I get back."

"Awgh. I really wanted to hang out with you."

"I'm sorry. I'll call you when I get there."

He Looked Like A Man, Until He Barked

"Ok. I love you."
"I love you too."

6

Asia was getting disgusted with Troy's job when he showed up. She came home with Lil' Tony and saw the BMW with ALL MIN on the plates parked out front. She pulled away from the curb and dialed Sheila.

"Hey Girl, can Lil' Tony hang out there for awhile?" Asia's excitement spilled into her voice.

"Sure, lover-man finally showed up?" Sheila wasn't feeling Troy. He was too mysterious.

"Yes. He's parked out front. I just drove off."

"Why? Lil' Tony?"

"Yes! You know how I am about my baby." Asia seriously joked.

"It's good that you love my nephew and all, but this is getting ridiculous. How long y'all going to continue like this? I bet he's comfortable with it."

"Until I'm sure. He wants to meet him. It's me." Asia lied.

"I don't believe you. He ain't thinking about nothing but screwing, just like the rest of 'em. You talk about me, but I'm keeping it real. I keep my head out the cloud and I ain't been hurt yet."

"I haven't either. Troy is not just into sex. We do other things." Asia was losing her confidence realizing that nothing else had been done. Troy always cancelled at the last minute.

"Like what? Never mind. I'm home. Just look at him good and start demanding to get out of the house. If it's all that—go somewhere. Let him see you fully dressed and hold your hand in public. Make his ass show the world he buys chocolates." Sheila was getting mad. Troy was occupying Asia's time according to his schedule and locking her in the house when he had the time. That sounded like marriage to Sheila.

"We're on the way."

"Asia, be careful. Troy sounds like the kind of brother that will be in your place butt naked when you return, then tell you about what he's got to do first thing in the morning. If it's something that you can't do with him, brace yourself for some Bull."

"Do you have PJ's for Tony just in case?" Asia needed to change the subject. She knew Sheila had at least a week worth of clothes for him.

Sheila accepted the "Pass Card" and let it go. "Yes. See y'all in a minute."

When Asia walked in with the baby Sheila hugged her. "I love you girl! I just want to make sure you're happy."

"Love you too." Asia left. Her stomach was unsettled. Sheila was right. Troy had done some very romantic things, but no one knew. She was a secret. She remembered her co-worker telling her, 'girl you still gotta check your man for a dog tag?' Her heart needed this to be real.

Discarding the negativity posing as love from her friends she rushed home to Troy. Asia's heart nearly fell, visibly, when Troy was sitting in the living room naked.

After making love they showered together. Asia held her composure until he shared "Babe, you want me pick you up something to eat before I leave or just give you some money?"

Her expression showed her feelings. She tried to settle her stomach. "Troy where are you going?"

"I'm going home and get ready for tomorrow. I have to work in Sacramento tomorrow." He did have to go to Sacramento, but not to work. He was interviewing for an interim position while another female Hospitalist took maternity leave.

"Oh." Asia's tears were evident. She turned and faced the shower letting the water dilute her tears. Troy saw them and he knew that meant that he had to start taking her outside before she started doing the math.

"Babe, it's actually a job interview. You want to ride with me? You can't go in, but I'll only be about an hour."

"Sure. I'll go." Asia felt like she had won. She could tell all the naysayers that she got out of the house. It didn't matter that it was in a city that no one she knew would see her, she was getting out.

"Let me go get my stuff together, I'll bring something back to eat. Get yourself together. We gotta get up early." He grabbed the soap. "Where's mine?"

"You are out. I'll pick up some."

"Alright." Troy tried not to draw attention to how upset he was, but he only used Irish Spring. He wore condoms and used Irish Spring. Keeping it uniform was easiest for him. He lathered his towel and reluctantly used the soap that was available.

He Looked Like A Man, Until He Barked

Deanna expected Troy to disappear soon. He'd been home every night for almost a week helping her with the baby. His announcement that he had a three-day trip didn't surprise her at all. She let him go. When he kissed her forehead the pregnancy enhanced sense of smell caught a whiff of Wild Berry-Extra Moisture, Caress.

Troy returned with a garment bag and a small duffel bag. Asia's little heart did a pitter-patter at the sight of the bag. She knew it meant he would be with her for a few days. *Married men don't stay away from home for days at a time. Wait 'til I tell Sheila about this.*

"Babe, I guess it's time for me to meet Lil'' Man. I'll be here for the next few days." Troy kissed her forehead and she smelled her soap on his body and smiled.

Sacramento was a wonderful time. Troy got the job. They walked around the mall. They went to Cold Stone Ice Creamery. They bought Lil' Tony and Ashley some gifts. Asia told Troy about her financial challenge of Lil' Tony's birthday celebration. She wanted to do something nice, but her budget dictated a small get together. She wanted to invite his daycare friends and some of her co-workers kids and make it a grand time. His first two parties were with Sheila and his cousins only. They were all still grieving, but everyone seemed to be doing much better and it was time to celebrate. Life was looking up, finally. Troy agreed and told her not to worry about it. He would help out.

His heart wanted to sponsor the party right then, but his account wouldn't allow it. Deanna needed pocket money this payday and Ashley wanted one of those electronic cars. So he'd have to budget Lil' Man in. He was grateful that Asia was the only woman he dealt with on the giving end. He wouldn't dare give another chick a dime.

On the drive home they held hands all the way. Troy went back to the apartment to get some rest and talk to Kelly.

Asia got in her car and went to pick up Lil' Tony.

Sheila was excited about her outing, but not completely sold on Troy. Though she didn't mention her feelings to Asia.

7

When Brian met Asia he knew that Troy had erred. He recognized that someone had been good to her. The man before him had made her his priority. She was accustomed to the real thing. Asia was wife material. Troy was not available that way and she was going to be devastated at the discovery of that.

He knew at first glance that she loved Troy sincerely. She reminded him of Gabby. Women that give that high school, talk on the phone all night kind of love. The love that Barry White sang about *Can't Get Enough of Your Love Babe*. It bothered him to think about what she was about to go through with Troy. Gabby's change came to mind, but he comforted himself in knowing, in the end he was going to exhaust himself in loving her. Just as her Dad did her Mother. Ms Esther wanted for nothing. She was reverenced in all things. Dad even called her "Mama". He couldn't wait to celebrate Gabby that way.

He hoped that Troy's behavior didn't destroy Asia. It was certain to shift her life.

Brian believed in the laws of karma. He believed that the women he dealt with knew he only wanted sex. They may have said something different, just to keep it ladylike, but they knew the game. Sometimes he would warn them 'if you play *pussy* you get fucked'. Most of them thought that was cute. Each time they were hurt by the games of love/Brian.

Brian thought of himself as a caregiver. He took care of women until the one for them showed up. Like the latchkey system. He was a female care provider. He provided them romance. He bought flowers. He made a few calls, returned a few calls and hung out with them occasionally. Sometimes he lent the base in his voice to a conversation with a kid or two just to fill the need. And always he let them go when they were ready. He deleted their numbers and picked up someone else. This was easy for him because he had given his heart to his wife. She truly was the love of his life.

"How you doing Asia. I'm 'B'."

"Hello. Can I get you something to drink?"

"No, thank you."

"Eat?"

"No thank you." Brian smiled back thinking *this woman is gorgeous. Damn!*

"Well, let me know if you change your mind. I'll serve you this time, but next visit you're on your own."

"Babe, you didn't ask me if I were thirsty or hungry." Troy teased.

"Boy please you know your way around the kitchen." Asia walked away from the door into the living room. She stuffed a bunch of sales papers and her nightclothes behind the couch; swept potato chip crumbs into her hand and then sprinkled them in a nearby plant. The room was instantly cleaned. She'd run two baskets of laundry up the stairs when she heard Troy's key rattle in the door. They were sitting at the top of the stairs. She figured he wouldn't be going up there since he mentioned that he was just dropping money for Lil' Tony's birthday celebration. She heard a voice in the background and got all giddy at the idea of meeting someone in his life. They had been seeing each other going on four months and she hadn't met anyone in his life. If he didn't spend so many nights at her house she'd buy into the mess that Sheila was always saying about his acting like a married man.

Asia was content with Troy, not happy like she was with Tony, but she was okay. She loved his generosity and attention when he was there. He never complained about her apartment, her cooking or anything. He seemed to like her just as she was. That felt real good.

Troy walked into the living room with Brian. They sat down. He made small talk with Asia. Then pulled out three one hundred-dollar bills.

"Babe, this should do it. Can you handle a gift or do I need to pick him up something?"

"This is more than enough. I will get the gift. He's only going to be three."

"Yeah, but he's going to want a jumper or a clown or something, they always do. Get it, whatever it is."

"Okay. You should come early so I can meet Ashley before the party. Don't want our first meeting to be public."

"Okay." Troy kissed her forehead and motioned for Brian to head to the door. His heart was pounding. Ashley wasn't going to be coming to the party. Deanna would kill him.

"It was nice meeting you Asia, See you next time."

"You too 'B', next time."

They exited. Before they got to the car Brian started.

Patriece

"Troy, how you going to pull that one off? Why and what does she know about Ashley? You shouldn't be flowing like that with nobody."

"I know. I used Ashley as an excuse for not returning a few weekends back. I told her that I rotate weekends with her Mom and we were switching. Now that puts Ashley with me on Lil' Tony's birthday."

"Well, you better think of something. Man you know that girl done been loved before? She ain't like a chick that ain't looking for nothing. She can see karats and veils and shit. You need to pull out as soon as possible man."

"Can't."

"What you mean, can't?"

"I just can't." Troy realized a few days ago that he really cared about Asia. He was trying to figure out a way to keep her and Deanna.

8

Troy's heart was committing to Asia without his permission. He missed her. He wondered what she was doing in the course of a day and he had begun to think about her even when he was with Deanna. He had labeled what they did in bed as "making love". No other woman had registered that way with him. With the exception of his wife who also enlightened him of the difference. And he and his wife hadn't "made love" in months. They had been together while he was with Asia and he had enjoyed her, but the closeness he felt with Asia was absent. In his mind he had two women. (He didn't acknowledge the women he picked up. They meant nothing).

He had broken a few player's rules too. He'd said, "I love you". And it wasn't always followed by "too". The rule was he wasn't supposed to say it at all. He called Asia for no reason. Troy never called women. He returned calls. Actually he treated her better than he'd ever treated Deanna.

With Deanna he did just enough to stay out of divorce court and make the marriage tolerable. If he were to be honest with himself he'd admit that he never loved Deanna. He cared about her. He didn't love her. He never did. He married her because she was comparable to Gabby. And he was Brian's protégé.

The things he did for Asia made him feel good. He took responsibility for her smiles. The flowers he bought yesterday were purchased because he wanted to see her smile. She smiled so wide and genuinely. After getting them she kissed him with her breast pressed firmly against his chest. Their lips locked which spoke "I love you, thank you! That was so sweet!" over and over again. It was the sincerity that he loved about her. She made him feel good. Returning to her was like picking up Ashley from school, the eyes grew wide and bright, the smile and then the sprint! That was the best feeling in the world. It made him feel whole and it defined unconditional better than Webster's Collegiate Dictionary.

Troy would never admit it, but he loved Asia with all of his heart.

Troy walked in the house feeling good. Everything was neat and orderly. He knew he was home. He had one fish in the bucket and two poles in the water, one on the line and one swimming upstream.

"Hi Baby, why you up?"

"Couldn't sleep."

"You look tired."

"I am."

"Ashley keep you up?"

"No. She's at Carla & Ron's tonight. We were supposed to be talking after you got off."

"Baby I'm sorry. I got caught up at the hospital."

"What's her name this time Troy?"

"What are you talking about?"

"I'm talking about the female that you are sleeping with this time."

He Looked Like A Man, Until He Barked

"Deanna the accusations are too much. I'm not going to kiss your ass for the rest of my life regarding my infidelity. I have already made amends for that. It will never happen again."

"Troy why do you think that statement is going to comfort me when I've heard it as least three times already? You must really think I'm a fool. I may not have a degree, but I don't need one to figure you out. You're a liar, a cheat and there is no good in you. I don't know why you're here because it's real obvious that you don't want to be. You are going to look up one day and me and the kids are going to be gone."

"Where y'all going? I provide very well for you and my kids, because I want to be with y'all. What do you mean kids?"

"While you were out building a relationship with the next 'B' your new baby is growing in me."

"Why didn't you say something?" His eyes dropped on her stomach and for the first time he realized that it was protruding quite a bit.

"I was going to tell you, but you rarely make it home. I'm okay though because I figure since you always at the hospital we'd just meet you there." Deanna said no more. She stood up and walked into her bedroom leaving Troy sitting in the living room, dumbfounded.

It took Troy a full ten minutes to retreat to the bedroom. He remembered that night about five months ago when he didn't use a condom. He also realized that that was the last time he'd touched Deanna too. He dropped his hand in his lap and fondled himself. He knew he needed to touch her. He was grateful that Asia thought he was in Atlanta for a while.

Troy climbed into the bed and his thang poked Deanna right on her butt. She didn't budge. He poked her again deliberately and then cupped her breast. Her body ached for his comfort but her heart just wasn't in it. Her heart loved *her*. It was *her* friend, even if her body was not. Her heart remembered the pain. She wanted to listen to it, but her body was winning. She let him grope her for awhile and then he touched her stomach and like a lioness protecting her cubs, she swatted his hand away. "How dare you lay up with some 'B' and then come in here like nothings happened and try to roll up in me. You have lost your mind." She grunted.

Troy grabbed her arm and pulled her into him. He held her as she struggled to get free. He never said a word. Tears just started to wet his arm and he knew that she was hurting. He loosened his grip just enough to see if she was still struggling. She lay limp in his arm. He turned her over and held her some more. She continued to cry. He let her.

"Dee, I'm sorry. Baby, I'm so sorry. No more okay?" He was sincere—his heart went soft for Deanna. He loved Asia. He wanted to get a piece of Kelly, but the tears were too much. Deanna had cried at their wedding. She had cried during labor with Ashley, but those were expected tears. Even when she busted him the first, second and third times she didn't cry. She didn't yell or scream. She expressed her disappointment. She distanced herself from him for awhile

He Looked Like A Man, Until He Barked

and eventually things got back to normal. Deanna crying was foreign. He decided to concentrate on home. It was time.

9

Brian had the perfect life. His wife loved him unconditionally and allowed him to do his thang. His baby's Mama's didn't force him to pay for his kids. They just wanted him to spend time with the kids. He didn't even do a lot of that. The third child's mother was different. When Brian asked her "whose baby is this?" She answered "mine."

Michelle was also a Realtor in the same company as him. Finding out about his wife was devastating. Finding out about her pregnancy was all she could handle. The challenging of his paternity forced her to remove herself from his presence. For his safety, she transferred to another office.

Brian was invited to witness the delivery. He opted to visit afterwards instead. Michelle's baby looked more like him than his other children. For good reason—her baby was an only child.

Michelle asked Brian one last time if he wanted to be apart of their baby's life. He knew that was asking him to sign her birth certificate. He wasn't doing that.

Brian hadn't signed any birth certificates. He had challenged the other two mothers with blood test and they came up with a *quality time remedy*. All they wanted was for him to spend time with their children and claim them in namesake. They would provide for them. He was needed, basically for show. Hoping to commit to quality time with this one too. He answered "Naw, I'm cool."

He Looked Like A Man, Until He Barked

She responded. "Brian Comier, I will NEVER give you a paternity test. I know you are her father. You will sign her birth certificate because you are her father or you don't have to. She won't die either way. But, you will not assassinate my character with your ghetto trips. I am a woman not a whore. So, there is no question as to the identity of my baby's father. You will not get me in the presence of a bunch of white folks and make a mockery of my integrity. I am still gainfully employed thus her needs will be met. Return to your wife, your drama and your ghetto mentality. We won't bother you at all. I will teach her about you, but I will not force you to be apart of her life. I'm a different caliber of woman and it's obvious that you are out of your league. Quality time is not of interest to me. I'm seeking parenting. Thank you for stopping by. I can take her away with a clear conscious now. In case you ever need to communicate with her, her name is Quetti Dave-Comier. It's pronounced K-wet-ty, my last name Dah-vay and yours Comier. That's all you need to know. Again, thanks for stopping by."

Brian was taken aback. He realized he'd erred, but he didn't bother to correct himself. On his exit he glanced at Ms. Quetti Dave. He knew she was his daughter. He felt it in his bones. He counted Quetti when he counted his children, but he hadn't seen her since that day. Two years ago.

10

"It's Dee". Deanna answered.

"Hey girl. The kids are sleep. You got a minute?"

"Yeah. Whew. I'm tired." Deanna slid into a chair.

Carla and Ron's house was beautiful. The color scheme was warm browns, rust and greens. There were plants everywhere. Tall plants with big vibrant leaves filled large ceramic pots. The sofa and chair were chocolate in color. They were plush and gave you the feeling of dropping into the balls in the McDonald's play area. There was a Plasma TV attached to the wall and stacks of coordinating pillows beneath it. The area rug had a few pillows sprinkled on its back as well. There were no other pieces of furniture save a few wicker baskets containing slippers and socks for guest. The walls were filled with family pictures. There was a poster size black and white picture of Ronika with her head leaning to the right between a picture of Carla alone and on the opposite side a picture of the three of them. It was amazing how much she looked like Carla. The only thing she shared with Ron was his name. Ron was light brown, golden even, with chestnut brown eyes and dark brown hair. Carla was medium brown with black/brown, round, eyes and thin lips. Ronika was dark chocolate with the waviest hair and round puppy dog eyes (more black than white). She had long curled lashes and thin lips like her Mama. Her fingers and toes were identical to her mothers. Her complexion was her only individual trait. In addition she had a bubbly, kind spirit—like her mother. Ron was quiet and introverted. Carla had become mild mannered since Ronika's birth. Ronika was Carla before she was born. She was loud and robust. She had pizzazz. To be in her presence was entertainment at its best. After Ronika she just quieted down, got serious about life.

"Deanna have you told Troy that you're pregnant, yet?" Carla broke Deanna's concentration on the pictures.

"Yes. Girl I hate Troy. I know my baby's going to look just like him because I hate him."

"Let's just hope he don't act like him." Carla chuckled.

"He won't. I'll see to that. You know Carla; sometimes I regret not having an abortion. I mean my family is about to be destroyed. I have no choice but to leave." Tears rolled down Deanna's cheeks. "My husband is a whore and I can't live with that knowledge anymore. He's never going to change. I'm four months pregnant and he's so preoccupied with the next 'B' that he didn't even noticed and he's a doctor." Deanna started to cry.

Carla's heart was breaking. She didn't know what to do for her friend. She hugged her.

Deanna looked at the pictures on the wall. "Carla, we don't have any family pictures. Troy ain't never available to take one. You know how Ron will do little things for Ronika, bring her home a toy or something? Troy never do that." Deanna sobbed.

Carla wanted to tell her that Ron didn't either. She had been lying about Ron's dealings with Ronika. Ron never touched Ronika. He didn't treat her bad, but he didn't treat her like she was his daughter either. Carla never pressed the issue because she didn't know if he were her father or not. She spoiled her baby and tried to overcompensate for his lack of interest. That was the purpose for the pictures. She wanted to give the illusion of happiness. The only person on the picture smiling was Ronika. She and Ron were posing. She used Ronika's infant picture because that picture was before her color came in and she had that in common with Ron for a time. The others were in black and white to eliminate the reminder that Ron was so much lighter than "his daughter."

"Deanna, you don't have any proof that Troy's fooling around. You can—"

"He smelled like Caress soap the other day. Wildberry Extra Moisturizing Caress, Troy uses Irish Spring. He is gone more than ever, now. I guess he really likes this one. He is trying to juggle me, keep me, but I've known for a long time that Troy doesn't love me. I guess I was hoping that someday he would. Now I got two babies and no Daddy. No job, no money of my own and no education. How did I get here?" She had pulled herself together. Deanna knew it was time to change her fate. She wiped her eyes. Her strength was evident. She was strategizing and Carla knew it.

"I can't argue with that. What are you going to do?"

"I'm going to take care of me. I'm going to wean him out of my system. I'll sleep with him when *I* want to. I'll maintain until I build a life for myself."

Carla smiled. She was glad that Deanna had a grip on her situation. She wished she had a grip on hers.

Her sex life was great. Ron had not missed a beat in years. He had become a great lover. The only problem now was the alcohol. There were nights when he smelled like a brewery. Carla would have to hold her nose as he pounded inside of her. Mentioning it to him changed absolutely nothing. Carla knew that Ron had crossed the invisible line into alcoholism. It hurt to know that her husband had inflicted such a disease upon himself.

Her pain registered on her face.

"Are you okay Carla?" Deanna asked.

"Yeah." Carla could barely grasp her composure.

"Here I am going on and on about my stuff. Are you okay?"

"Yeah." Carla's tears slipped out of her eyes. She was fighting to hold them so hard her bottom lip was trembling. Her hands were shaking. Yet, she tried to stand and busy herself as if she were fine.

"Carla. You need to share this time. I'm always crying and opening up to you. Talk to me. I'm your best friend too. You're not just mine."

Carla fell back into the chair. She let lose a torrent of tears. Deanna cried too. Her heart was heavy. She didn't know what to do. Helplessness was heavy on her. She went to Carla and held her while she cried for a few minutes more. Finally Carla lifted her head.

"Dee, please forgive me." She broke down. "I'm soo—sorry for how I've treated you. So sorry."

"Carla you haven't done anything to me." Deanna reassured.

"Yes I did."

Have you been with Troy? Deanna's eyes asked.

"No. Dee. Nothing like that. I've been lying to you for a long time about my baby."

She's not Ron's?

"I don't know if Ron's her Dad." Carla turned away. She hated the way she would be looked upon in this situation. Not all women that are confused about paternity are sluts. Carla certainly didn't think she was a slut. She made a mistake. A bad decision, but she wasn't a slut. It had only happened once.

"Carla, what happened?" Deanna forgot about her own problems and focused on her friend. It was her turn to be a friend.

"Ron wasn't satisfying me at the time and well this guy, John, at my job was giving me attention. I had fanaticized about him, but it didn't go any further than that. Then one day our office had training across town and we carpooled over. Well, it so happened that he and I got left out of the carpool. So we decided to ride over together. We made small talk and I thought he was a decent guy. We were both married so I thought we were safe. The seminar let out earlier than expected. Management told us to go home from there. Well, that left us almost two hours of free time. We talked some more and ended up at a hotel, screwing like two teenagers. He drove me back to my car in silence. Later that night Ron came home and he was feeling frisky…how do you tell your husband no? I couldn't so we were together that night too. I haven't had a problem out of John at all. Even during my pregnancy he asked me once. I said no; this is my husband's baby. Neither of us have spoken of it again." Her lips trembled some more and she leaned into Deanna. "John and Ronika are the same complexion." Tears burst from Carla. She was still sobbing when the babies entered the room.

"What da matta you?" Ronika asked as she joined her mother in crying.

Ashley was crying too. She climbed up in Deanna's lap.

Carla sat up. Ronika climbed up in her lap too. All four of them cried while the adults tried to calm the little ones.

"I'm sorry Deanna."

"Don't worry about it. We'll figure out something."

"I don't want to know. I'm scared."

"I understand. I've got to leave Troy and you got to find out about Roni's dad. Even if you share it with no one else. You need to know."

"I'm so scared. That 's why I take so much off of Ron. He's cheating too. Cheating, drinking, probably cracking. He's changed so much. I think it's weighing on him as well. It would do my heart good to find out that it's his baby. Maybe he'll change if he knew for sure."

"He has doubts?"

"He hasn't said that, I feel it. I know that's why he won't fool with her. I do everything for her. Everything. Once when she leaned on him he moved."

"We are going to be okay. All of us." Deanna reassured.

They talked into the night while watching the girls play and feeding them raviolis. It was no big deal. Neither Ron

Patriece

nor Troy made it home that night. Deanna and Ashley arrived at their empty house at 10:30 pm.

11

Troy compared Asia to Deanna on his way home. Asia had gotten comfortable and let her guard down concerning her apartment. Looking for her keys, purse—bag was apart of her morning routine. She always had a pile of papers somewhere, a laundry basket of clothes that she smelled to determine if the clothes were clean or not. Dishes around the house. The dish drain was always full. She never washed dinner dishes until time to cook again. She used plug-ins to add freshness. She was completely opposite Deanna, yet he loved her.

He was ready to go home today. Three days was enough. He needed a break. Deanna cleaned, paid bills, cooked daily. She cooked 'pretty food', the kind you paid good money for in five star restaurants. And it was damn good. She read cook books like they were novels. She watched the cooking channels and she loved it. She read fashion magazines and was up on the latest fashions. Sometimes Troy didn't know if she wanted to be a chef or a designer. She was going for her AA degree when he met her. Instantly he knew she'd be better at taking care of him. Convincing her to quit school was a cinch. After a shopping spree, a dozen long-stem roses with a few mind-blowing compliments and some serious lovemaking, he proposed, knowing his presentation was irresistible. She fell easily. However Troy realized immediately that Deanna was not a punk. Her mother had simply yelled so much in her childhood that she refused to yell at all even when she was livid she talked in a moderate tone. Troy hated that. He preferred outburst that afforded him walkaway time. He never got that from Deanna, he just left. Sometimes he had to. She had the ability to make him feel real bad about most things.

She had done so recently and he knew it was time to stay home some. He'd already set things in motion with Asia. She believed he was going to be in Atlanta for a week and a half, possibly longer. He'd given her the number to an Atlanta Hotel where his friend at the front desk took messages for him and paged him whether he was there or not. *I'm sorry Dr. Arlington is in a seminar, I've been asked to collect his messages rather than have you them on his voicemail. May I relay your call?* Troy had used this hook up for many years. Tamara covered his butt without a heads up. She just liked him like that. That was great in case he could not make the call, he still had no worries.

Deanna had that "I'm getting tired of your mess" look when he walked in at a quarter to one in the morning last week. She didn't say a word, but he knew it was time to set Asia aside for a minute and take care of home. He wanted to offer a lie, but decided against it. This pregnancy had taken her patience down to nothing. She ate and slept when she wasn't taking care of Ashley and Ronika. Roni had been over more than usual. The truth is he'd gotten off of work at banker's hours. To secure his relationship with Asia he stopped by her apartment. She greeted him naked and made love to him until he was exhausted. He fell asleep and then at 12:00 am his Blackberry alarm woke him. He had set it to call a nurse in the ER and bid her a good night.

He Looked Like A Man, Until He Barked

She had a nice pair of hips siting on some slightly bow legs and he wanted to experience that—which meant he had to show some interest. He knew he'd have to work on her a little bit; she was hiding behind principles. He triggered his alarm again and pretended it was the hospital paging him. He left Asia at the door longing for his company.

"Baby, go back to bed. You don't need to be up. I'll be back. Nothing, but patients would pull me from *here.*" He touched her there and smiled. Then kissed her and bid her a good night.

Troy drove home feeling pretty good. Kelly was pleasantly surprised to hear from him. She even told him she knew he was married and she doesn't do that sort of thing.

"Technically I am married, but I'm also legally separated. Would I be watching you get to your car safely if I were in my marriage?" He flashed his headlights to make his presence known.

"What are you doing?"

"Making sure you got to your car safely. Women are not safe walking alone this time of morning." He knew she smiled. He knew she liked that. He knew she felt special.

"Thank you Dr. Arlington. Thank you so much. It does get scary sometimes, but I have my mace."

"I feel better this way." He smiled.

"Me too." She laughed aloud.

"Well, good night Nurse Kelly." He flashed his lights again and drove off.

Kelly buckled her seatbelt and pulled away from the curb. *Damn! I'm going to have to experience that up close and*

Patriece

personal. Only this time I won't let him get away before the ceremony or a baby, this time I'm doing the playing. She smiled.

12

The living room was a mess. The kitchen was a mess. The bedroom was a mess and the hampers were full. Asia was lonely again for the first time in a long time and she didn't like it. Troy's presence had become apart of her and she missed him. He'd called her back within 2 hours every time she left him a message with Tamara. The really nice desk clerk at the JW Marriott at Lenox Hotel, Atlanta, GA.

Troy had told her he'd be back in three days. The two weeks away had been hell for both of them according to his phone calls. Asia planned to clean up the house, at least pick up the house before he came home. Troy was different than Big Tony in that way. Big Tony complained and complained about her cleaning practices until she cleaned according to his standards, but it only lasted a week—max. Asia just wasn't into wiping on a house all day. She planned to LIVE her life, not *clean* her house all of her life. She was comfortable curled up on the couch watching LIFETIME Movie Network while a few dishes decorated the coffee table and a basket of clothes crowded the walkway with a pile of paper clutter sitting on the end tables. She could relax in the clutter as long as she had a blanket thrown across her body; where it came from the basket or the closet or the bed itself didn't matter. She just didn't trip on stuff like that. She was grateful that Troy didn't either. The only thing she obsessed over was the bathtub. She made sure it was clean at all times because she didn't want Troy to think she didn't take care of her personal hygiene. She did that very well. Tony always had a bath and clean, pressed clothes too. Where those clothes ended up at the end of the day was unimportant. On more than one occasion their clothes had mildewed right in the washing machine because Asia neglected to put them in the dryer. Once her dishwater was so thick it looked like mosquito larva because she'd put off washing dishes so long. It was near that again because since Troy left for Atlanta she'd been eating at Sheila's or eating out which meant that she had no need to wash the dishes.

Tonight she had Sheila's girls too and she still wasn't cooking and she certainly wasn't washing the dishes. Sheila had called and said she was going to pick up the girls in the morning because her date was better than expected.

Asia ordered pizza, requested delivery and curled up on the couch. She made a mental note of the book that slid behind the couch when she sat down, but she didn't bother to pick it up. Asia monitored the kids playing by ear until she heard silence too long. When she went upstairs they were asleep. Lil' Tony and Janay were on the floor and Jada was in the bed. Their little faces and hands were greasy. There was pizza on the floor and gummybears (jellybeans) smashed into the carpet. Jada was holding a Capri Sun container and what was left of it was spilled onto the comforter. The DVD was finished and just the blue screen was showing. Janay and Troy had no socks on and they were both drooling. Janay reminded Asia of Big Tony as she approached her. Her little eyelids didn't quite touch so she slept with her eyes open, as did Big Tony. Tears welled up in Asia's throat as the doorbell pulled her from the moment. Her heart hoped it was Troy, but she sensed that it wasn't. As she approached the door she heard Sheila talking on her cell phone.

Sheila came in and moved the blanket out of the way then flipped the pizza lid up. She retreated to the bathroom to wash her hands and on the way back she noticed the kitchen.

"Asia are you trying your odds with West Nile Virus? Girl you better wash them dishes."

"I know. I haven't felt like doing much since Troy left town."

"Well, honey if you want to keep Troy you better clean up this house. Men will tell you they ain't tripping off of this and that, but the minute you piss them off you're going to be a trifling bitch and you know it. So clean this mess up." Sheila grabbed a piece of pizza and slipped off her shoes and curled up on the other end of the couch after moving last weeks Sale Ads. The movie Love and Basketball was starting. "Turn it up. Let's watch this."

"What happened to your date?"

"Oh he wore a size 10 shoe. You know I like'em 12 and up. It wasn't worth my time. I didn't feel like having nobody playing with my girl tonight. I hate that!—start a fire and can't put it out, so I passed. He'll call again. Maybe next time."

"Let me put the kids to bed. They up there on the floor in pizza and toys."

Sheila rose to help her. When she saw the kids laying in piles of toys and the room a complete mess and their little hands sticky and faces greasy she laughed. "That's why the girls love coming over here. Every baby needs an Auntie Asia. You just let kids be kids. Girl I'd kill them about my room and their little butts eat at the table."

"They were watching a movie. Leave'em alone. I'll clean it up."

"Yeah right. I'll help you because when ol' boy get back he gon' leave you for this. This place looks like something on a "Cops" episode."

"It ain't that bad!"

"PLEAASE!"

They placed all the kids in Asia's bed after wiping them off and dressing them for bed. The kids slept through the whole procedure. Sheila thought briefly about her brother. He'd shared with her that Asia could let the house go, but she had no *real* idea what that meant until he passed. She often came and cleaned when Tony was a baby. She knew Asia loved her baby and would literally die for him, but she had no concept of cleanliness and babies. To look at Asia you saw a beautiful, free-spirited woman with energy and happiness that was contagious. She smiled all of the time. Even at the funeral Sheila remembered Asia smiling and thanking people for coming. Sheila was hurt at first, but her mother told her that Asia wasn't happy, she was nurturing. She wanted to comfort everyone else. She meant no harm. Sheila accepted that wholeheartedly a month later when she got the screaming call from Kaiser Hospital and learned that Asia was 13 weeks pregnant. Asia confirmed her love for her brother by her response to that pregnancy. She had no man, the baby had no father, her apartment was small, her job was

He Looked Like A Man, Until He Barked

not secure, her medical coverage was mediocre yet she was ecstatic about having Tony's baby. That memory brought tears to Sheila's eyes.

"What's wrong with you?" Asia asked reaching for her wine cooler.

"Just thinking about when you called me and told me you were pregnant."

"Oh. That was the best day of my life. I was so grateful to God that I got a piece of Tony. I needed him, even if he was in baby form. I needed that man."

"You don't need him now. (?)" Sheila tried to make it sound like a statement, but it was a question. She was not quite ready for Troy or anyone for that matter to replace her brother.

"Yes, I need him. Can I have him? NO. It hurts like hell, but it's my reality. I had a moment just before you came. Janay sleeps with her eyes open and I missed him."

"I know! I can't look at her asleep sometimes, it hurt so bad."

"I thought having someone in my life would stop the pain, but it didn't it just diverted it. This relationship is more contemporary. We live separately. We screw a lot. We don't argue, correct each other—nothing. I mean I know Troy does nice things and stuff, but Tony and I were friends. Tony was real good to me. We were that old fashioned kind of lovers. Tony and I used to have some knock out arguments and then race for the refrigerator trying to get the last Pepsi. Tony could tell me the truth and I could tell him we would be hurt or whatever, but we didn't say nothing at the moment. Like when he told me that my breath was foul and I should go to the dentist. I was so embarrassed. I wouldn't tell him though. I went to the bathroom and cried. When I did go to the dentist they took the tooth out and told me it was rotten beyond the root and was infecting other teeth. Tony never said a word to me, but he kissed me again and I felt loved all over again. I couldn't kiss him if he was ever yuck mouth." Asia laughed.

"You crazy girl. What's up with Troy?"

"He's in at Atlanta on business."

"Oh. Why didn't you go?"

"You don't like him do you?"

"I guess he's alright. I just…just… feel like something's amiss with him."

"All men are not dogs Asia. James wasn't a dog, he was an addict."

"The fifty or so brothers I've been with since he's been gone are. Forty-nine of them were married and the remaining one had nothing to work with. He couldn't cut the mustard or lick the jar."

"SHEILA! You so nasty." Asia tossed a pillow at her and a sock flew with it. They laughed until the movie soundtrack stole their attention.

Sheila and Asia slept on the couch, one on each end.

Asia missed Troy's pulse. She yearned Tony's love.

Sheila regretted not staying on the date. She craved the feeling of security and feeling like she was home, like she was loved, like her life meant something to someone besides her babies. The warmth of a man, his arms, his legs and his chest sheltering her for that while was worth it. So worth it she kept chasing it and no matter how long it lasted it wasn't enough. At some point every man let go. Sometimes he let go at the point of climax, sometimes he held on until morning, but always he let go. She wanted someone to hold her until it was all right, until her fear subsided. Until she felt safe, until she was sure, until she was calm, until—until—until…

13

Deanna's heart wouldn't let her believe that the two weeks that Troy came home no later than 6 p.m. weren't planned by him. In the past he'd told his mistress that he was out of town whenever he stayed home. She figured he was probably still doing it that way. Deanna couldn't shake that thought from her mind. The last time she busted him, she confronted the woman he was with and learned that information. His mistress was a gorgeous woman that could chose any man. Initially her beauty intimidated Deanna. Deanna approached her victim to victim, woman to woman, sister to sistah even, but the woman was so rude and obnoxious Deanna stayed with Troy just to spite her. In short she charged Deanna with his infidelity and told her *"If you were doing what you were supposed to be doing, I wouldn't be with him. I'm staying as long as he wants me and if that means permanently, eventually I'll wear that ring."*

Deanna didn't flinch. She excused her victim, her sophistication and summoned her ghetto persona. She laughed a hearty laugh then explained to Mistress, in her calm and stable tone, *"I— am his wife, you— are- my- helper. Let's not get it twisted. What-evah—I don't feel like doing, I let—you do. I'm not one to give head, so I leave that for you. I don't do feet and I don't rub backs, that's for you to do. I spend money, mingle with the family and friends, get all the reverence due a wife and you Cinderella stay in the dark, cold motel room waiting on MY HUSBAND, your chore. Whenever you get tired of helping me, and serving him, leave. I'm not going anywhere. And if you want a ring for*

He Looked Like A Man, Until He Barked

your services I'll—get you one. You're a good helper." Recalling that thought Deanna could hear the phone slam down all over again. Troy didn't have to leave that one alone. She dismissed herself. Deanna was really through with Troy then, but the thought of letting that one have him forced her to move forward with him. She was in a place of acceptance now.

She accepted that her marriage was over. She needed to position herself to take care of her babies. It was time to embrace the idea of single parenting. She hated the fact that she was pregnant, but she didn't hate the baby.

Troy had been attentive this past two weeks. Their lives resembled normalcy. They ate dinner together, watched TV, went shopping; he even went to Walmart. They took Ashley to the movies. He went to the Ultrasound appointment. He was even glad that it was a boy. They celebrated. He massaged her back and called on his way home from work so that he didn't have to go back out. Troy always looked for ways to get back out. Deanna almost believed that he loved her and that she was wrong about the mistress thing, but her faithful loving heart wouldn't let her.

"Hey Babe! What time do you arrive?"
"I'll be landing at 6:17 pm California time."
"Do you want me to pick you up?"
"No. No. That's too much trouble to have you coming to SF during commuter's traffic. I'll be straight there."

"Okay, but I don't mind. Tony's at Sheila's."

"No. Just relax. I'll see you in a little while. Let me finish packing."

"Okay love you."

Troy pushed the hang up button on his phone. Nurse Kelly was approaching and he couldn't let her hear a response like that.

"Hey Lady. How are you?"

"I'm good and you?"

"I'd be better if you dine with me."

"How do you know it's lunch time for me?"

"I checked your schedule."

"Isn't that some type of violation?"

"Only if you don't go to lunch with me?"

"What's the violation?"

"You'd be guilty of breaking a grown man's heart and sentenced to repairing it."

"What if I can't?"

"You can. You're a nurse."

"A nurse, not a doctor."

"I'll coach you over lunch, come on." Troy was comfortable swaying her by the arm into the parking lot and to his car. She didn't resist. They drove through Jack-N-Box due to the limited amount of time they both had. Troy promised her a real dinner tomorrow if she were up to it. She confessed that it was her day off and she had plans. Troy requested that she break them this one time.

Kelly had no plans. She was playing with his mind. She knew that Dr. Arlington was a good catch. He was handsome, well groomed, polite and mannerable. He got rave reviews from his patients and their families. She had even seen him cry once at the news that a child couldn't be saved. He wasn't sobbing, but he was human and he cried with that child's mother. She didn't know that he slept with her for a bout six months after that, just to help her cope. The mother knew that he didn't really care about her. She didn't care about him either. She just needed a man, any man to hold her through all of her pain. When she didn't want to play anymore she stopped calling and he stopped coming, that simple.

Kelly agreed to dinner the next day. She also planned to whip it on him like no other woman had ever. She was going to trap that man.

Troy dropped Kelly off and went back to work. At the end of his shift he stopped and got some flowers and some Chinese food. Two separate orders because Deanna was craving Chinese food. She'd left him a message earlier. He got two small bags of cookies for Ashley and Tony.

Troy walked in and stumbled over Asia's briefcase. The house was as neat as when he first met her, but not clean like home. It was tolerable. He sat the food down in the kitchen and Asia stepped from behind the door butt naked under a sign that said WELCOME HOME TROY. For a minute he shuddered at the word home. He wasn't home. He was at Asia's apartment. He knew things were getting out of context that the friendship was changing and he preferred it stay as sex buddies. That's what his head told him, but just like he couldn't resist Deanna's tears he couldn't resist Asia's sincerity. She really liked him. She liked him with the same strength that Deanna started with.

Troy lay on Asia while having the thoughts that he needed to pull back some. She was getting too close. He didn't realize that this time he was the one becoming attached. Kelly was fun, Deanna was convenient, Asia was the one he needed.

"Babe I gotta go."

"What?" Asia had just fallen asleep. It was 9:00 pm.

"I gotta work in the morning. You know how it is when you return from a trip. You gotta get settled in. I need to do a couple of things before work in the morning. Tomorrow I'll stay here."

"Okay." Asia threw the covers off of herself to see him out.

"Don't get up. Get your rest. Love you."

"Love you too." Her stomach quivered with intuition. Common sense told her *something ain't right here.*

"Hey Babe. I'll be there in a minute. The place was packed."

"Just come on Troy." Deanna was pissed.

"Okay. Love you."

"Love you too."

Troy dropped that lie on Deanna to justify the food being cold. He turned up the radio and sang with Chris Brown.

He Looked Like A Man, Until He Barked

Wendy's came into view *this will kill all questions*. The drive-thru was empty. Troy bought a large Frosty which would further explain his timely trip. He was close to two hours going to pick up an order that he called in before he left.

14

Deanna struggled to believe the things Troy told her. She knew he was a liar and a cheat and could not be trusted, but she had no solid proof that he was at it again. Her gut told her to position herself to take care of herself and her children.

This time it didn't hurt. It didn't feel like anything. She simply accepted that it was over between her and Troy. The decision to leave had been made—and when she busted him she was leaving period. She wasn't going to explain anything, talk about it or make any effort to stay. When it was over it was over and finally she was okay with that. She sat on the couch watching the cooking channel and taking mental notes on how to prepare a gourmet meal in 30 minutes. Suddenly out of nowhere it came to her. *I will be a Chef.*

Deanna scheduled an appointment for Wednesday. She got all the information, filled out the financial aid paperwork and turned it in. When the school called and informed her that she wasn't eligible for assistance and it would cost her approximately $9000 to attend she enrolled anyway with a $2000 deposit. It would cost her approximately $450 a month. Troy allotted her $300 for her pocket so she just need $150 more to fulfill her dream and take care of her children.

"Troy I need an increase in my checking deposit. The economy is changing and things are costing more."

"How much?"

He Looked Like A Man, Until He Barked

"I don't know, A hundred, two hundred? Can we afford that?"

"Yeah. I can handle that." He walked past her and sat on the couch. He was trying to focus his thoughts to home because earlier he almost called Asia "Kelly" and he couldn't afford to make a slip with Deanna at all. He was still thinking about Kelly now. She had seduced him and left him with his imagination. And even though he stopped by Asia's and relieved himself, he couldn't stop wondering what Kelly would have been like.

Deanna came into the living room and served him roasted chicken breast Dijon with Japanese breadcrumbs, Dijon mustard & Parmesan—roasted golden brown. With a tossed green salad of baby tomatoes and English cucumbers, coffee and warm double chocolate cake and a scoop of vanilla bean ice-cream for dessert. She joined him while Ashley sat in her highchair eating a plain hotdog and chips. She didn't like the day's special. Troy watched the Discovery channel and Deanna sat next to him bored. When the meal was over she cleared their trays started the dishwasher and retreated to the bathtub with Ashley in tow. Her waddle was beginning. She was entering her final trimester and counting down. She would start school two months after the baby was born. Carla had agreed to keep him and Ashley. Deanna would be going to school at night. In her effort to finish in one year instead of 18 months she would be going every night from 5-8 pm. Troy wouldn't even miss her. Rarely did he come home before 10 pm. She would have the kids in bed by the time he arrived. Unless he looked closely he wouldn't notice that anything was going on.

It wasn't that she was sneaking, but in her quiet time she reasoned that Troy liked her because she was easy to control. He suspected that as long as he provided for her financially she'd have to stay. And in some ways he was right. If she were to be honest with herself, she knew that she had turned a blind eye to his prior indiscretions because he provided so well for her and Ashley. She enjoyed maintaining a house and cooking as her sole responsibility. It afforded her unlimited quality time with her baby. Carla worked and barely got to see Ronika in comparison to how much time she spent with Ashley. Sometimes it unsettled her to know that her son wouldn't have that type of bond with her because she'd be on her own by the time he was able to realize what was going on. Daycare frightened her. That's why she propositioned Carla about keeping her babies. She trusted Carla. Carla had leapt for joy at the idea especially since they were exchanging services and she wouldn't have to pay daycare anymore. She needed the income because Ron was contributing less. Things were getting tight and she was starting to suffer when Deanna offered to start keeping Ronika now, before the baby came.

Carla pulled the covers over Ron and went to her bedroom. He'd been sleeping on the couch, every couple of days, for a few weeks. The alcohol was reeking and his conversation was slurred and random. Carla was hurting, but forgiving. She knew that people made mistakes. She had made a grave mistake herself.

15

Brian walked into the house lit by the light from the TV and smiled. Gabby was as predictable as the engine of a new car. He opened the refrigerator and found a plate covered in Saran wrap. The freezer held a Pepsi. Brian put his plate in the microwave then walked over to the other counter and grabbed a slice of cheesecake. He carried his plate into the living room where his TV tray was already set up.

Half way through his meal Gabby cracked her eyes open.

He smiled "Hey sleeping beauty? This is good. Did you make the cheesecake? "

"Yes. I got a recipe from Deanna."

"She can cook her butt off. You did good too."

"Thank you."

"You okay?" Brian noticed that Gabby seemed more down than usual. He decided to take her to the concert at Yoshi's this weekend. He had already gotten the tickets. He was debating on whom to take. With Gabby looking so down it must be her turn.

"I'm okay." Gabby tried to smile. She wanted to scream I am miserable! I am lonely! I am tired of living like this! And Deanna's pregnant again and I'm still not!"

"Come here."

Gabby pulled her blanket back and walked over to him. He moved the tray and offered her his leg. She sat down on his lap and he held her for a minute.

He Looked Like A Man, Until He Barked

"I love you so much." He squeezed her tighter. "We are going to be just like your parents. I bet they still do it." He chuckled into her neck as he kissed her repeatedly.

"I guess so." Gabby couldn't respond lovingly. She was thinking we're like them now. They started out with Daddy acting the same kind of fool as you and Mama being the same kind of fool as me. Gabby couldn't remember when their change came, but it came. The hope of Brian's change was fading fast.

"Baby, what's wrong?"

"Nothing." Tears began to fall from her eyes. She couldn't talk to Brian; he never did anything about her feelings. She'd grown hopeless in the area of communication. Gabby had started isolating and neither of them recognized it.

"Is it Deanna's pregnancy?" Brian figured it was. He knew how bad she wanted a baby. He wanted her to have one too. She was the reason he didn't deal with his children unless he absolutely had to. Once there was a baby in his marriage, maybe he'd acknowledge the ones he had outside of their marriage.

Gabby needs a baby. She would not be alone when I'm away if she had a baby. Mama Esther coped better with Dad's indiscretions because she had Gabby. A baby would make things so much better for me. He pondered.

"Brian I want a baby too. Everyone is having babies. I am in the world all by myself. I'm lonely. I'm depressed and I'm unhappy." She sobbed.

"Gabby you are not alone. I'm right here. Baby, I love you with all of my heart. I love you so much."

"Brian, pray with me. It will be okay if we touch and agree. Pray with me. You don't have to say anything, but 'amen' when I'm done. Amen means you're in agreement with everything I just said." Gabby was pleading with urgency. Brian didn't want to hurt her, but his belief system was not the same. He believed in a power greater than himself, but he didn't exactly deal with him like that. He just respected that he was real. Not exactly real for him, but he was okay with her believing and relying on God. His heart melted for his wife.

"Okay baby, okay." Brian soothed her with his voice.

Gabby dropped on her knees in front of Brian and immediately began to pray. She pleaded with God for a baby. She asked Him to restore her marriage and help Brian to be the husband she needed him to be. "In Jesus name, Amen".

"Amen." Brian mumbled.

Gabby heard it and she was glad. That was the first time Brian had prayed with her. The first time she stepped out on faith and requested that. In her heart she felt hopeful again. Brian got down on the floor with her and kissed her. He told her again how much he loved her and he wanted her to have his child. He said things that comforted her. She felt good all over. They talked for about thirty minutes with her in his arms. Both of them were at home and at peace. With the exception of Brian's plans to continue his behavior until he was forty, they were on the same page. She loved him and he loved her.

Gabby was hopeful that this was the beginning. Brian was hopeful that this feeling lasted longer than a few days for Gabby. She was starting to grow depressed or sad more frequently and it bothered him. He wanted her to be happy. Finally he told her about the concert tickets and she was happy. They laughed a little then finally Brian said, "Let's go to bed."

Gabby woke to an empty bed. The bathroom light comforted her. She knew that he was near. After a while she got up to check on him. As she approached the door she heard him talking. "I'm not coming over there for awhile. You know damn well, I have a wife and I'm staying home this week. Do what you gotta do." There was silence, then "kiss the baby goodnight and get yourself together. I'll see you when I can." More silence. "Okay. Bye."

Gabby ran toward the kitchen and hit the light switch as he opened the bathroom door. Within minutes Brian was standing behind her as she used a bottle of water to force tears back down her throat.

"You okay Baby?"

"Mhmp." Gabby was aching.

The rest of the night Gabby lay awake in her pain. She didn't know how to stop the pain, but she didn't know how to live with it either. She didn't want to die; she just didn't want to live.

16

Deanna was 8 months pregnant. There was no mistake about it. She and Carla and Gabby were going to lunch as opposed to having a baby shower. The fact that she wasn't going to be continuing her marriage took the joy out of public announcements.

Deanna didn't have any gas in her Volvo this morning so she took the Beemer.

"Troy, you are not going to believe this. Some kids have keyed your car."

"What!?" Troy tried to act like he didn't know the car was scratched. Not only did he know, but he knew the woman that keyed it. He'd contacted her and broke it off too. She was upset that he stopped seeing her when he got with Asia. He planned to leave her anyway; Asia just pushed it up a few weeks.

"Yes. Babe, it's bad. It's like they used it for scratch paper. They just scribbled all over it. Not like a scorned woman that basically is costing you money in a paint job, but scribbled like some grammar students."

"Motha—" He yelled rather convincingly.

"Troy, turn it in to the insurance and try not to be upset. It's done now."

"Alright. Try to enjoy your lunch."

"Okay, bye."

"Bye."

He Looked Like A Man, Until He Barked

At lunch Deanna and her friends chatted about their husbands. No one cried, but the pain was visible in each of them. They tried to have a good time. They really did.

Deanna finally said "Okay ladies, we are all in bad situations and we all deserve to remove ourselves from it. We only get one life and we should be happy."

"After this life, I don't want another one. After-life my butt." Gabby teased. No one heard the seriousness in her tone.

They joked with her.

"I think I'm the only one here that wants out. I don't love Troy anymore." Deanna admitted. "I care about him. I don't wish nothing bad on him, but I'm so done. Sooo done."

"I love Ron."

"I love Brian too. So much." Gabby starred into space.

"Okay, well what are you going to do to stop your pain?" Deanna tossed it out there. The waiter picked up their dishes and brought more coffee.

"I'm going to get a paternity test, but I'm so scared that Roni is not Ron's. I risk losing him either way."

"I'm going to be patient. Everyone says it'll get better and that Brian loves me too."

"I think Brian does love you, he's just a dog." Deanna offered.

"I think he loves you too. Brian is just playing cause its recess. When it's time to buckle down he will. I can tell by the way he looks at you it's love. Yours is easy. You just have to be patient." Carla stated. Deanna nodded in agreement.

"You just need a DNA test."

"How am I going to ask for that? Ron don't even know I slipped." Carla responded.

"You don't need to ask. You can send in their toothbrushes and they will test the saliva in them. I saw it on TV. In your down time google it. Finding out is not the problem. The results are what you need to ponder. Are you going to tell him if she's his? How you going tell him? What if she's not?" Deanna gently proposed.

Gabby faded out. She sat through the rest of the evening in silence. Smiling occasionally. Her friends were so preoccupied that they didn't realize that she wasn't participating in the conversation. Deanna gave them details of her plans to leave and how she was going to leave. She had already kicked the ball. She went to school for three hours a day. When she got out of school she picked up Ashley. In the morning she kept Roni so that Carla could go to work. It was working out fine.

"Deanna your food is so much better than this. I can't wait for you to graduate." Carla offered, pushing her desert aside.

"Are you going to open a restaurant?"

"If I do it will be called *Off Day Café* we all need a day off from cooking."

"That's cute. I like it."

"I do too, but it probably won't happen for a long time. Troy ain't going to put me through school and buy me a restaurant." They all laughed.

He Looked Like A Man, Until He Barked

Asia turned around when she heard Troy's name. There were only three women in the restaurant. One of them was pregnant. All of them wore wedding rings. All of them were good looking. Asia smiled at Gabby who smiled at her first. Then she paid for her and Sheila's food and left.

Struggling to control her imagination, she sat there. Wondering all kinds of things. She wanted to cry, but couldn't. She wanted to ask, but didn't want to know. It hurt to even consider that this was the same Troy. The courage to leave came too late. The women came out of the restaurant. They walked over to Troy's silver BMW with the ALL MIN license plate and the pregnant woman sat in the driver's seat as Asia's heart plopped into the pit of her stomach.

17

Asia couldn't bring herself to tell anyone what she saw, not even Troy. She needed to process it for herself first. Jumping to conclusions is always the wrong thing to do. Flying off the handle and making accusations is not the answer either. Her goal was to communicate her feelings and get a truthful answer. She didn't want to breed mistrust, start an argument or taint their relationship. She simply wanted to know who was this pregnant woman driving her man's car and why? In addition her heart wanted to know if he fathered the baby she was carrying?

Their relationship had been going on for close to 4 months and she looked about 8 months pregnant, which meant that her pregnancy was too close for comfort. The baby may have been conceived before Asia, but so close it didn't really matter to her. No woman is going to have a baby with a man she's not with. Asia wondered what was going on. She couldn't work. Her desk was cluttered and she was falling behind schedule. Troy had reached out a few times, but she ignored him, politely. She was careful not to show that she was in pain, careful not to indicate that anything was outside of normal concerning them. She decided to get through Lil' Tony's birthday celebration before she dealt with her feelings surrounding what she'd witnessed and Troy. Her first instinct was painful. It said that Troy wasn't whom he said he was, that she was going to end up hurt and that he'd made a fool of her. She crumbled at that thought. If that were the case it was such a cruel thing to do. She'd given him an escape. She was already willing to sleep with him. She recalled explaining to him that behavior was unnecessary. *Why? Why? Why?*

Troy had been spending all of his spare time with Kelly. It amazed him how things worked out for him. He didn't even have to dodge Asia while he pursued Kelly. He'd been seeing Kelly for almost two months now. It was time to start spending some quality time with her before she started tripping too. She wasn't as docile as Asia. Someone had hurt her before, possibly every man she dealt with. She showed signs of possessiveness. The signs didn't concern Troy because in his heart he'd resolved to ending things with her this weekend anyway. This was her last rendezvous.

Asia was the reason for his ending things with her. He wouldn't admit it, but he wasn't willing to lose Asia for dealing with Kelly. He blamed it on player's convenience instead of love. Asia was logically the best choice, because of her docile nature. Kelly was wild and unpredictable. Asia was easier to keep and maintain his marriage.

Sex was the thing that drew him to Kelly. It was the thing that drew most men to Kelly. She couldn't count her lovers, even if she used borrowed fingers and toes.

Dr. Arlington was the end of that part of her life. She intended to conceive and get married in that order.

Kelly hadn't swallowed a birth control pill since her last lover. She knew that her next lover would also be her baby's

Daddy if nothing else. She had monitored her ovulation with home ovulation kits for well over six months. Everything was in place. Her only problem was getting Troy to sleep with her without a condom. He explained to her that he used them for *her* benefit. And not one time in the two months did he forget or come unprepared.

"Babe, do we have to?"

"Yes, we have to." Troy reached into his wallet for the condom and tossed it on the nightstand next to the bed.

"Why? It's been so long. I want to feel you inside of me. How can we get closer with a condom between us." She pulled away from the kiss.

"That thin piece of latex can't stop me from getting close to you." Troy's erection was growing. Kelly turned him on. She was a different kind of nasty. She was unladylike with it and that was new for him. She didn't look like the typical slut. He never would've guessed.

"Dr. Arlington, I want your skin on my skin, your heat on my heat. I want to feel the friction between us, I want you to do me like a dog does his bitch." She purred.

Troy entered Kelly without warning. She knew it was coming, but she didn't know how abruptly. In two minutes it was over. Troy was embarrassed and couldn't believe that a few words stripped him of his experience. He knew to pace himself. He knew the *Ladies First* rule. Troy tried to redeem himself as he reached over and touched her there and then drew her nipple into his mouth.

He Looked Like A Man, Until He Barked

Kelly smiled. She had her moment before he touched her. The ovulation test was blue, and she hoped the pregnancy test would be positive.

18

The apartment was filled with balloons and streamers. Bob the Builder was the theme. Tony even wore an outfit similar to Bob the Builder's. "Happy Birthday to you! Happy Birthday to you! Happy birthday Dear Tony! Happy Birthday to you!" They all sang. Everyone was there. Asia's co-workers and Sheila's neighbors too. It was a grand party. Right before the opening of the gifts Troy strolled in with Ashley and Brian. Brian had two little boys with him also. Ashley was precious. She looked a lot like the lady driving Troy's car.

Asia had told no one of that incident. She'd gone home and cried her heart out. Troy had called several times; she had called him none.

He noticed that she was pulling back. He wasn't sure why, but he was expecting it eventually. He had been pursuing Kelly in their down time. Today he came to the party and brought Ashley, Brian and his boys too. This was the first time he'd seen Asia in close to a week. She was busy with the party planning every time he called or attempted to stop by. He realized again that he loved her when he made up his mind to risk bringing Ashley around her. Deanna was resting because the baby (TJ) was sitting on her sciatic nerve. He made it seem like he was considering her feelings when he took Ashley. Truth is he was trying to convince Asia that he was who he said he was.

Asia smiled. She was glad to see him. More so she was glad to see Ashley. The deal she made with her heart was

He Looked Like A Man, Until He Barked

that if he didn't bring his daughter to the party she would conclude that he was a liar, he was married and it was over. Ashley's presence meant (to her) that she was correct in not saying a word because there was a good explanation for his ex-wife, Deanna, driving his car.

"Hello, 'B'. These must be your boys." Asia greeted.

"Hey Asia. Yes, this is Brian and Bryant."

"You guys want some cake?" They nodded yes. Brian walked them over to the table.

"Hey Lady." Troy leaned in for the kiss. He pecked Asia's cheek and then introduced her to Ashley.

Asia picked Ashley up and walked over to the cake table without acknowledging Troy. Her pain was rearing its head and this was not the time.

They stayed for the entire party. Asia and Ashley were like a mug and some coffee. They fit perfectly. Ashley cried for Asia when it was time to leave.

Brian noticed Sheila. He was into her like plant roots are into soil. He liked her. She reminded him of Gabby when she was stronger. Lately, Gabby appeared frail, weak and blah.

Sheila had a body that made him think sinful thoughts. He eased over to her and introduced himself. "Hello, I'm B. How are you?" He extended his hand.

"I'm 'S', and I'm fine. You?" Sheila smiled.

"I'm good. Did you say S?"

"Yes. You're B, right?" Sheila flirted with her eyes.

"Ah, man. You tripping."

"No I'm not. I'm playing the game too."

Janay walked up crying. "He hit me! My happy birthday! My happy birthday!"

"Who hit this baby?" Sheila bent down and picked her up.

"Ony! Hit me!"

"Nay-Nay it's his birthday. You have to wait." Sheila cooed while walking away from Brian. It wasn't that she wasn't attracted to him; she didn't know how to handle the attraction. 'B' was the kind of man she could love. Sheila was out of the business of loving a man. The attraction tickled her keloid. She knew that she would end up hurting if she fooled around with him. His smile represented pain to her. Sheila dealt with men she wouldn't be able to commit to.

"My happy birthday! My happy birthday!" Janay stretched out in Sheila's arms.

Brian was undisturbed by her walking away. He had enough women in his life already. The truth is he didn't want them. He wanted to love his wife. He wanted to ease her pain; it was becoming so evident in her life. Observing her deterioration made him wonder if he should change his behavior now. Actually he had tried several times without success. Pursing women had become a habit for him. The funny thing is, it was no longer enjoyable. He was ready to settle down. His intuition told him that Gabby needed him to settle down. Immediately his mind told him she was fine.

His love for her brought him home two times a week as oppose to one. Gabby needed seven days a week if she were to save herself, yet she couldn't articulate it.

He Looked Like A Man, Until He Barked

She was functioning in a robotic state. She appeared normal. Yet, she had slipped into an unreachable place. The scary thing is she wasn't afraid; she was comfortable there.

Brian gave Troy no grief about bringing Ashley to the birthday party. He recognized that Troy loved Asia in return. His hope was that she would be there when he was ready, as his Gabby would be there for him. Brian was glad that Sheila didn't give him the time of day. He made up his mind to start releasing his women and love his wife. Troy's expression of love for Asia freed him.

After the party Troy realized that Asia really was pulling back. Her behavior indicated distrust. He thought that he was willing to let her go. Women had left him before. Leaving was a part of the game. Kelly would simply fill the gap when Asia finally did break away.

Whenever he thought about things coming to a close with Asia, he ached. The ache was foreign because he never really cared about one person before. Troy had never been in love. The feelings he had for Asia were real. He fought to label it as something different, but it was love. It was different with Asia—she was under his skin. So many times he'd heard his uncles and friends bragging about *the one that got away* and how, if they could do it over again they wouldn't let her go. He knew Asia was everything he needed in a woman. She made him feel good. Her love was safe. She was missing that bitterness that most women had. He was grateful that Big Tony had been kind to her. Tony's kindness afforded him the kind of love most people dream about. Asia trusted him. She didn't question him or look for loopholes in his statements. She had no scar tissue to remind her of past pain that would make her tense up in the relationship. It was bliss.

As Troy pondered these thoughts, feelings rose up in his spirit. He smiled. He loved her. Without warning he dialed her number.

"I miss you, Baby. What's up?"

"Nothing." Asia responded. She missed him too, but she couldn't shake Deanna's image from her head.

"You sound down. You okay?"

"Yeah," she sniffed. "Uh-uh. Troy I saw a pregnant lady driving your car last week."

Troy's heart plunged into his gut. The panic he felt was unexpected. Urgently he scrambled his Brian for a logical explanation. The end was threatening to begin and suddenly he wasn't ready. Desperation found a lie and started trying to sell it.

"That was Ashley's mother, Deanna. Her car was broken, and she was meeting friends for a little baby shower. I was keeping Ashley while she went, so I let her use my car." He crossed his fingers hoping that he'd kept his tone confident and believable.

"Why couldn't she get her car fixed?"

"It stopped in front of my house, when she was dropping off Ashley. She was already running late. I didn't think anything of it."

"Did you fix it too? "

He Looked Like A Man, Until He Barked

"Yeah. Her man is out of town. She's pregnant. She could use the help. I didn't think anything of it. We are adults and we are both with other people. She's getting re-married."

Asia started to calm down. "Troy, that didn't feel good at all. You can't let me stumble on stuff like that. The right thing to do in those uncomfortable situations is let me know, even if it is after the fact. Don't have me looking stupid. I thought you were her baby's father."

"Baby I'm sorry. I'll keep you posted from now on."

"It's okay. I was so scared. I thought all of this was a game."

"No games. Just Your man helping a friend. Deanna and I are better friends than spouses—we know that."

"Troy I'm so glad that isn't your baby. That's the one thing that was hurting the most. She looks about 7-8 months pregnant, and I've been with you at least 4 which would mean you were with both of us at the same time."

Troy didn't realize she was keeping track.

Deanna was due any day. "I'm Ashley's Daddy."

Troy jerked in fear. There was a little tap on his thigh. Ashley had apparently awakened.

"Iwana go. Mommy go. Daddy go. Atley go. Iwana go. C'mon. Iwanago." Ashley whined.

Troy handed her his forbidden pen. His heart was beating like a drum roll. Deanna's footsteps could be heard coming down the hall. Deanna stopped—the bathroom door closed. While the baby was fascinated with the pen, he ended his call with Asia. "Babe I gotta go. There is money in my sock drawer, treat yourself." He hung up.

Patriece

If it were anyone else Asia would have been mad about the hanging-up in her face. Troy was at work so she understood his urgency.

"Troy you ready? Ashley is. She woke me up." Deanna entered the room.

"Yes. I'm ready."

"Thanks for taking the day off to go with me to the doctor and take this little lady to the movies."

"No problem. He's my son too. I can't wait to see him. Thanks for meeting me half way on working things out." He kissed her.

"No problem." Deanna mocked. Today, this moment, she was okay with her marriage. *Don't trust him. You can't trust him. You'll get hurt again if you do. He's a liar. Don't trust him.* Deanna kissed him back. The Arlington's buckled up and headed to the obstetrician to make sure TJ was okay.

19

"Deanna, how do I get Roni tested?" Carla was crying.

"Are you okay? I'm on my way." Deanna hung up and bundled up Ashley. They loaded into her car and drove straight to Carla's.

Carla opened the door. Tears stained her face. Sobs burst from deep in her gut. Deanna just hugged her. The girls cried and screamed for attention at their knees. Neither woman addressed them. It was a time for healing. They needed to help Carla, not Roni, not Ashley.

"What's wrong baby? What happened."

"Ron is using drugs. I found a syringe in my room. He has condoms in his pant pockets and inside jacket pockets. He's been staying out all night. He goes to clubs almost every day, even on Sundays. This is my fault. I know the question around our baby turned him away." She cried.

Deanna started crying too. "Carla, that's not your fault. Ron is a grown man. He made the choice to do all of that stupid mess. We are over thirty. Anybody that starts using drugs this late in the game is doing it because he wants to. He saw as many crack-heads for as many years as we did, he knew better. He made a conscious decision to get involved with that. Ron needs help, true, but don't blame yourself."

"I feel like if I come clean and prove Roni's his child, we will be alright." Carla reasoned.

"Maybe, maybe not. Men don't accept babies the way we do, but I agree you need to find out."

"Is Ron using drugs or drinking or both?"

"Both, I guess."

Carla went to the bathroom and got some tissue. Roni followed her. Deanna picked up Ashley and laid her in the middle of the floor with a "Dora the Explore" video. Ashley started watching. When Roni came back she ran and sat on the pillows too. Carla got them some puzzles and dolls and dropped them on the rug with them. Deanna sat at the kitchen table. She was having some vaginal pressure and knew that TJ would be here soon.

"Where's your laptop?"

"In my room."

"Get it."

Carla came back with the laptop and sat it on the kitchen table. The kitchen was also brown and cream and copper. The pictures were beautiful.

She sat down. Deanna GOOGLED *"Home DNA Testing Kit"*. Finally they found a company that carried the home testing supplies. Everything was done via mail. Upon receipt of payment, the buyer would receive two biohazard bags and two sterile Q-tips. They are instructed to return the Q-tips or toothbrushes of the testing parties with the bags and receive your results. Deanna ordered the kit. She had them delivered to her house. The evening was spent soul searching, venting and problem solving. Carla understood that she had nothing to do with Ron's behavior. She loved him with all her heart and while talking, she prayed for his safe return from his nightly excursion.

He Looked Like A Man, Until He Barked

God please let Roni be Ron's baby and deliver him from drugs and alcohol. Restore my marriage in Jesus name Amen.

Ron unbuttoned her blouse and kissed her breast. She moaned and groaned like they were in a bed and not in an alleyway. When it was over, he walked back toward the club. A minute later red and blue flashing lights blinded him. Cops ran past him and into the alleyway where her next patron was receiving oral sex. Ron watched, as they were both placed in police cars. It sobered him. He realized that that could have been him. He dealt with these women to build up his esteem around sex. They didn't care how long it lasted just that they were paid. He couldn't deal with them without drinking, and he couldn't face Carla after dealing with them without another drink. Drinking was the root of his problem, not his sexual abilities. He stayed too drunk to realize that his wife enjoyed being with him.

Ron loved his family—his Roni was the most precious thing in his life. He'd die for his baby. He made up his mind the minute she plopped out. Sure his buddies had given him a hard time about her complexion, but he didn't care. His Daddy, Roni's granddaddy, was ink black too. Most people forgot about him because he was such a hell raiser, and he'd been dead for at least 34 years. This was as many years as Ron's been alive. In his mind, she simply got her color from his Daddy. Ron ached at the recollection of pushing her away to keep her from smelling the scent of another woman on his body and alcohol on his breath. When he looked up he saw Carla watching, and he knew she misunderstood his moving away from Roni. It was in her face. He couldn't explain it so he left. He went to the club and got drunker.

The thought of being arrested and the humiliation that would go along with that hit him so hard, he prayed. *God, help me get my life together. Help me satisfy my wife and be there for my daughter. Restore my marriage in Jesus name, Amen.*

Carla and Ron's prayers were prayed simultaneously. Each of the prayers was heard. Neither of them was aware of the love they shared or the strength of it. Theirs truly was love.

Carla saw Deanna and Ashley to the car. It was almost midnight. Deanna offered to stay over, but Carla insisted that she go home. She couldn't handle the embarrassment of Ron staggering in any minute. Deanna didn't argue. She figured as much, and the baby was giving her major vaginal pressure. Her contractions were coming 45 minutes apart. Her due date wasn't for another two weeks.

Troy was home when she arrived. Deanna walked over and felt the hood of his car, and the hood was warm. The car had recently been painted so her handprint on the hood was evident. She wiped it off with the sleeve of her jacket and proceeded inside. Troy was in the chair with one shoe on and his eyes closed. He pretended he was asleep. Deanna knew that she had walked in just before he could finish getting undressed. "Troy, you better get to bed if you're that

He Looked Like A Man, Until He Barked

tired. I saw you pull in a minute ago." Deanna lied. She just wanted to nip his lie in the bud. She went upstairs and laid Ashley down without any further thought. Troy chuckled at her. She was so up on his mess.

Deanna packed her bag for the hospital.

The room was darker than usual. It was the height of night. Deanna was writhing with pains. Her plan this time was to wait until she absolutely had to go before she left. She'd gotten up and showered. For some reason she plucked her eyebrows and made sure they were perfectly arched. In between pains, she applied her natural tones of make-up. She lined her lips and used her clear gloss. When she looked in the bathroom mirror, she was pleased.

Ashley and Troy were still asleep. Troy had the cover pulled up to his waist with the top of his body exposed. He was not a model, but he did have a nice body. His wheat colored skin was noticeable even in the dark. Deanna reached the foot of the bed and retrieved her bag. She tiptoed back into the bathroom and slipped into the clothes that she planned to wear to the hospital. A maternity dress that buttoned up the front and a pair of slides. She brushed the edges of her hair back and put mounds of gel across her hairline, front to back, then brushed her hair into a ponytail. She decorated her ear lobes with her diamond studs. With the exception of her exaggerated nose size, she looked normal.

This time Deanna opted to attempt Lamaze. She settled in downstairs on the couch. Her technique required her headset. Earlier in the month, she and Carla had burned some CD's for the occasion. The CD's started out upbeat, then eased into jazz and ended in encouraging gospel beats. The gospel songs relayed the message of strength and triumph. They even made one for the ride home. It included songs of celebration and clarity. Deanna plugged in her headset and listened. She repositioned herself repeatedly. Never staying in one position for longer than fifteen minutes. For hours she endured growing pains.

The sun rose, and she decided to call Carla.

"Hello?"

"I think it's time."

"Oh my goodness. You want me to come get the baby or are you taking her to your Mom's?"

"Can you come. My Mom wanted to go to the hospital."

"Sure I can come. Now?"

A pain ripped through Deanna. Her legs quivered even though she was sitting down. She couldn't answer.

"I'm on my way."

"Okay." Deanna whispered.

Troy rounded the corner from the hallway into the family room. He smiled at Deanna sitting on the floor amidst a mass of pillows. She had it looking like the linen section at Walmart. As he approached her, he saw the familiar look of pain. "Is it time?"

Deanna nodded yes. "Call my Mother and 'em"

"Okay. What about Ashley?"

"Carla's on her way."

"Where's your bag?"

" By the door."

"Can I tape it this time?"

He Looked Like A Man, Until He Barked

"I don't care." Deanna was trying her best not to yell out, but it was hard. The pain was ridiculous. "Hurry up, please. Hurry up."

Troy had never seen Deanna like this. She started crying. Again he went soft. He raced up the stairs and put a coat and shoes on Ashley. That's when he heard the knock on the door. Assuming it was Carla, he opened the door and started to run back up stairs to tend Ashley. Instead of Carla, a rather tall man entered the house, and a petite woman was on his heels. Next to enter was Carla. Everyone was moving swiftly. The paramedics followed the moaning sounds straight to Deanna. Carla directed Troy to Deanna, and she ran upstairs to Ashley.

"I pushed." Deanna tried to explain.

The gurney and more paramedics were coming in at that exact moment. They lifted Deanna up and saw that her water had broken. "Mam are you still pushing?" Deanna nodded yes. "I can't help it" she whispered.

They ripped open her dress and cut her underwear off. To everyone's surprise TJ's head was lying in the crotch of his Mom's panties. Deanna started to push again. TJ's head moved forward enough for the paramedic to see that the cord was wrapped several times around his neck.

"Don't push. Stop, stop, stop." She called to Deanna.

Deanna kept right on pushing. There was no stopping, her body had a mind of it's own. The gurney started rolling quickly out the door. Everyone ran. Troy, Carla and Ashley were already crying. Troy couldn't get in the ambulance before it drove off. He jumped in his car and followed. Carla

Patriece

rode home with Ashley with a heavy heart. No one realized that the front door was left wide open.

20

Sheila had gone to church out of desperation. It was time to ask God for deliverance from anything that wasn't of him. She had been to church before and she promised God that if He let her out of her marriage without drama, she would surrender to His will. Once she received her divorce decree, she went to church twice to settle that debt. After that, she went on to enjoy her freedom, thus ending up sitting across the table from a woman with a confirmed appointment with the Grim Reaper.

The meeting place was Apple Bee's in Hayward. The stranger sat in the corner near the exit sign. The lady was nice looking. She was in professional attire and appeared sensible. She explained to Sheila that their lover, whom they also shared with his spouse, was a carrier of the Aids virus. The woman had contracted the virus from him. His wife also had the virus and was currently hospitalized. He apparently is responding to the disease better than his partners are. Aside from his sleeping an unusual amount of time, it is not detectable in him.

Sheila had just begun dealing with him. They had yet to graduate to the no condom comfort zone. She'd slept with him three times and each time with a condom. The frightening thing is that she had decided that tonight she wasn't going to insist that he used protection. (She had plans to see him tonight). He always smelled nice and, she'd never seen dirt under his fingernails or smelled his feet. So, he'd passed her "cleanliness" test.

The thought that she was dealing with a man that was infected with a lethal disease made her break down at the table.

The stranger told her "Don't be so hard on yourself. You came to hear me out. I called three other women in his phone book, and they were unwilling to meet with me, I left messages with this information on their answering machines. I feel that he should've told them, but if not him, then me. They needed to know." The lady cried.

Sheila was in shock. She couldn't believe it. Maybe this woman was lying? There was something about the sadness in her soul that came through with seriousness, urgency, fear and truth. Sheila knew that she was telling the truth— in the back of her eyes she held regret.

As if she could read Sheila's mind she started "All I did was neglect to protect myself from something that I wasn't supposed to have anyway. I go to church faithfully. I know better. I ain't married. Sex ain't even for me; it's for married people. That's all I did. The cold thing is everybody else is doing it too."

Sheila nodded in agreement and lost a tear of recognition and empathy. This woman was dying for partaking in a liberty that wasn't hers to partake in. Finally Sheila spoke through her tears. "I'm so sorry. I appreciate you calling me; God knows I do. I was about to neglect to protect myself with him too. He looks so clean."

"It ain't his body that's dirty; it's his blood. How could you know?"

He Looked Like A Man, Until He Barked

"I didn't need to know. I needed to keep my legs closed." There was silence for an uncomfortable moment. They embraced and Sheila paid the tab. Their goodbye was brief, and the stranger disappeared as quickly as she appeared.

On the way home, Sheila had to stop curbside and compose herself. She couldn't let her girls see her like this and Asia either. Asia had warned her to be careful, because she could catch something that did more than 'stank and itch'. She'd laughed then, but now it wasn't funny. She realized that what started as pleasure had become a near death experience for her.

As she approached the traffic light just before the turn that led to Asia's, apartment, her cellular beeped. At first glance, she recognized his number and following it was 700, which meant the time he'd be by her house. If she dialed back and typed in 700 then he'd know it was okay. If not he'd try later. Sheila dropped the phone back into her purse and made a mental note to get a new number tomorrow.

Sunday morning, Sheila and her girls were at Truth and Light Holiness Church. She was trembling with fear. She walked into the church and slipped onto the last pew. An usher approached her. "Come on baby. We reserve our front row for visitors. We want to make sure you have a wonderful time in the Lord." The light from her smile warmed Sheila. Her eyes were so enduring. Sheila became embarrassed to be in her presence. She and the girls stood and followed the little lady that she guessed was 4'10" tall to the very front row. She sat down. There were no distractions for her. Her only view was the pulpit. She thought to herself, I just wanted to slip in, ask for help and forgiveness, and go home. This is too close for comfort. The woman next to her seemed as intimidated as she was by the front row seating.

The organ began to play. The church was coming to order. There was singing and praising and then the introduction of the Pastor. When the Pastor graced the pulpit, Sheila was taken aback. The Pastor was so fine. He was the direct cause of the sin, Lust, attending service every Sunday morning. He was an Adonis—the picture of perfection. It seemed as if he were chiseled from Beauty itself. It seemed sinful to look at him.

Pastor Knowit opened his mouth, and the church fell silent. His voice commanded your attention. His words of wisdom dripped with experience. He knew; had experienced first hand, the things he preached about. He was definitely a biblical scholar, but he also knew the streets of Oakland just as well as he did the gospel. Pastor Knowit was more than an ex-everything. He was a sinner of the highest rank. His hands had touched six of the seven sins at some point. The only sin that he had not committed was murder and even that he came close to. It was the gift of grace that kept him from it.

Sheila had to check her motives for attending service. Realizing that it was her sexual behavior, lust and irresponsibility around her body that got her there. She tuned in to the message.

Ironically Pastor Knowit talked about near death experiences. How they are a call for change. Sheila was all ears. She fished a piece of paper from the bottom of her purse and

He Looked Like A Man, Until He Barked

wrote the scriptures on the back of it below a male's phone number. She doubled back and scribbled through his number until it was completely illegible.

She wept during church. Her gratitude was shameless. Her babies cried with her, but only because she cried. They did not know why they were crying, nor did they know that this was the beginning of the answer to their little prayers.

21

In the beginning, having two women was great. When he added Kelly, it was mind-blowing. Everything was going smooth for him until his job started demanding more of his time. Now, all the juggling was wearing him down. It seemed like the women in his life were pulling at him at the same time. A lot of energy went into safeguarding Deanna because of her marriage license. He had respect for "half". It seemed to him that the system favored women, especially, women with children. He also knew that Deanna thought things through and would probably end up with 60%, knowing her. It just wasn't worth it.

He felt his time with Asia was limited. He didn't think she would have him once she learned the truth; the truth was near. If she left—Kelly simply got promoted.

Kelly blowing up his phone while his son's life hung in the balance helped him to appreciate that something had to give. As soon as the crisis around his son was over, he was going to dump Kelly. Hopefully, she would go quietly. He didn't know what to expect from her. Troy hadn't bothered to investigate her character. They got together for the sole purpose of having sex.

The back to back calls revealed to him that Kelly was going to be trouble. She couldn't grasp the concept of "unavailable" in spite of his selecting "ignore" on his cell phone every time it rang. TJ was his focus. Not even Deanna, but TJ.

He Looked Like A Man, Until He Barked

Kelly couldn't think of anything more important than her baby—joy kept her from anger. She hoped it was a girl so that she could continue her love affair with the color pink. Her entire home was pink. The kitchen's window treatment was pink scarf style curtains accentuating custom wooden white shutters. The appliances were chrome. The table was chrome with a glass top. The chairs were covered with custom-made pink upholstered pillows. The pictures were hand drawn stills that Kelly had drawn her self.

The living room was a spin-off of the kitchen. She had a soft pink sofa and a mint green chair with white striped throw pillows. The stripes were pink, white, green and cinnamon brown with the cinnamon stripe being the smallest. The table in this room was also chrome and the walls were covered in watercolors painted by Kelly herself. The paintings burst of the same color scheme and rested in silver or chrome frames. Above the sofa were four pictures, two on top and two on bottom. They created a perfect square. One picture was of a pair of lips with pink lipstick. The one beside it was a pair of hands with clasped fingers wearing pink polish. The one below it was a pair of feet dangling from crossed legs with toes polished in pink. The fourth picture was of a pair of eyelids with long lashes and shades of pink, silver and green eye shadow.

The bedroom and bathroom were also pink. The plans she had for her daughter's room was in the makings. Even

Patriece

the EPT that she purchased indicated a positive result with the show of two pink lines.

This was her sixteenth time in a row trying to call Troy. She dialed Troy again. This time the phone went straight to voicemail, which meant his phone, had been turned off deliberately. *Where is he? He's not at the hospital. He's not answering the phone. This is not the time to start trying to distance yourself. This is our beginning!*

22

Brian had made a similar decision regarding the women in his life. He had gotten rid of all but one in the past two weeks. The decision came after finding Gabby at home ill. She managed to take care of Brian as if nothing was wrong. All his needs were still being met. The only difference he'd noticed is that she smiled less and less. He overheard a conversation on the phone one day where she jokingly said, "Girl, I'd get his undivided attention if I were dead, if but for a moment." Her laughter was so brief it scared him. For the first time he saw her pain, felt it and wanted to do something about it. Love for her swelled so big in his chest, his breath was caught up in it. He inhaled deeply and stayed home that night. Gabby didn't even realize he was there. Apparently after that conversation she swallowed a couple of sleeping pills and laid on the couch. Brian's clothes were laid out for tomorrow, his dinner was made and tray set-up in the living room before she had the conversation. All she had to do was take the pills and relax.

Brian had no idea that the days that Gabby stayed home were spent watching divorce court, negative male-bashing movies on television, and listening to music that validated her state of hopelessness. He got his tray and watched TV in the living room with her. He loved her from across the room all night. She never knew he was there. That morning his lips touched hers several times. Each time harder than the last as he bid her a good day. Gabby never even flinched. She was under the influence of 6 sleeping pills. The directions sug-

Patriece

gested two, but two no longer worked for her. Brian had no idea of her addiction to sleeping pills. No one knew.

On his drive to work his phone rang. "'B'. Man I'm at the hospital, Kaiser Oakland. TJ's coming and the cord's around his neck." The phone went dead.

Brian turned his Benz around and headed towards Kaiser Oakland.

Gabby woke up, made a cup of coffee and swallowed two more sleeping pills.

23

Troy's phone went straight to voice mail for Asia too. Her heart broke. Troy had promised to take her and Lil' Tony to the movies to see Cars. Lil' Tony was so excited. He was wearing his Cars tennis shoes with the lights. He was carrying his Cars backpack too.

At twenty minutes 'til the start time of the movie the phone rang. Asia answered immediately, hoping it was Troy.

"Hey Lady. What y'all doing?" Sheila sang into the phone.

"Getting ready to go see Cars."

"We are too. Yall going with Troy?"

"Nope. Just us." Asia tried to sound upbeat. She knew Sheila would give her a hard time otherwise.

"Wanna go together?" Sheila asked. In her studies of the bible she'd learned that it wasn't necessary for her to slap Asia with doubt. Especially since she discerned that Troy had already done that. (Neither of them knew that Troy really was going to take them to the movies.)

"We'll met y'all there. The movie is about to start."

"Okay." Asia smiled. She was grateful for Sheila's pass, plus she wanted to see her. Lately Sheila had been at church one night a week and on Sunday. Entertaining had come to a complete halt. Sheila had even changed her telephone number. She'd always dressed nice, but her new look was very classy. There was nothing provocative about it, yet it was still attractive. She seemed calmer and collected. It was as if she'd changed. Sincerely changed. This was different than her encounter with the church after her divorce. This time she was genuine.

By the middle of the movie Janay and Tony were asleep. Jada was nodding.

Asia was hurting. She couldn't believe that Troy stood her up again. He always seemed to have a hospital emergency when it came time to make good on a date. A public appearance. Asia's intuition always reminded her of the pregnant woman driving his car. She had let it go, but she had not forgotten it. The woman was so comfortable in his car.

If they were about to leave, why was she using his name in a sentence? Why was she still talking about him at the end of her gathering? It didn't make sense. If it were a matter of her using his car and they were just friends like he said, then she would have informed her friends when she got there about her car and why she was driving his. She would not still be talking about him at the end of the day. Is that Troy's baby? But why would he lie? Asia thought.

"Are you ready?"

"Yeah."

"You okay?"

"Yeah."

"Thinking about Troy? Men will be men. He can only hurt you if you let him, Asia. I used to think I was protecting myself by using them before they used me, but I was foolish. Girl, all I was doing was subjecting myself to fatal diseases.

He Looked Like A Man, Until He Barked

Placing my kids in position to be raised by someone other than me and living without a Mother's love."

Asia blinked back tears.

"We don't have to talk about it, but if you ever want to I'm here." Sheila leaned over and picked up Janay and balanced her on the floor. Then she tapped Jada and balanced her too. Asia stood up Lil' Tony. Once the kids were fully awake they walked out of the theater. "Next stop McDonald's!"

"E-I, E-I-O!" Lil' Tony sang while jumping up and down. The adults laughed. He always screamed the Old McDonald chorus when he heard the name McDonald.

24

Having worked in the hospital before got Dr. Arlington no special treatment. He double-parked in front of the ER as the Security Guard yelled that he couldn't park there. Troy was not a staff Dr. today. Today he was a frantic family member behaving irrationally. How was the ambulance going to get through with other patients, just as important as his TJ, if he didn't move his car?

"Dr. Arlington, you gotta move man." The guard sympathized, but insisted. Troy tried to rush past him.

The guard stepped into Troy's path. "Doc, it'll be towed or wrecked in thirty minutes or less. You gotta move. I'm sorry about your baby Man, but you gotta move."

Troy looked at the parking lot, he knew that his car couldn't stay there. He looked at the guard. Without his asking the guard responded. "I can't leave my post. Man, you can't do nothing for him now. Just pray and hurry back to be with your wife."

Troy turned around and jumped in his car. He rushed out of the parking lot as the words rang in his ear, *Man; you can't do nothing for him now. Just pray and hurry back to be with your wife. Man, you can't do nothing for him now. Man, you can't do nothing for him now.* A park came available just outside of the ER driveway. Never were there parks right there. Troy took that as a sign and swooped into it, cutting in front of oncoming traffic. Vehicle horns blew and brakes screeched. He didn't even notice. *Man, you can't do nothing for him now.* He attempted to enter the medal detector. The buzzer went off.

He turned around and ran back to the double doors. When a nurse friend saw him she hit the red button inside to open the ER doors. The button was for the Paramedic's delivery of patients on gurneys. Troy ran through. Right there in the middle of the floor, TJ was being delivered. Troy could see his little face. He was an ashy pale color and his lips were a shade darker. Deanna was still pushing in spite of the directives. She struggled not to, but she was pushing.

"STOP PUSHING, Damn it!" Troy screamed.

Deanna looked at him with half open eyes. She wasn't trying to push, she wasn't trying to kill her baby, but she could tell by the expressions of everyone around her that she was killing TJ.

There was a clipping sound.

"Hand him to me."

An incubator had been summoned. A Pediatrician was there and an obstetrician. The obstetrician consoled Deanna. "It's okay, Mrs. Arlington. You did a good job. You did a good job. Refraining from pushing when the baby is coming that fast is a very difficult task, you did good." He rolled his stool into position and began the process of delivering her placenta. One more push and it was over.

Troy was attempting to see TJ. He was already being rolled quickly to another area of the hospital. Troy was trotting alongside. He hated Deanna.

"Can I see my baby? Is he alive? Please tell me."

"Mrs. Arlington we don't know the status of your baby. I don't even know if it's a boy or a girl, Your baby was taken to Pediatrics where he can be better cared for."

Patriece

"Did he cry? Did he cry out?" Deanna pleaded for information.

She could see Brian entering the ER door. "Can you get my brother. That's him. Please get him."

A nurse got Brian. Brian's heart ached at the sight of Deanna.

"Go to the pediatrics find Troy and TJ. Tell me Brian, please tell me if my baby's alive? I need to know. OH GOD!!!!!!!!!!!!!!!!!!!! Help TJ, Pleaaassseeee!!!!!!!!"Deanna cried out with a blood-curdling wail, then collapsed on the gurney. Exhaustion had taken over her body.

Brian was given information about where she was being taken within the hospital and directions to Pediatrics. When he left the paramedics, nurses and a few hospital staff joined hands in a small prayer, in a chapel room, for the little baby. They knew that the baby needed a miracle. Blue lips were a sign of no oxygen.

"I'm a Doctor and I'm his dad. Let me help." Troy wanted to work on TJ himself. He knew that he would do all that he could. He knew that he would save him.

The doctors ignored him and worked on the baby. There was sweat beading up on the forehead of the Pediatrician as he tried to resuscitate the infant. He was concentrating so hard on his lip color that he missed the fluttering of his eyelids. Finally, the baby cried. Everyone in the room gasped and tears were shed for this little girl that upset the ER just two minutes earlier. Troy wept. He didn't even care that she was a girl. She was alive. He looked at her, and he knew that he would love her forever. She was his baby. "I love you, TJ."

Brian met him in the Pediatrics lobby. He told him that the baby was fine. "They are keeping her in the ICU for observation, just to make sure there's no brain damage and stuff like that. They're not exactly sure how long she was without oxygen."

"You Ok?" Brian asked.

" Yeah. I'm okay." Troy looked beat up.

"Deanna's on the fifth floor with the other mothers. We need to go tell her the baby's okay." Brian was glad that it was over. He changed his position concerning adoption.

"Alright." Troy's heart began to soften towards Deanna.

"Did you say she?" Brian chuckled.

In Deanna's room, Troy explained, "The baby is alive. She's in ICU for observation. Are you okay?"

"Yes. I'm fine. I thought he was dead. Did you say she?"

"Yeah, it's another girl."

"Wow! I thought it was a boy."

"Me too. Now let's pray that she's okay. Odds are against her there too."

"She's fine. I already prayed. Now, all we have to do is believe."

Troy turned his cell phone back on, on his drive home. There were 25 missed calls. The last one was from Kelly. She demanded a call back. The next one was Deanna's mother and her Sister. Carla and Ron, too. Asia and Tony had left one message.

"Troy we gotta go to da movies. See you later." Lil' Tony sang into the phone. His excitement grabbed Troy by the heartstring. Troy had not forgotten. Life had prohibited their trip to the movies.

"Troy we're at Kaiser Oakland and we can't find y'all. Call me. This is your mother-in-law."

"Troy congratulations. We just talked to Deanna. She told us that the baby was in ICU, and you were going to shower and stuff. We have Ashley as long as we need to keep her. Just let me know if you need anything. A girl huh?" Carla laughed. "Oh, I cooked; it's not as good as D's, but it's a meal." Carla said.

"Dr. Arlington, You need to call me as soon as you get this message. This is Kelly."

Troy called his mother-in-law back and as expected they had located Deanna. Next he called Carla and simply said he'd be in touch. He was going back to the hospital in a few hours and to work tonight. Last, he called Kelly. He decided to stop by there and inform her that it was over.

"Hey Kelly, its Dr. Arlington. I'll be by in about thirty minutes if it's okay?"

"Of course it's okay. Are you okay? You sound a little beat up."

"We'll talk when I get there. See you in a few." He hung up.

25

Brian didn't like the way his wife was looking. He'd ended it with all his women friends except one. His expectation of her response caused him anxiety. He confused her personality with her residence. She lived off of International Blvd in East Oakland amidst a barrage of makeshift stores and storefront churches. The area was high in crime due to the drug activity, but Brian wasn't afraid. He was a product of that community. He lived there when the kids swept porches, skated in the street and washed their parents cars. The mentality of most of the people there now was less than prideful. The apartment building she lived in always had litter all over the yard. Some of the numbers in the addresses were missing, and no one bothered to replace them. Her carpet was old and worn. The exterior needed painting. Inside it was cheaply decorated. None of the furniture even matched, in a half-hearted effort to coordinate multi-color throw pillows were tossed on the couch. No attention had been directed toward the apartment.

Her apartment décor misrepresented her style. The way she put together outfits with such class and flavor was proof that the apartment simply was not her priority.

Brian walked in. "Hi Shaniquah I need to talk to you. I know I haven't been around in a minute, but I didn't want to leave it like that."

"What are you talking about?" Shaniquah walked provocatively in Brian's direction. She pushed him gently down on her worn hand-me down sofa. This was how things usually transpired between them. Brian had dreaded this visit for that reason. The sex was great and hard to resist, but he knew in his gut that it was time to be a husband. He gently coerced her to sit next to him.

"Shani, I seriously need to talk to you. You know I'm married."

Shani's hands folded and her lips tightened. Brian recognized that he had a fight on his hands.

"My wife and I are going to work it out." He started.

"What?! Don't talk to me about your damn wife after you been jumping around in my tail for almost a year!"

"It ain't like that. You knew this wasn't no permanent situation. I'm doing you a courtesy by even telling you I'm through."

Shani started crying. "Brian how you gone use me like that! How come every man just want to screw, then when y'all ready to redeem yourself you dump me." She had never seemed more human to Brian. "Brian I believed you even though I'd heard the same mess from other men. My instincts told me that you were lying on your wife—just to get next to me. You lied "B". You lied and you didn't have to!" Tears were streaming down her cheeks.

Brian tried to console her. He reached over and pulled her into his arms. "I'm sorry. I just grew up in the course of this thing we had going. I can't speak for the others, but for me, I just matured. Before it was about my reputation not your feelings, not my wife's feelings. I wanted to look good in the eyes of my peers. I didn't want to be put on blast for loving a woman. It was all about status and reputation. I wasn't trying to hurt you. I was too damn immature to do the hard thing, you know? I'll be honest with you I was scared too. Love ain't just hard on y'all, it's hard on men too, and we don't have the luxury of crying and venting to our peers all day. I hope you understand."

"Well I don't! Did you really expect me to? You are so full of shit it's ridiculous! You have a bible in your glove compartment 'B'. It's not in there because you're a God-fearing man, but so that women like me that are starving for love will find it. You know we snoop, you planted it there!" (Brian hung his head in shame. He had done so many things like that.) "When I started dealing with you, I told you that I didn't want to be hurt anymore. I told you that! So why would you sleep with me anyway?" Shani cried.

Brian couldn't answer the question. Shani wouldn't let him get a word in. "You visited my mother when she was sick! You helped her refinance her house. You told me that you loved me! YOU LIED TO ME BRIAN!"

"You lied to you! You knew I wahn't shit. You'd heard about my reputation. You are responsible for your feelings not me!" Brian couldn't deal with her accusations without lashing out. It hurt to think that he'd done all that to her. *If Shani's this hurt my poor Gabby must be near death.*

"I'm not responsible for your lies, 'B'. You deceived me. Why?" Shani's voice was calm and soft again. "Why?"

"Shani. I'm sorry."

"I love you Brian. I really do. I love you enough to let you go. I'm not going to bother you at all. I just pray that your wife loves you back. Karma is a *motha*— Brian. The one you love, just may leave you too."

"I know Shani. That's why I'm trying to fix this mess."

"Stop playing with women's feelings, Brian. I can see that you love your wife. I can see it. I hope it's not too late for y'all for your sake."

"Shani, do you forgive me?"

"Not today, but I'll work on it. I'll work on it for my sake. I think it's best though if you just make like you don't know me, even on the streets."

"Okay." Brian stood up. He was grateful for her not acting a fool with him.

"Brian do you really want to make it right with your wife?"

"Yes."

"Test your boys. Word on the street is you're being played."

"Thank you. I never knew you were such a beautiful person." He was sincere. Everything looked different when looked at through truthful eyes.

"Bye Brian." She stood up and hugged him. A well of tears sprang onto his shirt before she let go. He walked out without speaking another word.

Brian's heart was light and heavy. Heavy because he finally realized that his behavior caused women serious pain. He was eager to make it up to Gabby. Light because if the boys weren't his, then he could eliminate that much more pain from Gabby's life. Even lighter because he no longer

He Looked Like A Man, Until He Barked

cared about what people thought, he was in love with his wife. There were no other women in his life.

26

Troy walked into Kelly's house with his key. He'd already removed it from his key ring. The key ring that he kept in his trunk inside the pocket of his emergency roadside kit. Asia's apartment key was there also.

There was a wave of relief as he entered knowing that he wouldn't have to deal with her again. Kelly was in his life only because he feared Asia was leaving him sooner than later. But, after the way she blew up his phone, he would take his chances of being with just Deanna for awhile if Asia left him. It was still his hope that somehow he could keep Asia and Deanna. His desire to keep Deanna was only because he didn't want to share his possessions. If it weren't for his car and his house and the rental property that he'd acquired since they'd been together he would allow the marriage to dissolve.

Kelly was sitting in the living room in a pair of blue jeans and a pink tank top. She had on a little make-up. She was striking. Behind her was a bouquet of pink and white balloons. One of the balloons had a baby rattle on it and another had a baby bottle. The largest balloons said CONGRATULATIONS. For a split second Troy was confused. *How did Kelly know about TJ?* He reasoned that the balloons had nothing to do with him. Perhaps she was planning a shower or someone in her family had just had a baby or something. He ignored the balloons and sat down next to her. He eased her key onto the coffee table and then looked her dead in her eyes. "Kelly, we need to talk."

"We sure do. See the balloons? Those are for you." She jumped up, grabbed the balloons and handed them to him. "Our baby is going to be so fine. I mean, look at us." Kelly beamed.

"Our baby?" Troy let go of the balloon strings. "Kelly, we ain't having no baby."

"Yes we are!" Kelly stood over him, speaking with a strange confidence.

"No we not!" Troy stood up.

Kelly stepped up on him again. "Yes the hell we are." Her nostrils flared and her lips tightened. Even her fist balled up. Kelly's eyes squinted with anger. "You are the father and I'm the baby's Mama."

"I ain't having shit with you. I just had a baby today with my wife. I'm here only to tell you I'm done. I ain't kicking it with you no more." Troy was livid. *A baby. A damn baby! He knew exactly when it happened. DAMN!* Troy gritted his teeth.

"Your wife—a baby—How you just gone do that to me?"

"Same way you trying to trap me with your baby. You begged me to sleep with you without a condom so you could get pregnant! Be careful what you ask for, sometimes you get it!"

"I didn't ask you to lie to me. I didn't ask you to use my body. I didn't ASK you to do any of this to me!!!"

"Do what???" Bitch you took your own clothes off?"

Kelly was already too close to Troy to begin with. In less than two seconds she was in his face. His ear was in her mouth, and she was biting him with all her might. Troy couldn't snatch her off of him without ripping his ear so he gut punched her. She gasped for air and fell to the floor doubled over in pain. While she lay there collecting herself, Troy walked out, holding his bloody ear and dripping tiny spots of blood onto Kelly's white throw rug. "Stay your crazy ass away from me!" He slammed her door so hard the picture window cracked. In his car, he wrote a personal check for Six hundred dollars. In the memo section he wrote Window–BAL Ø. Troy slid the check into the mailbox and walked away. In his haste he didn't realize that his home telephone number and address were on his checks.

Kelly reached for the piece of paper that dropped on the floor via the mailbox. *Don't worry baby, Mama not gone kill Daddy, but I'm going to get his ass, if it's the last thing I do.*

Troy drove to work. He was in shock. At work he received one stitch in his left ear lobe and a Tetanus shot. He told his colleagues that a patient at another hospital bit him and he didn't realize it was that bad. In light of TJ's birth he was granted the next three days off.

He couldn't believe that Kelly was having a baby. That his beloved TJ was in ICU and that Asia was probably feeling slighted again. He knew that it was only a matter of time before Asia cut him off. When she told him about seeing Deanna in his car and he lied his way out of that, the line had been drawn and he knew it.

He Looked Like A Man, Until He Barked

Kelly's pain subsided when she read the check. She snatched her car keys off of the key hook in the kitchen, grabbed the outfit that she intended to give to Troy when she announced the baby, but forgot to and rushed out the door. She knew exactly where Elysian Fields was located in Oakland.

Troy stopped and chatted with a few co-workers, but headed to his car. He wanted to eat, shower and get back to the hospital to be with TJ and Deanna. He knew that was the right thing to do.

Kelly did not see Troy's car. There were trees and lots of greenery. His home was very nice. Professionally landscaped, dual pane windows with wooden shutters and a solid cherry wood designer front door with brass handles that just happened to be wide open. Kelly walked in with the confidence of a burglar.

Inside she was consumed with hatred. The home was gorgeous. It had tile floors; granite counter tops with recessed lighting. It made her homeownership seem mediocre in contrast. Voltaire St. was a nice area, but Elysian Fields was the place to be. The stairway drew her upward. Kelly didn't even realize she still had the baby's boxed outfit in her hand. It was a white dress with the ruffled panties and tie-on booty socks. The lettering was pink embroidery that spelled 'DADDY'S LITTLE ANGEL'.

Troy got in his car and started home.

Kelly walked into Troy's room. She dropped the outfit on the California King sized bed that he shared with Deanna. She looked at the pictures that were actually art. She glanced at Deanna's designer clothes. Then she went into Ashley's room. She toured the entire home.

As Troy exited the freeway, Kelly searched his desk. She stole checks number 1801-1849 from the bottom of a box of checks. She swiped the unopened Nextel bill and jotted down his email address, which he had not disclosed. At the door she decided to leave it open. Heartache wouldn't let her leave as she looked around the house one last time.

Troy drove the 500 feet to his destination.

Kelly's hand was on the ignition. Troy pulled into the driveway. Less than two minutes separated their paths.

The front door was wide open. He entered with caution. After checking under the beds and in the closets, he concluded that it must have been left open during the commotion of TJ's delivery.

In the shower Troy tried to relax. He wanted Asia. He needed her comfort. Brian called while he was eating Deanna's lasagna. The food was prepared the day before. It was vegetarian spinach lasagna and it was delicious. Troy's nose was tickled by Kelly's perfume in spite of his shower. He could smell her. It was if she were in his house. The conversation was about Brian's decision to commit to Gabby and letting go of everyone, including Shani. Troy didn't say so, but he understood—his time had come for change also. He did not disclose Kelly's pregnancy. There was no need to since he was absolutely through with her. The relationship, the pregnancy, the baby—all of it was behind him. Brian told him that he and Gabby would meet him at the hospital later.

He Looked Like A Man, Until He Barked

Outside the Beemer had been egged. Troy stood in front of it, took a deep breath and closed his eyes slowly. He pulled into the driveway and rinsed the egg from his car. That's when he noticed the note on his windshield. It read: Congratulations Daddy, love Baby Mama. Troy looked over his shoulders for Kelly. His ear started to throb with pain. After snatching off the note, Troy got in the car and headed toward the hospital.

The desire to call Asia grew more intense, but he didn't know what to say. Truth is he didn't want to hear her disappointment. He couldn't handle being yelled at anymore today, maybe tomorrow, but no more today.

Kelly sat in her car watching Troy wash her breakfast from his vehicle. She rubbed the checks and the Nextel bill, not quite sure why she'd taken them or how she was going to use them, but confident that she'd find a way.

At the hospital Troy stopped in the Gift shop to get Deanna a token. The cashier was good-looking and flirtatious. With ease Troy ignored her. The habit to respond was present; the energy was absent. Exhaustion kept him honest for the moment.

Brian and Gabby entered the hospital room at 7:50 p.m. There were only 10 minutes left of visiting hour. Both Troy and Deanna understood that that was all the time Gabby could muster in the company of a newborn. Their hearts were empathetic to her pain.

The room was a little on the chilly side. Deanna had three blankets on her bed. TJ was in her arms. Her hair was pulled back into a ponytail. She looked normal, not like a woman that had just survived a traumatic delivery.

Gabby's appearance concerned Deanna. As she sat on the bed to hold little Troi Jasmine, TJ, she looked more than barren. More than empty. There was hollowness in her soul. There was pain in her eyes, sadness in her mannerism and defeat that communicated surrender. It was clear that Gabby wasn't present. Her body was in the room; her voice made the appropriate cooing sounds, she smiled in sync with the conversation; but she simply wasn't present. If Deanna didn't know better, she could easily mistake Gabby for a patient. Her beautiful eyes were outlined in black circles. They were also a storehouse of pain. After looking at Gabby Deanna glanced at Brian. He was well groomed and happy. There was a freedom and hope dancing in his spirit. He was very affectionate with Gabby, more so than usual. He stroked her arms and shoulders; he kissed her head and looked at her with warmth and pride. Whatever happened between them had changed them both.

Brian began "Baby, we going to do this real soon, even if we have to adopt. You know they say as soon as you adopt you get pregnant."

"Okay." Gabby gave a half smile.

Deanna was sure that something was wrong. In the past, Gabby would die for Brian to consider adoption. The fact that he was sincerely considering it should have made her heart jump. The "okay" was a red flag for Deanna. She made a mental note to talk to her soon. Just check on her.

He Looked Like A Man, Until He Barked

Troy walked them to the elevator and returned to Deanna and TJ. His thoughts returned to Asia. He was consumed with how to get back in her good graces even while sitting at Deanna's bedside. Deanna was asleep. TJ was doing fine and showing no signs of the day's trauma. Troy was relieved. TJ lay in her crib alongside her mother. The TV was on. The lights were out. It was finally evening. Troy sat listening to the sounds of hospital monitors and beeps. A nurse offered him a chair that let out into a bed and he accepted.

Brian held Gab's hand on the way to the car.

"I love you Mrs. Comier. So much."

"I love you too." Gabby's heart didn't receive the love from Brian. It no longer trusted him. The pain from disappointment was too great. To accept his love again meant to risk that pain. Gabby's emotional fiber was too thin to weather another storm. Too thin to hope, so she didn't. Hers was a hopeless situation and she respected that. Numbness was her coping mechanism. The sleeping pills helped her to stay numb. It didn't matter what was going on around her. Her feelings were asleep. She popped two more in her mouth while Brian walked to the driver's side of the car.

While they all rested, Asia was on the other side of town in unbearable pain. *Asia this is going to leave a scar. You know this man is married. Stop being a fool. You deserve so much better.*

27

Carla woke up frustrated. Ron was drunk. He didn't even take the keys out of the ignition and his car was not in the driveway. This morning Deanna was coming home with the baby. Ashley wanted to go home. Two days at Auntie Cowa were enough. She was becoming whiney, and her patience was wearing thin with Roni.

By the time Ron woke up Carla had contacted the police department and the insurance. The girls were dressed. They were headed to see the baby. Troy was back at work, which is where Ron should have been, but he was calling in sick today. The stolen car provided him two excuses one for staying home and one for having a beer.

Carla arrived at the house to see the baby. Troy was pulling out of the driveway with the strangest look on his face. He looked scared and angry combined. He didn't notice Carla waving at him.

"Hey girl, we in here." Deanna called. Troy had made the den into a baby haven for the time being.

"What's wrong with Troy? He looked like he just saw a ghost that pissed him off." Carla teased.

"He tripping. He bought TJ the cutest outfit and left it on our bed. When I found it, all the color left his face and he started acting strange. Who knows?"

"Must be something in the water. Is Gabby okay? I can't reach her." Carla asked.

He Looked Like A Man, Until He Barked

"I haven't talked to her. I've been calling her, no answer or return call." Deanna said.

Carla noticed the girls hovering over the bassinet. "Watch her head. She not a big girl, y'all. Let me put her up here so you can see her." Carla picked up TJ and let the two little ones get a closer look. They were playing over her head in the bassinet trying to see her. Deanna went to get the package from UPS delivery that Troy left on the table by the front door with her name on it. She knew he wouldn't suspect anything because she got packages all the time.

It was the DNA testing kit. Carla had the girls follow her. After putting them into the playpen, she and Deanna read the instructions. Carla's reality stung her. Confusion spun around her head. She leaned back on the sofa and closed her eyes. *God please let this work out in my favor. I need for Roni to be Ron's daughter. I'm sorry. Please help me. In Jesus Name, Amen.*

I'm not taking another drink. Next I'll be losing my family, not just my car. Ron thought.

28

Sheila entered the church. Sister Esther greeted her. The same little usher that brought her to the front row last month.

Sister Esther, or Sister Usher, as the girls called her smiled real bright when she saw Sheila come in. "You remind me of my daughter, Gabby" she escorted her to the second row.

Sheila sat down in anticipation of Pastor Knowit's sermon. He had a way with words and the scripture that really reached her. She always knew exactly what he was talking about. When he referenced the Bible after his anecdote, the message became very clear.

The church was packed. By the time church started, it was standing room only. A mass of people had come to the 7th annual revival.

Pastor Knowit took the pulpit like any other Sunday. He delivered a word that had every adult in the congregation on their feet, clapping, stomping and jumping. A couple of people were running circles around the building. Some of the youth were on their feet too. Pastor Knowit was young enough to speak their language. He made it plain where they could all receive the message. Sheila couldn't recite his sermon word for word, but there was one thing he said that stuck out in her mind. The message was *removing yourself from temptation*. Pastor Knowit grabbed the microphone, and he walked briskly from one end of the pulpit to the other. "You know it helps a whole bunch when you REMOOVE yourself from temptation, while asking to be *delive-ah—ed—*

You might want to stay out of the bakery if you have a problem with pastries. Amen. It don't make no sense for you to be fooling around with temptation. Amen. You asking for *trouble*— when you do that. Amen. Young folk, you ain't got to dance with Satan— jes' 'cause he's at the club! Can I get an Amen." The congregation roared "Amen!" "Preach Pastor!" "That's good stuff!"

Sheila knew that meant that she was doing the right thing, changing her phone number and respecting herself. Her commitment was to deal with men in the forum of marriage. She no longer desired the false safety of promiscuity or the single life. Sheila was a wife and this time she wanted a husband. This time she would pray for a husband not choose one with her flesh.

After service Sheila by passed the crowd. A burning desire to go by Asia's house brewed within her. She loaded the girls into her Prism and buckled them in. Once inside, she dialed Asia.

"Hello." Asia answered the phone.

"Hey. What you doing?"

"Nothing."

"You have company?"

"Uh-uh." Asia fought to hold her tears. Troy was doing to her the very thing she'd asked him not to do.

"Feel like some company? We're leaving church now."

"Sure."

Sheila knew Asia was hurting. She also knew what she was feeling. Too many nights, she'd ached for a sincere man in her own life. A man of the old days. A man with some gumption, one that prioritized his family and knew what "forsaking all others" meant. Sheila wanted a man that wasn't afraid to love her back.

The house was a mess. Asia was laying on the couch under her blanket. Lil' Tony was sitting on the loveseat. They were watching cartoons, only he was watching alone. Asia wasn't focused at all. Sheila came in and kicked off her shoes. She moved items and made a seat for herself. The kids ran to Lil' Tony's room.

"You okay?"

"No. I haven't talked to Troy in two months. I haven't heard from him since the day we all went to the movies."

"Have you called him?"

"No. He's called and come by, I've been avoiding him."

"Why?"

"I don't know."

"Think about it. Be honest with yourself and it'll come to you. When I was out there. I didn't call men back, because I didn't want to hear what I already knew was a lie. I even knew that the motive for the lie was to keep things as they were. It was easier for me to live with my behavior if I didn't know the truth. I could place all the blame on him. I could be the victim instead of a butt-hole myself." Sheila slipped tissue into Asia's hand.

"I hear you, but I love him. I feel that little inkling that it ain't right. I feel that he's married, but I can't let him go. I can't. I was listening to the radio, some old school, and my song came on. Whitney sang 'love gives you the right to be

He Looked Like A Man, Until He Barked

free'. I've heard that song a million times, but I finally heard it. He has a right to be free."

"I know, Boo, but, ask yourself, does he have a desire to be free?" Sheila said as lovingly as possible.

Asia didn't answer. She just laid her head on Sheila's shoulder and cried until she nodded off. Sheila eased from under her and cleaned the house.

I'll just stop by on my way home. Deanna's doing fine. Kelly's quiet. Asia, my sweet baby, please be home.

Troy missed Asia and Sheila by fifteen minutes. They were walking into the night service, at Truth & Light Church when he entered Asia's empty apartment.

29

Carla couldn't bring herself to return the envelope. She'd managed to get samples for both Ron and Roneka. It was time simply drop the envelope into the mailbox. She sat in the living room with her feet in the couch and Roneka on her chest. She didn't know what to do. Roni just being "her baby" was no longer enough. She wanted to know and she didn't want to know at the same time, if Ron was Roni's father. The confusion was familiar. It reminded her of the abortion she had in high school. She was sixteen. Her mother was single parenting and constantly pleading with her not to get pregnant. Carla didn't mean to get pregnant. She didn't even mean to have sex. It was an unconscious decision. Her inability to say "no" in ninth grade and in route to the motel room was the reason she was faced with the same dilemma all these years later. In ninth grade, with all the information and sexual education, she didn't think she would get pregnant the first time. It took six months for it to happen. Six times. Carla still remembered the visit to Planned Parenthood to find out.

Roni stirred in her arms. Carla kissed her on the top of the head. *Oh I love you little girl. Soo—much. I love your Daddy too. No matter what happens. Ron is your Daddy. I'm sorry that I risked your family like that. I'm so sorry. If the results divide our household please forgive me. I never meant to hurt you. I was selfish and irresponsible. Just believe with me that all is going to be all right somehow.*

He Looked Like A Man, Until He Barked

God please forgive me and help me to forgive myself. Give me the strength to drop the envelope in the mailbox and help me to do the right thing. I confess my first thought is to not tell either way, but I don't want to live another lie. I'm already holding my first baby and the affair. Whatever happens, keep us a family and deliver Ron from drinking. Amen. Carla spoke aloud.

"Amen." Roni whispered. She had not heard any of Carla's thoughts/prayer. She responded as taught.

Carla squeezed her tighter. Her little 'amen' gave Carla hope.

Putting the envelope in the mailbox was easier than Carla thought. Afterward they stopped by Deanna's to see the baby.

They were sitting in Deanna's kitchen, which burst with red, green and cream colors. It was very well lit. Everything was clean and you could smell pleasant fragrances. The kids were in the family room playing. TJ was in the kitchen with the lady's. She sat on the kitchen table in a bouncer. Her little feet just kicked and caused her to bounce until she fell asleep.

"I can't believe you're back to school so soon."

"Yes. I want to get out of here before I fall for another of Troy's lies. I don't know if TJ's birth caused him to feel the need to stay home or what it was, but he's here every night for the past two months. I didn't expect him to keep it up this long. A few times when I came home from picking up the girls from your house he was pulling up. I had to tell him we were shopping or something I was out so often. He has no idea that you're keeping the girls in the evening. He knows that I keep Roni in the mornings. That offsets Ashley's stories about Roni."

"I just don't think I could ever do it. I mean you made up your mind almost a year ago to leave and you are still focused that way." Carla was surprised.

"Carla, I don't love Troy anymore either. Not like that. The only time we are together that way is when I have a need. You can only trust a person for so long. I don't trust Troy at all. The cheating is like a drug for him. I honestly don't think he can be honest."

TJ drooled. Deanna dabbed her little mouth with the corner of her bib and stood to prepare Ashley and Roni some lunch. Vienna sausages, chips and mandarin oranges with milk.

"I need to stay the course because it's only a matter of time before he is back to his old habits."

"Maybe he's changed Dee." Carla offered.

"Carla, to find that out I'd have to trust him one last time, and last time was the last time. I don't have it in me."

Deanna was trying to be honest with herself. What she wasn't telling is that the Executive Chef had eyes for her or so she thought. He had no kids. He was single and he loved her cooking. He'd even offered her a position in his restaurant when she graduated. She had nine months to go. It wasn't that she was doing anything to provoke his attention. She was just being herself. Once they had sat after class and talked. They shared intimate details about their lives. Deanna had shared her belief about Troy cheating again, his record of cheating in the past, as well as her belief that he never loved her.

Kenneth shared that he'd never been married. He wanted kids. He loved cooking. Loved seeing people eat. He owned/inherited his grandmother's restaurant. It was in a nice location, but it was run down. It needed a woman's touch. He also wanted to gradually upgrade the clientele to include all classes of people. Soul food is not restricted to Styrofoam and flytraps. He wanted chandeliers, tile flooring, art-filled walls, jazz musicians, window dressings and customer service oriented staff. His was a vision. Deanna had grabbed the vision and embraced it with him. They both knew that they were attracted to one another. Ken didn't advance because he respected her marriage regardless of the condition it was in. Deanna didn't welcome an advance for the very same reason. Too many times she'd watched Murphy's Law win a feat like theirs. She didn't even tell him her plans of leaving. She wanted to let things happen naturally. If they still had the dilemma of attraction after her divorce, great! Deanna accepted his offer of adding a woman's touch to his restaurant. Often she'd stayed after class for an hour or less to talk about it.

"You really are going to leave him huh?" Carla asked snapping Deanna from her daydream.

"Yes. At some point in my life I want to be happy. I'm not happy. I have two children, a husband and I'm miserable."

"I understand. I just don't think I could walk away from Ron. I hope Ron don't walk away from me. I mailed the Q-tips on my way over here."

Patriece

"You talked to Ron?" Deanna sat the plates on the table for the girls. She was about to call them to lunch until she heard that.

"No."

Deanna called the girls. "Ladies come eat lunch."

"How did you get his saliva on a Q-tip."

The girls rushed in. They sat at the little table next to the big table. It was a Playskool kitchen set. They fit perfectly.

"I caught him with his mouth open after a drunken bout. I hope it can be tested. But I included their toothbrushes just in case."

"Good. Are you okay?" Deanna walked toward Carla.

"Yes, for the moment. I pray it work out in my favor. My biggest problem is lying. I'm so tired of lying and secrets. Part of me wants to keep it to myself if the test says she's Ron's. My logic is why mention it if I don't have to? Then my conscious starts eating me and I start to feel like I need to confess either way." Carla was crying at this point.

Deanna sat down. She handed Carla a tissue. She knew what it was like to keep a secret. "Carla I have a secret too. There's a guy at my school, actually the Executive Chef and I'm digging him. I know he's digging me too. That's the hope that has sustained me this year. During my pregnancy I felt so guilty about caring about this man while I'm married. It feels horrible and good."

Carla began to cry harder. "I know what you mean." Carla could not bring herself to share about her first baby. She wanted the freedom that truth gave, but she couldn't risk the judgment. Originally she thought it would get better

He Looked Like A Man, Until He Barked

in time, but it never did. Keeping it to herself was getting harder to do. The smell of the Vienna sausages were growing intense. She wanted one.

"Carla, I want this man so bad. Once when I was *with* Troy I closed my eyes and imagined it was him, Ken. I was disappointed when I opened my eyes and saw, Troy lying next to me." Deanna hung her head in shame. This feeling was embarrassing.

"After my incident I douched and still didn't feel clean." Carla sniffed. "You know what else?"

"What?"

"I missed my period. The only good thing is I know this is Ron's baby. My fear is the baby won't look like Roni and then what?"

"Are you sure?"

"No. I haven't tested, but I know my body."

"I have a test. It's old, but pregnant is pregnant. You want to use it?"

"I don't care."

"It's under the sink."

"Okay." Carla needed to use the bathroom anyway. In the bathroom she used the test, waited the three minutes and got the results.

Deanna had pulled out the tent for the girls in the family room. They crawled in and started playing.

In the kitchen Carla sat down with a half smile. "It's positive."

They tried to rejoice while sitting there contemplating the weight of their marriages.

Patriece

Troy had no choice but to go home to Deanna every evening. He'd been calling Asia for well over a month. She was never home. Even when he stopped by she wasn't there. The last time his key didn't work. Troy felt vulnerable. He loved her and wanted to be with her.

Kelly had finally left him alone. He'd seen her a few times at work and there was no acknowledgement whatsoever. She seemed to accept the situation. There was a buzz around the hospital that she was pregnant though.

Troy sat in his car opening his mail. His checking account was overdrawn for the second time in two months. He couldn't understand how or why. He was the only one on the account. Overdraft protection was covering his checks. He made more than enough money to make his ends meet. This was the second time he'd gotten an overdraft notice. He intended to call the bank at his first opportunity.

Troy dialed Brian. "Hey 'B', man what's up?"

"Nothing. Working, getting ready to go show a house."

"Do you have one I could use for the weekend?"

"Man who you running game on now?"

"Asia. She's starting to pull back too far man. I need to show her that it's all good."

"Let me check." Brian's stomach knotted up. He was uncomfortable with Troy's behavior. He didn't want to see Asia like Gabby. Gabby was a wreck. Brian had taken her to the doctor and nothing was wrong with her. He made an appointment for marriage counseling. She had always wanted

He Looked Like A Man, Until He Barked

to do that. He hoped it brought her out of her depression. Sleeping all day was a sign of depression according to his research. He still didn't realize that she was taking 15-20 pills per day. "I have one that I'm showing on Friday. The owner's are vacationing until it's sold. It's not too far from your house though. It's on Thunderbird CT. That's close man."

"I'm desperate man. I gotta get Asia back. After I secure things with her I'm going to go ahead and free Deanna. She know it ain't what it could or should be. I care 'bout her, I love Asia." Troy sat in his car talking to Brian. Kelly entered the building and she had a little pouch. He looked away. As long as she stayed out of his way he was fine.

"Stop by and get the key. Man you can only play house for a few days. I gotta put the house on the market by Tuesday, no later than Wednesday."

"Alright. Let me get the address."

Troy hung up and dialed Asia.

Brian was consumed with guilt. Gabby came to mind. *I can't do that no more.* He thought.

"Asia before you hang up, let me talk, please."

In spite of sitting in the pews of Truth & Light and listening to Pastor Knowit and even relating, Asia couldn't resist the temptation of talking to Troy. She didn't answer she just held the phone. Her heart felt good.

"Babe, I know you are feeling slighted and probably like I'm a liar and married and God knows what else, but I'm not. I'm in love. Asia I love you. I had an emergency on the day we were supposed to go to the movies. I am sorry for being a no show. I called you as soon as I could, but you wouldn't talk to me." Asia was on the other end allowing her tears to flow smoothly down her cheeks. She'd pushed 'mute' on her phone so that she couldn't be heard making a sound. "Asia, I love you. If you love me meet me tonight at my house, here's the address." As Troy rattled off the address Asia wrote it down. "I love you baby, Bye." He hung up.

Asia said "I love you too, Troy. If only you knew..." the mute feature prevented Troy from hearing her.

Troy called Deanna on her cell phone and told her he had to go to Atlanta for four days. Deanna said okay, wished him well and called Carla. She asked Carla if she could watch the girls for an extra hour. Carla agreed.

Deanna accepted Ken's offer to discuss his restaurant after class.

Troy rushed to Brian's to pick up the keys to the vacant house on Thunderbird CT.

Asia thanked God that Troy called her.

"Sheila, he called. He invited me to his house. I wanna go, can you keep Tony?"

"Sure." Sheila began a prayer. She discerned that Troy was no good.

Brian came home to dinner; his clothes for the next day hung on the bedroom door next to a sleeping Gabby. Weight loss was evident. *I'm sorry baby. Hang on. It's going to be okay. I love you so much.*

30

Kelly wrote the check to the Fatherless Children Foundation for one thousand dollars. She knew that Friday was payday and the check would clear. She had written a check every payday after each doctor's visit. A total of five checks to charities assisting children less fortunate. She had her first ultrasound today. The baby was fine. She was twenty-two weeks pregnant. She was glad to be having a child, mad to be doing it alone. Her plan was to have a family as opposed to a baby. She struggled to wrap her mind around the acceptance that her and her baby were a family.

After getting a clean bill of health and knowing that she was out of the danger zone Kelly decided to mess with Troy some more. In Target she bought a bib that read *I Love My Daddy*. Later she mailed it to Troy's house. It was addressed to Beloved, from???

Kelly stopped at Popeye's chicken and ordered her usual before going to work.

The teller asked Troy to have a seat and told him that the Branch Manager would be with him shortly. He waited. The manager showed him the statements with the checks that he'd written totaling $4000. The checks were out of sequence, but everything else was correct. He signed an affidavit of fraudulent activity. At Troy's request copies of the checks were ordered. An investigation was begun and his account was closed. A new account was opened. Troy was baffled at who would tamper with his account like that.

It was a long day. Asia was bugging him about coming over so tough that he told her the house was on the market. He wanted something that they could have together. He told her that the house held memories of his marriage and he wanted something that was theirs. He promised to take her house hunting that weekend. Things were back to normal with them. Both of them were as happy as happy could be. The sex was good and the loving even better.

Sheila and Sister Esther were becoming the closest of friends. Sheila was thinking about joining the usher board at Sister Esther's leading. They'd talked in detail about Sheila's past behaviors. They'd fasted and prayed together for Sheila a good man. Sister Esther knew the dangers of loving boys posing as men. She cautioned Sheila to beware of men that took more than they gave.

"Baby, if you meet a man that is willing to give you his check that's great. But if you meet one giving you his check plus his bills and the bills are longer than the check, let him stretch his own check." Sister Esther compared Gabby. "My daughter is sick right now. Depression. She has a good husband though. He takes care of the finances. In the beginning it was hard. I tried to explain to my Gabby that men will love you before they trust you. Their "trust test" will kill you if you let it. Most men want to see how deep your love runs for them, before they'll show you the love they have for you.

He Looked Like A Man, Until He Barked

Chile, men will have you dealing with all kinds of drama. Set yourself some boundaries and you'll be fine. Baby, when you love a man, do right by him regardless to what he's doing. His love'll catch up. Men folk just as vulnerable as we are. They jes wants to be loved too."

Sheila tried her best to process the teachings of Sister Esther to her relationship with Asia. Part of her wanted to take a break from Asia's friendship until this thing with Troy was done. Sheila knew Troy wasn't the one for Asia. Yet, she listened to Asia telling her all about the house hunting and the homes that Brian had shown them. She listened when they were pre-qualified, per Troy. Every once in awhile she would ask a thought provoking question. A week or two later Asia would casually slip in the answer, Troy's explanation, during conversation. Sister Esther's advice was to be her friend until love ran its course. Listen, gently and lovingly advise, but stay out of it. As long as he wasn't abusing her or the baby Sheila was to stay out of it.

Asia walked in with Tony's backpack. She was dropping him off again. Her and Troy were going to Atlanta for four days. He had finally got some time off from work. Asia had never been anywhere so when he asked she rattled off Atlanta.

"Sheila. Thank you for watching Tony again. I'll get them all for the weekend when I get back. After this Troy's going to be really busy. I'm learning his routine."

"I'm okay with keeping the kids. They give me something to do."

"That's right you don't have company anymore. Did I tell you I'm proud of you?"

"Girl, get out of here." Sheila shooed Asia away.

Asia wouldn't budge. "I really am. You seem so much happier. You're not risking your life and you are glowing. Your life seems so much more organized."

"I'm much happier now Asia. I get lonely sometimes, but I'd rather wait on the right man than waste my time on the wrong one."

"Wow! Are you going to remarry? I remember when that was out of the question."

"Yes. There's no other way. You betta get out of here before you're late." Sheila hugged Asia. The kids circled around them and hugged her waist. They were growing.

31

"Hey Lady, your package is in." Deanna handed the package to Carla. The fact that Carla was unprepared showed in her face. Despite her mailing in the final payment and expecting the package in five to seven working days she was shocked. Today was day five. Fear rose in her; it revealed itself through tears.

Deanna came over and hugged her. She ached for her. The anxiety was thicker than the thickest fog. "Sshh. You don't have to open it today." Deanna cooed.

"Yes, I do. For everybody's sake, I need to know. This stress is too much for this pregnancy."

Deanna agreed. She could see her belly rising. "Have you told Ron yet?"

"Yes, Last night. He celebrated with a drink. He even had the audacity to bring a few drunks home. Girl one of them peed on the side of my toilet." It was evident that Carla was stalling.

"Carla, you may as well get it over with." Deanna eased.

"Can we pray first?"

"Sure. You pray though. I'm not good at it."

"Okay." Carla picked up the envelope and handed one end of it to Deanna. Deanna held the two corners offered her and without warning Carla began to pray. The emotion in her voice was heartfelt. She pleaded and begged God for Roni to be Ron's daughter. She asked forgiveness about things that Carla didn't even know had happened like the abortion and the lying and the manipulating. She asked for comfort and direction and all kinds of deliverance. By the time they arrived at "Amen", both women were able to handle the outcome either way. They were stronger.

Carla didn't' hesitate. She just ripped the envelope and began reading 99.9% positive. Ronald Wilson is the father of Roneka Wilson. The second test concluded 99.9% positive that Ronald Wilson is the father of Roneka Wilson. Carla dropped the paper fell on her knees and sobbed. She couldn't even answer Deanna. Deanna picked up the paper and read the words for herself. She almost screamed only she didn't want to wake the babies. All of them were napping.

Carla was so elated that she didn't know what to do. It was the best day of her life, the absolute best day of her life.

"Do you have a lighter?" Carla asked Deanna.

Deanna walked over to the junk drawer in the kitchen and fished out a cigarette lighter. "What do you need a lighter for?"

"I'm burning these papers. I don't need them anymore." Carla responded. "I'm okay now."

"I'm so happy for you."

"I am too. God is so good. So awesome!"

Deanna reached over and answered the phone.

"Hello?"

"Hey Dee, is Carla there?"

"Yeah. Hold on." She handed the phone to Carla. "It's Ron."

"Hi Babe, what's wrong?"

He Looked Like A Man, Until He Barked

"I'm in jail. Can you come get me?"

Ron knew that he probably shouldn't keep company with prostitutes during the daytime, but he was feeling bad. Yesterday, Carla had told him about the pregnancy. He was so excited he wanted to celebrate. He went to the club with intentions of having one drink. Before he knew it, it was morning. At home Carla dismissed his guest, but didn't say a word to him; her tears and silence spoke volumes.

When she left to go to Deanna's, she drove the new car. That was a statement within itself. No longer did she allow him to drive the best car. His drunken behavior made her too nervous. He agreed because of the pregnancy.

The pregnancy...a baby...I'm going to quit drinking. That was his thought when he left the house. He walked into the bar for his last drink and was comforted by the darkness. The darkness made him feel invisible. His character defects were blotted out by the blackness. The only part of him that could be seen was the "cool" part. His peers admired his ability to drink with them, do the things they did and maintain his lifestyle. He was amongst the few that were still married, owned vehicles, and had a place to call home.

Ron's mind was made up to go home and rest when he spotted a "regular". He wasn't feeling in the mood for sex. The reason he stopped was to fill up on self-esteem. The moaning sounds accompanied by the Oscar performance of satisfaction he got from prostitutes drove his self-esteem to the highest. When he left the bar, he decided that this was his last time. Less than ten minutes past and he was arrested.

The officer was a man of God. His heart went soft at the sight of Ron. He discerned that he was a good man with an addiction to alcohol and prostitutes. Another patrol car arrived on the scene. A female officer searched the prostitute. She handcuffed her and drove away with her. The arresting officer placed Ron in the back of his car.

"Are you married?"

"Yes." Ron mumbled.

"Does your wife know that you keep company with prostitutes?"

"She will now."

"What's that about? I'm just curious." The officer was writing while talking to Ron.

Ron didn't answer for a moment. He was down to the first layer of humility, and it didn't matter anymore.

"I deal with them to make-up for my shortcomings at home." Ron tossed his comment at the officer with no embarrassment.

"Does your wife complain?"

"Naw."

"Then what makes you think there's a problem at home?"

"I just know."

"Does she or has she ever cheated on you?"

"Naw. Never."

"Man you might want to sober up. All of this could be for nothing. You need to leave this alone."

"You right. I'm done now. This is going to kill my wife. "

"Well, that should be motivation enough. When we get there, you'll be charged and booked then you can call your wife."

"Alright."

Ron sat in the backseat hoping against hope that he could somehow spare Carla from this embarrassment, not to mention the pain she was sure to feel. Ron couldn't think of one person other than Troy, who probably wouldn't be available, to come bail him out. The weight of his burden rounded his shoulders, and he hung his head. He was thirsty for a drink or a cigarette—anything, with the exception of a woman, to take the edge off.

The officer pulled into the station. As he coerced Ron out of the car, he asked "Do you know that where there is good, evil is always present?"

"Naw."

"Think about that next time you need to make a decision. You might make a good one as a result."

"All right man. Thank you. I 'ppreciate you talking to me like a man. I'm not a bad guy, just made a bad decision."

"I hope you heard me. I don't want to see you back on my beat. It won't be this easy next time." The officer dropped some papers on a counter and told the officer behind the counter "Public Drunkenness". He patted Ron on the back one time and walked away. As he walked away Ron heard him say "Evil is always present."

Ron sobered. After calling Carla, he rejoiced in the reality that he wouldn't have to admit his interaction with the prostitute. *Public drunkenness. Thank you God.*

Patriece

Carla fussed at Ron, and she even cried some. Ron listened. He realized that in spite of her disappointment, he still had a family. He vowed to change his behavior. They picked up Ron's car before picking up Roni. Carla got the baby from Deanna's and left. She was surprised when Ron pulled in behind her. More surprised when he showered, shaved and sat in the family room with them for a movie. After the movie, he laid Roni down for the night. Carla washed the dinner dishes. Ron eased behind her and whispered in her ear "I'm sorry. I want to change. I could use your help."

Carla nodded okay. Ron took her hand and led her into their bedroom. They were both praying for forgiveness of their secret sins. Ron knew he would never tell of his encounters with prostitutes, and Carla would rest in her grave with the knowledge of her affair. Both were glad things were behind them. *Some things are best left unshared* they thought, as they joined hearts in the most sacred manner any two people could experience.

Deanna thanked Troy for the bib and asked him why he didn't write his name on the package.

Troy hunched his shoulders. He knew Kelly sent them to provoke a call from him. He decided to ignore it. It had been close to six months since he heard from her. Eliminating her gave him enough time to manage both Deanna and Asia. He hadn't gotten a complaint from either of them in about three months. His life was back where it needed to be. He and

Asia were doing well. They had gone to Atlanta and had a wonderful time.

Deanna wasn't tripping on Troy at all. He wasn't doing such a good job juggling. She was doing an excellent job letting go. She would be graduating in two and a half weeks. Her divorce papers were filled out. To complete the process, she simply needed to file them and have Troy served. Her evenings with Ken gave her hope beyond hope. She was still respectful of her marriage and so was he.

Kelly dressed for her appointment and went to the doctor alone. Resentment had swelled in her as large as her protruding stomach. Several times she'd watched The Arlington's comings and goings. Sometimes Troy was with them. Whenever he was he was carrying that baby. Kelly had watched her grow from a baby, supported when held, into a baby carried on the hip. She was a darling little girl.

Kelly had learned that Troy closed his account through hospital gossip, so she shredded the checks she had left. They were of no use to her now. She would have given anything to be a fly on the wall when he realized that he'd donated close to $4,000 to orphaned children.

Suddenly it came to her. Halloween was near. Will it be trick or treat for Troy Arlington?

32

The desire to be a man swelled within Brian and filled him with righteousness. He knew he had to clean up his act. While at the hospital visiting TJ when she was born, he fell deeper in love with Gabby. In the past few months, he had been coming home regularly. He had been cuddling with her and openly loving her. She was unresponsive. When he went to Esther with his problem, she told him to give her some time. Gabby was always slow to heal. Esther was glad that the time had come for Brian and Gabby. She encouraged him to continue to get his affairs in order and just shower Gabby with love. "She'll learn to trust you again." She told him. The statement unsettled him. It made him aware that his behavior was no secret. He apologized to Esther for his behavior. She accepted his apology and hugged him tight. Their love was genuine.

The first thing Brian did was contact his son's mothers and requested a DNA test. Shani was right. Brian had no sons. Suddenly, Quetti popped up in his spirit. He was confident that she was his. Her mother, Michelle, was a good woman. In addition, Quetti looked like him. He couldn't keep his mind off of her. A few phone calls later he was on the line with Michelle.

"Hi Michelle, how are you?"

"I'm great Brian. How are you?"

"I'm good. How's Quetti?"

"She's good too. Her birthday's coming up. She'll be four on Saturday."

"Wow! That was fast." He chuckled.

"I'm also having a baby, and I'm married."

"Congratulations. You know Michelle I didn't mean to hurt you. I was just immature. I'm glad you came out of it alright."

"Me too. It's all behind me now. I'm happy. I survived. It only made me stronger." Michelle was honest. She was much stronger now.

"So, does Quetti know about me?"

"Yes. She calls you her other Daddy. It would be awkward for you to step in now, but you do have a right to."

"I appreciate that. I'm not calling to cause problems. I'm just trying to finally do the right thing. I'd love to be there Saturday, but I don't know if that's appropriate."

"Things are certainly different now. We need to share this conversation with our spouses. Saturday might be a little soon."

"Can I call her Saturday?"

"I really need to get back to you. Let me process all of this. Perhaps we can all get together and discuss what's best for Quetti."

"Sure. Let me give you my numbers. Call me."

"Thank you for taking an interest in our baby. This feels so much better." Michelle sniffed. She had prayed that Brian showed up before Quetti was too old to care.

"It feels good to me too. Take care. Talk to you soon."

Patriece

Gabby walked into the Psychologist's office with a bottle of sleeping pills. She told the doctor that she'd been abusing the sleeping pills due to depression. She opened up and a flood of hurt and insecurities filled his office. After her one-hour of therapy was over the doctor referred Gabby to the chemical dependency recovery outpatient program. She walked two blocks over and made an appointment to return tomorrow. On the next day, Gabby opened up again to the Psychiatrist. This time, she was given a prescription to help wean her off of sleeping pills. She felt alive, well and empowered.

The phone rang as she walked into the house.

"Hello?"

"Well, hello Ms. Thang! We've been calling you." Carla screamed into the phone. "What are you doing?" Deanna chimed in.

"Just getting in from the doctor. Where are y'all at?"

"We on our way to Apple Bees. You wanna go?" Deanna asked.

Gabby was hesitant. She wanted to go, but she was looking so unhealthy.

"We'll be there in fifteen minutes, and you better open the door!" said Carla.

"Okay! Okay!" Gabby smiled a genuine smile. She loved her friends.

Brian walked in with a half smile. He wanted to share his news about Quetti, but he didn't know what kind of mood Gabby was in or her availability.

He Looked Like A Man, Until He Barked

Gabby walked out of the room in a pair of blue jeans that used to fit tight, but now they fit. She wore a green T-shirt and a silver belt, with silver slides and jewelry. Her hair rested on her shoulders and her wedding ring sparkled from across the room. She wore make-up for the first time in almost three months. Her radiance was strained but present. She grabbed her silver Coach bag and headed for the living room. Brian was standing there.

"Wow!" Brian was pleased to see her up and dressed and looking like her old self. There were still traces of insecurity and pain in her eyes, but she looked a thousand percent better.

Gabby blushed. She hadn't drawn a response of that magnitude from Brian since before they were married. It felt good to see his desire. Gabby dared to hope that this new Brian; this man that was so attentive and thoughtful was here to stay.

"Where are you going?" Brian asked.

"I'm going to lunch with Deanna and Carla."

Deanna knocked on the door. She'd managed to leave TJ and Ashley with Troy. Carla had left Roni home too. Ron was taking her to the zoo. He'd been so helpful these days. He'd gotten drunk once and got right back on the horse. Carla had been going to church again. She committed to praying for her family. Things had been well.

Gabby initiated a kiss from Brian and walked out of the door with her friends.

At lunch, Deanna gave more and more details about her cooking teacher and her acceptance of his offer to partner with him in his grandma's restaurant. They both gave Deanna ideas on how to decorate. Gabby was especially good at interior decorating and design. She lit up with fresh excitement as Deanna described the place. Gabby was her old self. They laughed and talked until they were hungry again. After finishing their dinner, they ordered to go meals for their spouses and kids.

Deanna held the door for the pregnant lady entering as they walked out. Kelly recognized her instantly because she'd been watching her, and she'd studied the picture that she swiped from their home months ago. Deanna smiled her friendly hello smile. Kelly spewed hatred at her with her eyes. Deanna wove her eyebrows together with confusion. Her gut told her that the woman's hatred of her was connected to Troy some kind of way. It didn't hurt at all. As she got in the car, she looked into the restaurant and it registered that the lady was pregnant. Deanna's stomach churned with discomfort. *Troy's having a baby with someone other than me. Wow.* She couldn't go forward. The car behind her blew it's horn. Deanna made a U-turn and went back to Applebee's.

"What are you doing?" Gabby and Carla asked, concerned.

"That woman in there is having Troy's baby. That's who he's been with!" Deanna started to cry.

"Dee don't do this. Don't embarrass yourself. Let it go. There's nothing you can do. You said you were done. Just be done." Gabby reasoned. Carla prayed, silently.

"How could he do that to me?" She cried.

He Looked Like A Man, Until He Barked

"I don't know, but you said you were leaving him. Just leave him."

"I'm leaving him because he's dogging me—Not because I want to. I can't stay. I can't take it!" Deanna cried.

"Let me drive Dee." Gabby got out of the car and came around. She helped Deanna into the backseat with Carla.

Deanna dropped her head onto Carla's shoulder and she cried.

Gabby backed out of the parking stall. She looked inside Applebee's and saw Kelly standing there with her hand on her belly and a nasty/hateful smirk on her face. It took everything in her not to drive the car straight through the restaurant.

33

Sheila was lonely sometimes, but for the most part things were going well. Her mind was certainly in a better place. She was growing closer and closer to Sister Esther; so close that the kids started calling her Grandma, even Lil' Tony. He'd been going to church with Sheila every Sunday.

Asia and Troy were hanging tough. They were looking for a house and everything. Sheila still couldn't get completely comfortable with Troy, but he did appear genuine. It was her hope that she was wrong about him. The bottomline is, Asia was happy.

Brian had given Troy a list of homes that were pending or simply no longer available. He informed Troy that he needed to find a new realtor. He would not accompany them on anymore bogus house hunts. After witnessing what that type of behavior did to Gabby, Brian wanted no parts of it.

The house game was yet another illusion that Troy used to keep his relationship with Asia alive. Periodically, he took her on a house hunt under the auspices that they were buying a home together. It was wishful thinking on both of their parts. Troy really cared about Asia and would have loved being with her full time. Whenever he was with Asia, he felt whole. She made him feel like he was enough. Enough everything—man, lover and friend. With the exception of his marriage and his lies, their relationship was good.

Asia picked up the list of homes off the floor in her bedroom. She was searching for her other brown shoe to wear

He Looked Like A Man, Until He Barked

with her brown suit. The paper was marked HOMES FOR TROY. She tossed it in her bag. The homes that had the red asterisk next to them were homes in Troy's neighborhood. Those were the homes that Troy should avoid. Asia got in her car and drove to work. After dropping Little Tony off she dialed the JW Marriott at Lenox Hotel, Atlanta, GA.

"Hi Tamara how are you? Asia asked. She was more comfortable with Tamara having met her in person a few months ago.

"Hello Asia."

"Hey. When you see Dr. Arlington can you ask him to give me a call? Just wanted to say good morning."

"Sure." Tamara hesitated. She didn't feel comfortable lying to Asia. After meeting her in person and seeing how beautiful she was and how genuine her feelings for Dr. Arlington were, she just didn't want to lie anymore.

"Thank you. Have a good day." Asia hesitated too. She picked up on Tamara's hesitance. *There could only be one reason why she'd hesitate. Troy is not there.*

Troy had spent most of the month of October with Asia. It was time to stay home. Deanna was strangely cooperative. She seemed distant in a scary kind of way. He wasn't sure where her head was at, so he pulled back and committed to staying home this weekend and a few days next week to see what he could see.

Asia let him go easily. She couldn't get off from work this time to accompany him to Atlanta. She kissed him at the airport and drove away. Troy waited until she was out of sight then walked to the parking lot and got his car. He loaded the clothes that he brought from her house into the trunk of his car, replaced both car seats and headed home.

Deanna wasn't home. She was at Carla's. Since her graduation, she'd been helping Ken in the evenings with the restaurant. It was coming together very well. Gabby was doing the decorating. She and Ken were planning the menu and Brainstorming about the direction of their business. CREAM OF THE CROP was opening in one month.

Troy walked into the house and went straight to the phone. He called Carla. She told him that Deanna had just left. When he hung up, he looked in the kitchen and dinner was already prepared. Everything was neat and in order. He was just about to make his own plate when Deanna walked in.

"Hi baby," She smiled wide and slipped into his arms.

Troy kissed her back. He loved her new disposition. "Hi baby. How are you?" He asked.

"I'm good. You ready to eat?" Deanna asked as she deposited TJ into her walker and directed Ashley to put away her shoes and her jacket.

"Yeah. I'm ready." Troy walked out of the kitchen into the family room and settled down.

Ashley jumped into his lap. Deanna chimed in, "Ashley give Daddy a minute to unwind baby. Come in here and keep TJ company. Read her a story for Mommy; can you do that?"

"Yes. I can read!" Ashley ran to get a book. She couldn't read, but she could make up a stroy to coincide with the pictures in the book. Deanna laughed at her and warmed the

He Looked Like A Man, Until He Barked

meal. She served Troy his plate, served Ashley, and made a plate to share with TJ. They ate and talked and when Troy wanted a second helping, Deanna sprang to her feet and served him again. Treating Troy like a king was harder than letting that pregnant lady at Apple Bee's live. She was comforted then by her plan, and it was her plan that took the steam out of her now.

After the girls were in bed, Deanna and Troy went to bed. He pulled out his faithful condoms, and Deanna craved Dramamine. Her stomach was so queasy she almost couldn't pull that part off. She thought about Ken and wished he was there. His image popped in her head, and she held it as Troy made love to her. She even managed to enjoy it. *Ken you've helped me in so many ways. I can't wait to be free to show you how I really feel. Please God let him still be available.* Deanna sometimes panicked when she thought about the two + years that she'd known Ken. *I hope he's still attracted to me.*

Asia missed Troy fiercely, and it had only been a day. Things were slow today at IMAGES Consulting, so she was given the afternoon off. Lil' Tony was at church with Sheila and the girls. Not really wanting to go home she turned onto Mac Arthur Blvd. She decided to take the scenic route home to kill time. Her car turned up 98th Ave all by itself. The next thing she knew she was referring to the listing of homes for sale and headed straight to Elysian Fields.

34

Saturday came and Saturday went. Brian was not invited to the party. Michelle had not returned any of his phone calls. His gut told him that her husband was the culprit. He played several possibilities over and over in his head. There was a part of him that was hurt by his exclusion now that he wanted to be apart of Quetti's life, and part of him reasoned that it was a good thing that he hadn't mentioned Quetti to Gabby.

Gabby was doing well lately. She was decorating some building or something. The assignment had her excited and feeling purposeful. As a result, they were making love on a regular basis. She had finally told him that she was in recovery around the sleeping pills. There were times when she struggled. When she suffered from insomnia he got up with her. Sometimes they played hangman, or she read to him from the novel she was reading. Sometimes they sat on the deck and watched the moon, stars or clouds. Sometimes they just listened to the night. This week Gabby slept. Every evening she slept sound. Brian was glad because he slept too. This morning he awoke well-rested and ready for work. Gabby slept in. She had a noon appointment with THREE-DAY BLINDS to discuss window treatments for the building she was decorating. Brian left a rose on the kitchen counter for her with a gift-wrapped box of business cards.

Interior Designs by Gabrielle
Commercial Design Specialist

He Looked Like A Man, Until He Barked

He closed the door gently behind him. In his car the phone rang.

"Hello?"

"Hello Brian. I'm sorry it took me so long to contact you. I had my baby Sunday morning." Michelle offered.

"Congratulations. What'd you have?"

"A boy, 9lbs, 3ozs. 22 inches."

"Good job. I know your husband is proud."

"Yes he is." There was a pause. "Well, we have decided that it's best for Quetti to learn the truth while she's young. We would like to sit down with you and your wife and discuss how to introduce you all into her life."

"That's fine. Anytime is good for us."

"Well, what about this evening?"

"This evening is fine. Let's say 6ish."

"Sure."

Brian gave Michelle his address and home phone number again. They both hung up feeling good about their conversation.

Brian dialed Gabby. He needed to tell her about tonight.

Michelle hung up and called her babysitter. "Hello, Granny. Is it possible to keep Ladybug until 8 o'clock? I'm finally meeting with her father. Pray that it goes well for us."

"Sure baby. She can stay the night if you need her to."

"Oh no, 8 o'clock will be fine. One of us will pick her up after we meet with him and his wife."

"Everything will be fine. Trust God." Sister Esther smiled. She hung up feeling good that things were working out for Michelle. She recalled when Michelle joined Truth & Light

Church. She had ministered to her just like Sheila. Now she's married with a husband and a new baby. Even Ladybug's father has finally come around. *"Amen."* Sister Esther smiled as she placed teacakes on a tray for the babies. Her day care was not a licensed facility. She was the old lady in the neighborhood or at the church that kept kids.

"Why isn't Gabby answering her phone?" Brian had dialed her several times. He cancelled his appointments for the day in the hopes of talking to her about Quetti before 6 o'clock.

Gabby sat in the waiting room. She smiled at her business cards. Brian was so supportive of her. It made her feel good. She loved him again. There were moments of fear that he'd revert back to his old behavior, but she managed to love him again.

The meeting with THREE-DAY BLINDS went well. They'd chosen a complimentary window treatment. Deanna and Ken both were satisfied. CREAM OF THE CROP was destined to be a hot spot. This was a soul food restaurant, not a soul food kitchen or a chicken shack. This was collard greens with smoked ham-hocks, fried chicken, hot water cornbread, green beans with potatoes and candied yams. This was roast beef, meatloaf, creamed potatoes with broccoli, baked macaroni and cheese and dinner rolls. The food was served on plates with cloth napkins and glassware. The ambiance was a down home setting. Shoes were removed; jazz played softly, the art wrapped around you like a blanket. The staff was as subservient as first-line workers—it was

He Looked Like A Man, Until He Barked

their job to provide you with comfort. This was a restaurant; a reservation appreciated restaurant. This was the cream of the crop in soul food dining. Gabby was proud of her contribution.

"Number 26." The nurse called.

Gabby stood up and walked to the laboratory. She extended her arm and gave her blood.

"Thank you." She rolled her sleeve down and left.

Her phone rang.

"Hello?"

"Hey Baby, where are you?"

"I'm at the restaurant."

"Still?"

"Well, I'm on my way home. What's wrong?"

"Nothing. I'm home. I need to talk to you."

"Okay. I'm hungry. You want something?"

"Chinese?" Brian suggested.

"Sure. I'll pick it up."

"Hurry up. It's 11:30 am already."

"Okay." Gabby hung up thinking what's the urgency.

She stopped and got the Chinese food.

On the way home she called Kaiser Hospital. A message was forwarded to her doctor. She was instructed to wait for a return call.

Gabby was hoping to talk to her doctor before she got to Brian, but it didn't look like it was going to happen that way. She parked, and grabbed the bag of food. Her phone rang.

"Hello?"

"Hello Gabby. This is Dr. Eastman. It's positive. Congratulations. I will transfer you to the receptionist to make an appointment as early as possible. I need to keep a careful eye on you. Whenever fertility is naturally lifted we need to be extra careful."

Gabby didn't say a word.

"Gabrielle?" Dr. Eastman asked.

"Yes. I'm here." She cried.

"Okay. See you soon. Congratulations."

"Thank you."

Gabby managed to get an appointment for tomorrow at 9 am. She reached in her glove compartment and got Brian's announcement card. She'd bought one earlier in the week just in case. Gabby had taken six home pregnancy test before going for the blood test. Dr Eastman had told her years ago that she needed to alleviate her stress to increase her chances of conception. Brian's lifestyle wouldn't permit it. She wanted to scream and yell and run and all of that. *A BABY! A BABY! MY BABY!* She whispered *"Mommy"* to herself as she entered the house.

Brian sat in the kitchen with an excited and scared look on his face. It was now a quarter to 1pm. Gabby sat the food on the counter and went into her purse for the announcement card. She handed it to Brian.

He took it and laid it on the counter. He nervously started making their plates. "Baby go sit down. Sit at the table. I'm going to fix your plate and I'll be right there."

A crushed Gabby walked into the dining room. She sat down. Brian appeared with their plates and left. He returned with their sodas. Gabby looked in his hands for his card; he didn't have it. He sat across from her.

"Babe, we need to talk." He started.

"First let me say, I'm so sorry about all the pain I've caused you over the years. I know you've heard rumors about all the relationships I've had and all the kids that I've fathered. Well it's not all true." Brian was trying so hard to find the words he didn't' even notice the tears in Gabby's eyes. He didn't notice that he hurt her feelings. He was busy looking at his plate.

Gabby held her breath. She just wanted to celebrate her baby today. She didn't want to accept his children. The selfishness was unlike her. She cried because she was ashamed of her feelings. She was hurt because she couldn't celebrate her baby, and she hated being in the situation overall.

He continued. "I hope you've noticed that in the past few months I've changed. I love you Gabby, more than I love myself. You are the reason that I'm the man I've become. I saw your pain one day, I really saw it—and I knew that it was time for me to be true to myself and openly love you. You needed to know that I love you. You needed to see, touch and feel my love. I couldn't afford to be hip, slick or cool anymore, not at your expense. The truth is; that wasn't me anyway. I've always wanted to romanticize you, do the things that other men label as corny and be faithful. My heart is good Gabby. I'm a good decent person that was more of a follower than a leader. When I saw that I was losing you I found the courage to be true to myself." He finally looked into her eyes. Her tears were flowing. "I love you so much, Lady." He starred into her eyes until she believed him.

There were two reasons for the tears. The first one was that she accepted his apology. The second was fear. *Is this real?*

"Baby, no. Don't cry. It's nothing bad. It's a blessing."

"How Brian? How is your past blessing me?" Gabby mumbled. Her pain was heavy and the announcement of her pregnancy was ruined.

"Gabby," Brian came around to her side of the table and pulled her from her chair. He walked her into the family room with his arm around her shoulder. Stiffly, she walked with him. They sat down on the sofa. The one that she'd slept on under the influence so many times. Her addiction stirred, she fought to re-channel her thoughts.

"Gabby. I'm sorry about that stuff. I love you. It's not a blessing in a sarcastic way. I have been cleaning up my mess and I wanted to share that there were three women claiming that I fathered their children. I tested the kids. Baby I didn't father their children. I know that doesn't ease your pain."

In spite of her goodness, Gabby's heart rejoiced at the understanding that her baby was Brian's only child. While composing herself, she redirected her energy towards him.

Brian started again. "Babe. Look at me. My past is going to be apart of our lives for a long time. I can change my behavior—I can be a better man, but some parts of it I cannot change. When I tested the boys I was glad that we were free from them. Their mothers were raunchy, classless women. Their results meant that we didn't have to deal with that type of ignorance for the rest of our lives. I'm not proud of my feelings of joy about that, but it's the truth. I'm glad we don't have to deal with them. But, there is one that I know is mine. Gabby I have a daughter. Her name is Quetti. She's four years old. I contacted her mother also. She's remarried, she has a newborn baby boy and we share Quetti. She and her husband are going to stop by tonight to discuss with us how to incorporate Quetti into our lives."

Gabby ached for her ruined announcement. She wanted to go to sleep. She wanted to avoid this information. She wanted to escape.

Gabby was numb. She sat there for awhile, with her head still on his chest, just listening to Brian's heartbeat. He held her and stroked her hair. Brian started again. "Gabby. I'm sorry this happened. When I said it was a blessing, I was talking about Quetti. Her parents are civil people. They are willing to share her. I know how much you want to be a Mommy. I thought you would be okay with it."

Gabby continued to sit there. Her tears fell like a leaking faucet. They were slow and constant. Brian leaned back, pulled her chin upward and looked at her. "Gabby, can you please forgive me?" She nodded and looked downward. Brian lifted her chin again. His tear dripped on her nose. "Gabby I am so sorry. So very sorry—I will never do anything else to hurt you. Never." He kissed her with passion he didn't even know he had. Gabby kissed him back. She loved him too. She was aching for her own pregnancy, but she remembered that she couldn't stress, so she *decided* not to—in spite of her pain. Finally, she wiggled free and walked away.

Patriece

She went to the bathroom and washed her face. As she looked in the mirror she realized that *Life is unfair and joy is short lived.* Gabby touched her stomach. *I love you! Thank you for coming into my life.* She walked out of the bathroom with tissue and a towel for Brian. Brian accepted it and looked at her with shame and pity in his heart that showed in his eyes. "Here." Gabby handed him the announcement card and walked back to the dining room. It was almost 3pm.

The card was blank, inside Gabby wrote:

It may be a girl, I'm hoping for a boy
But either way it will be ours.
Congratulations Daddy,

Love Mommy

Brian read the card twice before he realized that Gabby was pregnant. He walked into the dining room with the card in hand. "Oh my God! Baby, I am so happy. So happy!" He pulled her up from her seat and spun her around. Then he whispered. "This is *my* first love child. This is our first love child. Thank you for loving me. I am so undeserving of you." He kissed her again. Gabby smiled. It wasn't how she wanted it to be, but she was having a baby. *Two babies in one day.* Gabby sighed. She was exhausted.

They ate their meal, lounged in the family room talking about their future with Quetti, and their fears around meeting her parents. Several times they kissed in celebration of

He Looked Like A Man, Until He Barked

their own baby. Gabby was trying to accept Quetti into her heart. She kept seeing Brian with another woman and them having sex and him on the phone talking about their baby. It was a bit much, not to mention she had to compose herself to participate in a discussion concerning the best interest of the child.

At 6:00 exactly Michelle, husband and baby knocked on the door. The awkwardness lasted but a moment. Michelle's warmth and humility took the sting out of the situation. Her eyes communicated that she didn't know Brian was married until it was too late. Gabby accepted her telepathic apology. Gabby held their baby, and Brian announced their pregnancy. They offered sincere congratulations. Michelle looked around their home and noticed the picture on the mantel.

"Is her name Esther?"

"Yes. That's my mother." Gabby responded.

"That's our sitter. Quetti is there right now. She's kept her since birth. She calls her "Ladybug". Quetti was too much for her to say."

Brian looked at Gabby, and Gabby tried to smile. Her pain was visible. This was too much for her. Michelle walked over and hugged her. "Gabby. We will take this at a pace that's most comfortable for *you* and Quetti. This meeting is about *your* happiness too. Thank you for agreeing to even help with her upbringing. I appreciate that. Brian stayed away from her all this time out of consideration of your feelings. No one meant to hurt you, especially not Quetti. What's done is done. Let's try to make the best of this ugly situation.

Patriece

I apologize. I never meant to hurt you. Please forgive me too." Michelle was crying too.

Gabby accepted her apology with a nod. It helped that Michelle acknowledged her feelings in all of this. She was overwhelmed. Part of her wanted to go to sleep. Part of her wanted to be adult about the situation. Most of her swayed between hurt and anger.

They sat down and talked an hour or so more. They agreed that they would get together, without Quetti, for a month or so and then introduce Quetti. The good thing is, she already knew Brian and Gabby from seeing them at Granny's house.

Gabby lay in bed awake. *Don't take a pill Gabby. You can get to sleep without that. Think about your baby. You are finally having a baby.* She got up and went to the bathroom. She looked at her stomach in the mirror and went back to bed. She fell asleep with her hand on her stomach.

35

Kelly had no friends, mostly because she would always ruin the relationships. She'd slept with more than three of her friend's husbands in the past. She'd slept with scores of married men, and her behavior was mentioned in over a dozen divorce preceding.

Kelly only wanted to be loved. She was head over heels in love with the idea of being in love. It never occurred to her that she was stealing the love, affection and future of other people, including innocent babies. This entrapment scheme she had planned against Troy would effect many lives including her own baby.

Each man she kept in her bed when his children could have gotten a good night kiss was a form of selfishness that was unforgivable in the laws of Murphy.

As she lay on the delivery table with no one anxiously awaiting the arrival of her son she realized that she had cheated them both. Instead of sharing the blame with Troy she blamed Troy, solely. Her grief turned to sorrow and her sorrow to hatred and her hatred turned to vengeance. Kelly pushed and this time she screamed too. The pain was indescribably excruciating. Her thighs were trembling as her body struggled to deal with the intensity of the pain. She knew that she was ripping in half. The space between her private and her butt was on fire. She longed for someone to stuff her ice chips between her legs or better yet spray the fire extinguisher or something and then it happened. The wail of a baby filled the room. He was the most precious, perfect and beautiful baby ever born. His face matched Troy's face. His eyes were open and they looked into the eyes of his Mommy and said "I love you, no matter what." With that said, everything in the world was finally good for Kelly.

O my goodness! Look how precious you are. Look how beautiful you are. I love you so much! You are so beautiful, and you're my son. I love you Jeremiah.

Kelly's heart filled with love for her son. In his brief focus of her, she felt his unconditional love in return. It was a refreshing feeling. With him, she knew that her past didn't matter. The fact that she'd tried to trap his Daddy didn't matter. The number of lovers she'd had, homes she'd destroyed, marriages she'd ruined, or lies she'd told didn't matter. Jeremiah was a mass of her goodness. He was everything that was good about her and Troy rolled into one perfect baby.

The more she thought about Troy walking out on her, a vengeful spirit swelled within her. There was some satisfaction in donating his money to charity. A small amount of satisfaction in mailing bibs to his home, but she needed more. Kelly lay awake in the hospital bed thinking about Troy. She spent the first night as a Mommy scheming on how to snatch Troy from his children's lives.

With the force of impulse Kelly reached over and grabbed the phone.

"Hello?" Deanna asked with a start. It was 3:12 am. TJ was resting on Troy's side of the bed. His pillows doubled as a blocking tool to keep her from rolling onto the floor. Troy was in Atlanta recruiting Hospitalist for an HMO firm.

"Hello? May I speak to Troy?"

"He's asleep. Can I take a message?" Without even knowing whom it was she answered; it was obvious that he wasn't with her either. Deanna wasn't about to let another woman get the best of her. She may have thought she was being cute by calling there, but she'd hang up regretting it.

"Sure. Tell him Jeremiah was born last night at 11:15 p.m., and he looks just like him." Kelly threw the words like they were darts.

"I sure will. Is there a number? Or does he have it already?" Deanna calmly responded. There was no need for pain or retaliation—For over a year she vowed to leave if she could prove infidelity.

"He has it." Kelly was stumped. She called to unravel the nerves of Mrs. Arlington, and it didn't seem to work.

"Okay, he'll call you in the morning. Congratulations on your son." Deanna forced a smile into her tone. Kelly heard sincerity.

She hung up. She couldn't believe that the lady she saw at the restaurant was calm about her calling her house with news of Jeremiah's arrival. She expected her to holler, scream, cry, and put Troy out. Kelly expected homelessness to lead Troy directly to her. Her effort backfired just as her plans of entrapment.

Deanna hung up the phone and dialed Ken.

"Ken. Can you meet me at CREAM OF THE CROP at 10:30 am?" Deanna pushed through the tears that she could no longer contain.

"Sure."

She hung up and dialed Carla.

"Carla can you come or can I bring the girls to you in the morning?"

"I can come over there. You okay?" Carla didn't want Deanna to see or smell Ron passed out in the living room.

"Yes, fine. It's time to implement my plan. I'm going to meet Ken."

"Ken? What are you doing Dee?"

"What's best for me. I'll see you in the morning. Troy's out of town for a few days. So I have plenty of time to do what I need to do. Thanks for helping out.'

"Be careful Dee."

"K. I love you."

In the morning Deanna slipped into a pair of jeans, a T-shirt and a pair of K-Swiss tennis shoes. When Carla got there, she left without any further information. She drove to the restaurant. It would be open to the public in five days. It was a beautiful venue. Coupons for low cost appetizers had been mailed to every business establishment, corporate office, hospital, fire station, private practice and small business within a 70-mile radius. There were 15,000 coupons circulating. A staff of 60 had been hired for the three shifts—most of them students or former students of Ken's and their families.

Deanna sat at a table in the corner and cried for the last time over her marriage. Ken watched her. Ken valued her.

He Looked Like A Man, Until He Barked

Ken desired her. It was so plain. It was undeniable. Without warning their lips brushed against one another. The salt of Deanna's tears tickled Ken's taste buds. He wanted to comfort her. She pulled back.

"Ken I want you. I want you so bad. We can't do this right now. I'm still married. I can't deal with you until I'm free." Deanna cried some more. That vulnerable part of her wanted him to hold her, make love to her, make it all better. There was something about being in the shelter of a man's arms that felt safe. She wanted to feel that, even at the expense of her self-respect and integrity.

"Deanna. I love you enough to wait."

"You wont' have long. I need your help." Deanna pulled herself together. She leaned back and told Ken her plan in its entirety. Then she asked, "Do you think you can do that?"

"Yes. I certainly can."

Deanna and Ken spent the rest of the morning together.

Troy's car sat in the driveway. If it weren't for the license plate, Asia would have not been positive. As she drove up closer to the house, she noticed that there were two car seats in his back seat. The shocking thing is that they had gone to dinner, to drop his car off at the airport and back to her apartment last night. They had made love and left out this morning as a family. On her way to work, she dropped him at the airport.

Asia had no idea that Troy's flight wasn't leaving until later. She didn't know that once she drove off he'd come out of the airport with his luggage and retrieved his car. He drove home. Deanna then dropped him off at the airport again. This time he boarded the plane and took his flight to Atlanta. Troy always added a few days to his trips so that he could spend time with both of them.

Asia couldn't leave Troy's house. She just sat and stared at it. Her emotions were running high. Shock was an understatement. Instantly her head started throbbing with pain as she tried to think of reasons for Troy's car to be at this house instead of the airport where he'd left it. Logistics forced Asia to accept that only two things could have happened. Either Troy has no business in Atlanta and he was here at this house, or he left the airport after she dropped him off and drove himself to this house. Either way it made her feel like a fool.

Deanna opened the front door of the home. Asia thought she was striking. Her eyes were tear streaked, and she looked as hurt as Asia felt. As she approached the car parked next to his, her cell phone rang. She answered as she got inside of the car. By the time she sat down Asia was in tears. Before Deanna could drive out of Asia's view, Asia's phone rang. Her heart leapt to the ceiling of her car. "Hello?" She answered in a startled tone.

"Hi Baby, how are you?" Troy asked.

Asia couldn't speak. *Did he just call her and now he's calling me? Is Troy crazy? What is going on?* Asia noticed that Deanna's call ended a moment before her phone rang.

"Asia?" Troy called.

"Yeah?" She mustered.

"Are you okay?"

"Yes. I'm uh-uh...uh—looking at a house."

Troy asked. "With Brian?"

"No. I stumbled up on this one myself."

"Where is it?"

"Oakland. Can I call you back?"

"Sure. I'm at the hotel. Leave a message with Tamara if I'm not around."

"Okay."

"Love you."

Asia hung up before he could finish his sentence. She couldn't bring herself to say, "I love you too".

What's going on? Deanna rushed me off the phone like she didn't want to be bothered. Asia hung up in my face??

The truth was glaring. Asia couldn't be a fool any longer. She had to find a way to steel her heart against Troy.

Deanna ripped open Troy's cell phone bill, something she had never done in all her years with him. She skimmed the outgoing calls and she noticed the repetitive numbers. She dialed the number.

36

Asia managed to get to work and function fairly well for the past three days. Today was more difficult; it was one day from Troy's return. He was due back into town Tuesday night. The original plan was for her to meet him at home (her apartment) on Tuesday after she got off from work. Tomorrow was Tuesday. Asia couldn't shake the fact that his car was at a home in Elysian Fields. The car that she took him to drop off at the Airport and then got up early the next morning and dropped him off at the airport again, to take a flight to Atlanta. *How could his car be in Elysian Fields? Did someone pick it up for him? Why? Did he double back on me?*

Asia had driven by the house at every opportunity. She drove by on her lunch breaks. During the night when she couldn't sleep she bundled up Lil' Tony and laid him across the backseat with a pillow and a blanket. She drank coffee and watched that house. She had seen a lot of the activity, but she didn't analyze it. Her heart was wrapped up in Troy's deceit. It hurt so badly.

In one hour's time Asia realized that meeting Troy at her house tomorrow night was going to be extremely difficult. But, there was a piece of her that wanted to hear the lie. She hoped it would be good enough to dismiss her common sense. Otherwise she would look like a fool. Sheila had warned her about him.

It was lunchtime, finally. Asia had not done a thing at work all day. Her mind was so pre-occupied with thoughts of Troy's lies, trying to figure out his motive for lying and deal with her own pain. She held a lot of personal guilt too. Asia knew that something was amiss with Troy. She knew that whole thing about his ex's car being broken etc. was a lie. Now she regretted accepting it. Yet in that secret place in her heart she did it out of fear. She didn't want to be alone. Her thinking was that if she could manage to pretend that he wasn't married and she didn't disrespect his marriage everything would be fine. Asia never found anything to indicate that he was married because Asia never looked for anything.

As the pain, guilt and need to know the truth pounced her, she dialed Tamara.

"Hello Tamara how are you?"

"I'm fine Asia how are you?"

"Good. Can you connect me to Dr. Arlington? I don't want to leave a message with you, no offense." Asia said.

Tamara was grateful that she was free to be honest with Asia. "He's not staying here at this time."

"Can you tell me when he checked out?"

"He checked out 2 days ago."

"Thank you Tamara. Have a good day."

The pain ate through her heart like lye on coarse hair. The realization that Troy had been in town for two days was jaw dropping. Asia sat at her desk too stunned to even cry, wondering how long he'd been playing her as his personal fool? She wondered what he was going to say when she told him about himself. Reality began to harden her heart like the transformation of a boiling egg. Her mind began to spin a vindictive web. *I should skin him and blow salt on him!*

Patriece

Kelly answered the phone on the first ring. "Hello?"

"Hello?" Deanna responded. She had no idea who this woman was but she knew that she had reached the right number.

"Hello?" Kelly answered as she laid Jeremiah in his bassinet. "Hello?"

"Hi. My name is Deanna Arlington, I'm returning your call from last night on behalf of my husband Troy."

Kelly smiled. Her day had finally come to have her say. "Did you give Troy my message?"

Deanna's heart paused. *If Troy's not with her then there is three of us.* She smiled *Troy's too much.* "Actually I didn't. It turns out that Troy's not home and since he's not there I think it's safe to assume that he's with Her." Deanna covered her sarcasm with politeness.

"What do you mean Her?"

"I mean if he's not with us, he's with someone else. I was simply calling to let you know your troubles are not with me, but some other woman."

Kelly's pain wouldn't let her hang up without striking at Deanna. "Well, whomever is my problem it will be solved soon. I have Jeremiah now and I plan to have his Daddy with him. Not your kids, not her kids, but his *son*. See rumors have it that the men make the girls and women make the boys so it's real clear to Troy who the real woman is. Real clear." Kelly pushed the words through the receiver with vengeance that could be heard.

"Careful now. The very trap you lay for someone else will catch you. Don't be foolish. God don't like ugly and He ain't crazy about pretty. You already disrespected my marriage you will not disrespect my babies."

"Your babies are your problem. My *son* is mine. He will have his father even if it means your girls lose theirs." Kelly liked the way that rolled off of her tongue, she smiled and felt a rush of pride for having hurt Deanna.

"The world is round I pray you can handle the wrath that you are putting out there, because it is going to devastate your world. And my children are the love of Troy's life. You're going to play hell keeping him away from them. As far as I'm concerned you can have him."

Kelly had no comeback so she hung up, but not before laughing an artificial hearty laugh into the receiver.

Deanna placed the receiver onto the hook and decided that Ashley and TJ would never be allowed to visit Troy in the presence of that woman. Then she smiled at her progress in implementing her plan. For the first time in a long time Deanna felt hopeful. Deanna's loyalty to her vows diminished.

Ken's help kept Deanna's emotions balanced enough to tie all her lose ends. Before Deanna left Ken, two days ago, she explained that things had to remain plutonic for awhile longer. She confirmed her attraction and assured him that she would hold it until she was free. Ken respected her integrity, though he hoped he could wait. He'd already waited close to a year for her to do something about Troy's behavior. It was his experience that she wouldn't leave Troy no matter what he did.

In her quiet time, Deanna made up her mind that even spending time with Ken before the divorce was final was inappropriate behavior. She wanted Ken to respect and trust her. In order to earn that, she had to do the right thing concerning their relationship. She had to exercise righteousness, self-respect and integrity. She had to display dominion over her body and emotions. For the sake of a lasting union with him, it was necessary for her to do those things.

She was confident that things would go smoothly between her and Troy. With no stone unturned, Deanna picked Troy up form the airport. She had planned to have sex with him. This time it was for her. Deanna figured that there would be nights when she had that itch, and there would be no one there to scratch it. She decided to sleep with Troy as a survival technique.

Troy stood on the sidewalk with his luggage. He wore a pair of slacks and boots with a silk sweater. His bracelet dangled from his wrist. His watch sparkled just so. Troy had manicured nails with a coat of clear polish. Deanna could tell that he smelled good. When he spotted her, he smiled. His smile was attractive; his bottom teeth were crooked. The flaw added sexiness to his smile. Troy had style. Deanna suppressed the phone call from Kelly, took a deep breath and greeted Troy.

"Hi Baby. How was your trip?" She smiled.

Troy smiled; confident he was a true player. *I got my women in line, even though Asia hasn't been available for a day or* so, I'm sure she's preparing to receive me too. She's not expecting me home for another two days. I'll call her when Deanna goes to bed.* "Hey Baby. It was fine. How are the girls?" Troy leaned over and kissed Deanna's cheek.

"They're good. They're with Carla. I wanted to spend some time with you."

"Oh yeah?"

"Yeah." Deanna reached over and stroked him there. Immediately he responded by making his zipper rise.

Deanna hadn't initiated sex in so long that both of them were surprised. She, however, was the only one privy to the knowledge that her heart wasn't in sleeping with Troy, but safe guarding her self-respect. Too many times she'd found herself vulnerable around sex and ended up miscommunicating her value. She wanted to scratch that itch before she began the process of waiting on her divorce decree. She was confident that during that time, she'd be spending time with Ken. Ken made her feel safe, special and appreciated—all of the things that made her want to be made love to. Deanna knew from experience that holding on to her body for as long as she could, would place her in a more respectable light in the eyes of Ken. She wanted the genuineness that she thought he possessed. This time Deanna planned to marry for love—not just her love, but reciprocated love.

At the house they began touching at the front door. It wasn't long before they were spread out on the living room floor. Deanna allowed herself the same freedom with Troy that she had in the beginning. This was for her. She made love selfishly. She took what she needed. With her guidance,

Troy satisfied her in a way that he'd never quite managed on his own.

This lovemaking went on until the middle of the night. They snacked, and watched movies naked, then were back at it like teenagers. Deanna even relaxed into an adult movie with Troy, something she had previously refused to participate in. Troy was impressed with Deanna's ability to relax. As she slept, he stared at her. Her beauty was so evident. Her caramel complexion, her paperclip shaped eyes, and "m" shaped top lip with a wide letter "u" as her bottom lip, made the beauty more evident. She was so sculptured with femininity it was mind-blowing. Her lashes resembled blades of the finest grass. His erection returned as he watched her. Normally she wouldn't take kindly to his awakening her with his needs, but tonight, she inhaled his need like a drag on a cigarette. Troy felt the familiar love of their beginning. He melted under her cooperation and passion.

Deanna imagined Ken with every motion. It was the only way she could prevent herself from being overtaken by the illusion of love that she knew she was dealing with. Troy was a good lover, but he had no emotional capacity. Deanna accepted that when Kelly called her.

Deanna realized that no matter what she did or endured Troy would never commit to her. It didn't hurt; it didn't even sting. It simply was. She cried as a response to his rejection. Troy's behavior communicated "I don't want you. You're not enough. You're not good enough. You don't satisfy me." in Deanna's head. He was so successful he'd started stripping her of her self-esteem. Little by little she started to feel like Gabby, then Kelly called. That phone call was the final bite. Deanna was done eating Troy's mess.

When Troy thought Deanna was asleep he went into the bathroom and dialed Asia. Her home number was disconnected. Her cell phone went straight to voicemail. "Hi baby, I wanted to say good night. I can't wait to get home. I miss you. See you in a few days. I'll take care of your phone bill when I get home. My plane lands at 4:15 pm California time. I'll be home when you get there. I love you."

Deanna heard every word. Her heart embraced her decision. She focused on her plan. When Troy returned to bed, she grabbed his hand and placed it there, then she coerced him downward until he found himself in the most vulnerable position of man. She enjoyed what Troy hated to give the most. Her climax was motivated by his submission.

Asia sat in front of Troy's house while he and Deanna were inside with no kids. She watched the bathroom light turn on as her cell phone rang. She checked her messages after the light went out, and she received the lies of Troy. Her pain was paralyzing. She wanted to drive her car into his house up the stairs and mow him to his death. She wanted to honk until he came outside. She wanted to bang on the door with her truths. She sat there and cried. Asia recalled the many messages she'd left with the hotel in Atlanta, Troy showing up at Lil' Tony's party with his daughter, his explanation of Deanna driving his car, the pattern of the days he was missing, the cancellations, no-shows, the hang-ups, and the showering of gifts to divert attention from his truth. If she had been honest with herself about what she was seeing and feeling, she would have accepted that Troy was a fraud from the beginning. She wanted so badly for him to be the real thing that she convinced herself that he was while the evidence showed that he wasn't.

37

Ron wanted to stop drinking. He just couldn't. After two weeks of not drinking, he relapsed. One day on his way to work, he was sitting at a traffic light and caught a sign out the corner of his eye that read The Town Pump. *I never knew that bar was there.* When he walked out of the bar, the sun was down, he'd missed a day of work as a no show, and there was a ticket on the car. His cell phone was on the seat of the car, and it indicated he had messages. With that thought, Ron returned to the bar for a little something to help him cope with Carla's response to the day's events.

At 4:00 am, Ron stumbled into the house. Carla sat in the family room with her feet in the sofa. Ronika lay on her chest. At the sight of Ron, tears began to stream from her eyes. Ron knew that he'd messed up. His thirst rekindled. He wasn't dehydrated but yearning.

Carla laid Ronika on the sofa. She held her breath as she walked over to Ron. She didn't say a word. She hugged him. She held him and he let her. The baby in her womb kicked and Ron felt it on his own stomach. "Carla, I'm so sorry." He mustered.

"So am I." She cooed. Then she began a prayer. Ron joined her, asking for his own deliverance and surrendering that he had a problem.

At 9 am, Carla dropped Ronika off to Gabby while she and Ron attended his first AA meeting. Without knowing the power behind it, Ron raised his hand in the meeting.

Patriece

Asia knew that she couldn't avoid Troy forever. At some point, she was going to have to tell him, that she was done. She had been to church with Sheila all this week to keep herself occupied. She would never admit it, but there was a solace within her when she entered the church. The members were inviting and friendly. There was a lot of hugging. There were even a few pretentious people, but overall the atmosphere was healthy.

Pastor Knowit was dressed in a suit today, no robe. He walked to the podium. "I had a text prepared for you, but as I was on my way this morning the spirit pulled me in another direction. Now we've already covered how to prosper—If I may change directions follow me to how to live righteous. Now I ain't always been a Pastor. Let's say I wasn't born this way, so I am qualified to head this discussion. In my day, I was what they called a rank sinner. See I had exceeded the trillions and billions of folks that commit them little everyday sins, even the millions that deal in the common sins. See I ran with the sinners that parlayed with the typed of sins that even an atheist didn't dare commit. I was ranked, you know, for bad, ruthless, heartless and foolish. After a few visits to the local facilities for those in need of incarceration, I took a safer route and became a gigolo. This was a lucrative business for me. It afforded me the finest food, shelter, and material things HER money could buy. Somehow I ended up in he hospital with 37 stitches in my chest and stomach, and my mother was told that I wasn't go-

He Looked Like A Man, Until He Barked

ing to make it, so she called the Pastor, my Daddy. Yes, I'm a PK. Anyhow, he knew exactly what happened, and he prayed over me. I can't remember what all he said, but I do remember the passage that he read and it changed my life. Turn with me if you will to Romans 13:13-14 and when you have it say Amen."

"Amen." Sprang from the congregation in unison with a few stragglers. As knowledgeable as Sheila looked, she had to reference the Table of Contents before she could turn to Romans. Asia smiled relieved she was looking on with Sheila because she didn't know the location of Romans or the Table of Contents.

"Now church when my Daddy read this passage to me while the tubes were drying out my nostrils and pumping oxygen into my lungs for me, I realized how close I was to death. I could see the hem of his garment. It was still not determined that I would live. As God would have it, the only thing I could do was listen. I heard them give me a 30/70% chance, thirty that I would live and seventy that I would die. I heard them saying things like we've done all we can. The rest is up to the body, and I screamed in my soul when my Daddy said 'No sir, its in God's hands now.' I remembered how bad I wanted God to remember me. Remember that I was a good child in spite of my adult behavior. I wanted God to take into consideration that I was the child of His faithful son and servant Pastor Marvin Knowit Sr. Then my Daddy whispered to my mother, 'he'll be all right. He knows how to pray, he'll be alright.'

Patriece

"I grabbed that with both hands." Pastor Knowit illustrated by grabbing the air and pulling it to his chest. "I couldn't move, I couldn't speak, but I could still pray and I PRAYED! I ain't gone stand up here and tell y'all no untruth. I didn't change that exact day, but I *BEGAN* changing that day. It took a while for me to hear the call on my life, but I finally heard it. See you got to first hear the word, then you got to *hear* the word with your spiritual ear, then you got to accept the word in your heart, and then you got to change your behavior. See the first time I heard the word, I was a child. The next time I heard it, I was teetering between life and death. The next time I heard it, I was being wheeled out of that hospital grateful for my life and respecting how I got there. I was determined to do things different, but that flesh....don't always cooperate, and it loves to beat determination. Consequently I kept looking at women, but I wouldn't touch'em. This here is what you gotta do, grab that word—Romans 13:13-14 and read it every night, every morning, every time he or she call. Read on your break, read on your lunch, but get that thing down in your spirit. Come out from under that sin with the victory!" Pastor Knowit wiped his brow with his handkerchief, then the corners of his mouth and put it back in his pocket. "Is there anyone here that wants to be delivered? Is there one? Please make your way to the altar and be blessed."

The choir immediately eased into a song. The organ soothed and wooed a few women from their seats as well as, one man. Pastor Knowit wouldn't let it rest there. He continued. "If you have children outside of wedlock, come. If he's

He Looked Like A Man, Until He Barked

got a wife, but you just can't let him go, come!" Pastor Knowit jumped up and down on the pulpit. His excitement of the deliverance was contagious. Asia involuntarily stood. Sheila stood too. Sister Esther shouted praises from her usher's post. Across the room Brian, Gabby and Michelle all stood. Michelle's husband sat with the baby. Quetti stood between Brian and Gabby until Brian picked her up. He milled to the altar, which was flooded now with both men and women; even teenagers with tear streaked faces. Some sobbing or crying while others were shaking and clapping and praising with hand waves.

Sheila and Asia got separated in the crowd. Neither seemed to care. The lady next to Sheila grabbed her hand and squeezed it. They held hands for most of the time they stood at the altar deliberately grabbing hold of the words from Pastor's mouth as if their ears had hands.

"We get into broken relationships with men and women 'cause we can touch them. They are what we call tangible, but we don't really need them. Imagine, if you can, reverting back to virginity with *this wisdom*—knowing just one man and just one woman and the two of you becoming one just one time. Imagine the blessing bestowed upon THAT UNION!" Pastor Knowit shook his head from side to side expressing his excitement of the glorious vision. His eyes rushed from person to person verifying understanding. He was hoping that they were making the connection. Again he wiped sweat from his forehead. "Those of you that are virgins, young people, see the pain of these that are here! This, is what sex is really about? It is not *All* feel good and good times. There's some pain involved."

Sensing that no other was coming; Pastor Knowit stepped into the crowd and touched the forehead and head of those in need. He blessed them.

As he touched them, Asia, looked at the man and his daughter standing next to her. It was Brian. Brian noticed her too. No words were exchanged.

Asia realized that she had to let Troy go. She had to regain her self-respect. It was time to deal with her guilt and shame surrounding having a relationship with a married man. Tears were flowing freely, as Sister Esther offered her Kleenex. For no reason, she cradled Asia in her arms until she was settled then escorted her to her seat with an encouraging smile and a tight squeeze.

After Asia was seated, Sheila reached over and held her hand. This was the first time the two had expressed unconditional love, without any kind of judgement.

The house was a mess. Asia had been crying all day. She had even read the scripture a few times. The knowledge that she had found out earlier that Troy was married was losing its substance. She struggled to justify his availability. It seemed impossible for him to spend so much time with her if he weren't really single. To help resonate his lies, she hopped in her car and drove to Sheila's. After borrowing Sheila's car she drove back to Troy's house. She could see him sitting in the living room through the huge picture window. He was dressed down and sitting on a sage colored sofa against a cappuccino colored accent wall. His feet were propped on the glass coffee table before him. He had a tall glass of something that looked like lemonade next to him on an end table. Asia dialed his cell phone and watched him answer it.

"Hi Baby." Troy whispered in a fake sleepy voice.

"Hi." Asia could barely speak.

"You okay?" Troy asked. When Asia didn't respond soon enough, he filled the empty space with "I miss you. I can't wait 'til tomorrow."

"Why?" Asia asked.

"So I can see you. It's cold and wet here. My bed is too big or you're just not in it."

Asia's stomach turned as she watched him through the window. He picked up his glass and sipped his beverage. As he put it down he smiled. Then a little girl toddled over to him. It wasn't Ashley. It was a baby, practicing its first steps.

"Babe. The Powers that 'be' are paging me. I'm going to have to go, but I'll see you tomorrow. After this meeting I'm packing, the shuttle will be here to get me first thing in the morning." Troy hung up.

Asia watched him pick up the baby. He kissed her and then sat her next to him. Hatred formed in the gut of Asia's stomach. Love made a good effort at dissipation, but its strength gave Hate a run for its money. In spite of the pain, disappointment and hatred Asia loved Troy. Her mind let go, pushed him away even, but her heart held on by an angle's hair strand. That strand contained just enough love to cause her to put her car into drive and return to Sheila's.

Patriece

Brian was so glad that he'd stopped showing homes to Asia. He had asked God for forgiveness when he saw her at the altar. It felt good to know that he had turned his life around. After service his party went to lunch.

Quetti loved Gabby. She cuddled with her at lunch. Michelle seemed okay with their budding relationship. In all honesty her heart was glad that they were so loving toward each other. She was grateful that Gabby was able to conceal her pain. Michelle felt safe. During breakfast Quetti called Michelle "Mommy" and then turned to Gabby and called her "Mama" no one flinched. Gabby's little heart fluttered. She recalled her suicidal thoughts and was grateful that she managed to hold on. The baby kicked inside of her and she smiled. Quetti smiled too. "My nother bruther moved!" "My nother bruther moved!" Her eyes were wide with excitement. She remembered her Mommy's stomach flinching that way with her baby brother just a few months ago. Everyone laughed and talked. No partner felt threatened. Quetti's little smile was precious to each of them. She truly had four parents.

38

Troy kissed Deanna, Ashley and TJ then walked out of the door. He wondered how he was going to manage making love to Asia. He and Deanna had done it enough to last him a few weeks if not months. She jumped him like it was their last time. She took him down memory lane, to their beginning. He wasn't sure what he did to deserve it, but it was truly good. So good that his heart loved her in an authentic kind of way that frightened him. He actually realized that she was ideal. These feelings were so strong that he processed his relationship with Asia and admitted that he cared about Asia, but he loved Deanna. Deanna had tolerated him unconditionally, forgiven him unconditionally; she'd been loyal and kept every one of her vows during their matrimonial ceremony. For the first time ever Troy felt the vulnerability of love. Instantly he felt the safety of Deanna's tenacity. There was even a measure of gratitude in him for the miracle of realizing his love for her and finally respecting hers. He made a mental note to call Brian and share the news. Brian had stopped hanging out with him for the most part. His love for Gabby had finally matured him as well.

Even with the realization of his ability to love Troy dressed for Asia's. His greed wouldn't allow him to walk away. At this moment in his life if she left he'd let her go, but his maturity was too young to initiate a break-up. In his mind he couldn't just let go of Asia. However, he could accept it if she left him. Of course he had Deanna so his pain would be minimal if at all. For the first time in his life Troy embraced the truth. The truth was that he was willing to commit to Deanna. His heart made the transformation. Going to Asia's today was habit. Yes he was emotionally bound to her also, but he could handle not ever seeing her again. Not that it would be easy, but he had chosen to allow himself to love Deanna. Deanna was his choice. She was a wife to the fullest meaning of the word. He wanted her.

Troy pulled up at Asia's and parked his car. He set there thinking of how their relationship would end. His love for Deanna wouldn't leave him alone; he dialed her.

"Hello?" Deanna answered, surprised it was Troy. He normally doesn't call her when he's with his mistress and his pattern was that he was with her now.

"Hi Baby. I was just calling to say I love you. I'll be home tonight. My trip was cancelled." Troy had decided that he wasn't going to spend the night with Asia.

"Ok. I'll see you when you get home. Bye bye." *Damn, I thought I had a few days. I better call Ken.*

"Bye Sweetie." Troy felt a rush of goodness over take him. He loved her more.

Deanna called Ken. "Ken, there's been a change of plans. Are you available right now?"

39

Sheila answered the phone on the first ring. She'd just finished reading her Bible and was feeling good about her place in life. Celibacy wasn't so hard. She'd come to value her body and knew that it was too precious to be given at every request. Things had really changed for her since she'd been in church. It wasn't that the preacher was so grand. It wasn't that the people were so perfect. It wasn't that she enjoyed the environment. The principles taught at the church afforded Sheila the discipline to be who she always wanted to be. She was comfortable in her own skin since having embraced the church. The logic behind the simple principles gave her a freedom that was unknown to her before. Sheila was happy. She was also glad that Asia had been attending church too. Their relationship was still close, but there was a wedge between them. Sheila knew that it was the changes in her life that placed the wedge there. She didn't drink anymore, she didn't sleep around and she didn't buy hot items or exploit every opportunity for self-gain. She didn't give her shopping list to drug addicts and then give them half the cash for stealing the desires of her heart. She didn't write checks that she knew would bounce. She didn't return items after using them. She was free from finagling. Sheila felt good. Things were not perfect, but her reaction was healthy. Sometimes she was lonely, but it always passed quickly especially when she thought of Asia. Sheila's gut told her that Troy was going to hurt Asia. She prayed for her nightly.

Patriece

The knock on the door was a surprise. No one was coming over today at all. Troy's return from Atlanta had bought Lil' Tony to her the day before yesterday and Asia was supposed to be with him.

Sheila approached the door with concern. "Who is it?"

No one answered.

"Who is it?"

"Me." He responded.

Sheila cracked the door. The voice was familiar yet unfamiliar.

"Who?"

"Me, James."

"James?" Sheila opened the door wondering how he found her. Not that she was hiding, but she had lost touch for these past two years. "What are you doing here?"

"I. Uh. Uhh. I'm hungry. Can I come in." He looked at the ground instead of Sheila.

Sheila's heart sank. James looked horrible. His hair was matted to his head in certain places. His hands were black. The dirt under his fingernails was as dark as used oil. His clothes reeked of urine and dirt. His skin was dark. He looked about thirty years older. He had wrinkles and lines in his face that weren't there just two years ago. He was looking bad during the divorce hearing, but Sheila had never thought he'd get here. She wanted to help him, but she also wanted him to go away. The hatred that she had in her heart when they broke up was replaced with compassion. Sheila wanted to hug her ex-husband; his condition wouldn't allow it.

He Looked Like A Man, Until He Barked

"Sure." She stepped aside and allowed James to enter her apartment. It was a three-bedroom apartment that she'd converted into a two-bedroom apartment with a den. As James stepped inside Sheila saw a shopping cart with bottles, plastics, aluminum and cardboard. There was some cloth and a flat pillow. She pretended not to see it, but she knew that those were James' worldly possessions.

"The bathroom is right through that hallway and to your left."

Sheila was going to go get the girls and Lil' Tony from day care in about two hours. Her plans were to fry chicken to go with the cabbage and rice she'd already prepared. They loved that meal as long as they could put sugar on the rice.

The aroma of the side dishes followed James to the bathroom. As he walked into the bathroom he cried. The bathroom was yellow, orange, green and white—mostly yellow. He knew his presence was going to ruin its cleanliness. He tried not to touch a thing. He unzipped his pants and relieved himself. Suddenly his bowels began to loosen. His detox had begun. His joints ached and his stomach was queasy. He sat on the toilet. He must have nodded off because when he opened his eyes, Sheila was standing in front of him. She'd run a bath and placed two dark towels on the counter top.

"James. James."

James couldn't talk. He was trying to focus. He wasn't loaded or high, he was exhausted. He'd taken his last hit nine days ago. Since then he relocated to an overpass way on the other side of town. He'd walked for four of those days.

Patriece

He'd walked from West Oakland to the mouth of Hayward. That's when he saw Sheila and the girls near the 99 Cents Only Store. He walked in the direction they drove and watched them for 2 days before he figured out which apartment they lived in. Today he said his prayers and walked to the door when Sheila was alone. Today he just wanted to see her. He just wanted to smell her. James loved her. It was never about love. It was about his addiction. He wasn't there to get her back. He was there because he loved her. He knew that part of his life was over.

"James. I have some food on. You can eat. You can also take a bath. I've run you some water. Let me know when you're out of your clothes. I'll run them through the machine." Sheila tried to hold her tears.

James did not hold his tears. He just raised his leg and kicked off his shoes, which were too big, and without laces. His jeans, which were also too big, fell to the floor. His underwear was soiled. At the sight of them he said. "I'm sorry Sheila. I'm so sorry."

Sheila reached down and picked up his clothes. She balled them up and waited while he gave her his shirt. Then he stood and stepped into the warm water. His body was so thin his penis looked larger than she remembered. His ribs, kneecaps, elbows, shoulder blades, hipbones and collarbones were well pronounced against his fat free body. James eased down into the water. Sheila gagged quietly as she left with the clothes. In the kitchen she double bagged them and took them with her outside. She tossed them into the trash while praying that James didn't rob her blind while she was gone.

He Looked Like A Man, Until He Barked

A few blocks away she stopped at the strip mall. There were two or three shops that carried cheap clothing. She decided on a store that advertised "NOTHING OVER $5". Inside she bought two pair of small sweat pants and two T-shirts with a pair of flip flop sandals. She bought a pack of underwear and a pack of undershirts. She then stopped at the 99 Cents Only store and picked up some deodorant, and razors and a comb.

When she arrived home James was still in the tub. She knocked and then tiptoed in. James sat in the tub with tears in his eyes. Sheila said nothing. She sat the clothes on the toilet top and left.

James had run a second tub of water. He had washed his hair and scrubbed his feet. This was his second bath. He washed everything again. His tears were flowing. James wept like a baby. He knew that Sheila was just being kind to him, but something in him hoped she was still his wife. When he got out of the tub Sheila sat in the kitchen thinking of ways to get him out of her house. It was time to go get the kids.

James entered the kitchen area. Sheila pointed to a plate of food. She'd fried the chicken and poured him a big glass of Pepsi. James sat down. His eyes were glossy with tears. He nodded. Then picked up his fork and began eating. Sheila stood to leave.

"Sheila, thank you. I'll be out of your way as soon as I'm done. I don't want to keep you from picking up the kids. I know it's time to get them. I've watched you all this week." He never looked at her.

Sheila looked at him. He looked more like James, but was still a stranger. She felt his love, but didn't acknowledge it. She didn't want it. She couldn't survive another bout of relapse with him. She just couldn't.

"Okay." She walked into the kitchen and started piddling around to avoid conversation with him. James walked into the kitchen a few minutes later and rinsed his plate then put it in the sink. His forearm brushed against her and her stomach danced a familiar dance. He didn't notice. His brokenness pushed him out the door. He wanted to leave without her seeing his grocery basket. "Thank you Sheila. I appreciate your kindness. I really do. I'm sorry I didn't call. I don't have a phone right now."

"It's okay. See you around." She didn't look at him.

"Bye." James turned the knob and walked out the door. Sheila had placed a blanket, a fluffy pillow and the other outfit in his cart. She also wrapped up the rest of the food.

She would buy the kids some McDonald's. They would enjoy that. She heard the wheels of the grocery basket rolling away and was compelled to look out the window. As she peeked out she saw James pushing the cart and tears falling with each step. Sheila wiped her own tears and grabbed her purse. After giving him a few minutes to be completely out of sight she left. It was her intention to leave him with a measure of dignity.

He Looked Like A Man, Until He Barked

Kelly grew angry with Troy. She'd been dragging a bassinet from room to room careful not to leave her baby unattended for even a brief moment while he was doing nothing for Jeremiah. She grabbed her digital camera and snapped some pictures of Jeremiah. She changed his clothes a few times.

Jeremiah looked so much like Troy that when a few people dropped by from the hospital to see him, they commented that he looked like Dr. Arlington. Kelly responded 'I hope he's a doctor too.' And smiled, she was grateful that he looked like Troy. It would make it hard for Troy to deny him when she slapped that child support order on him.

Kelly searched for the cord to her PC that connected her digital camera to the computer so she could download Jeremiah's pictures. She was going to send them to Troy's email. Then she'd put a hard copy in the mail to his wife.

Jeremiah cried out. Kelly stopped everything and rushed to him. "Hey Man, good morning sleepy head. What's da mattah? What a matta wit Mama's big boy?" Kelly touched his nose with her own, while maneuvering her breast from her bra to nurse Jeremiah. He latched on and she continued to talk to him. "Mama, gone make Daddy leave dim utta babies and come be wit you. You da baby now. You da baby now. You da only boy. It's your turn now. You da baby." Kelly grew more vindictive as she imagined Troy at home with his daughters, playing and laughing and him buying them little stuff. What about Jeremiah? What about her baby? Kelly was hurt and disguising it as anger.

Patriece

After nursing Jeremiah, he drifted back to sleep. She held him in one arm while she connected the camera to the PC. Her mouse pad was pink, her room was decorated in pink, and the camera was silver with a thin line of pink outlining it.

Jeremiah looked just like Troy. Kelly looked at him and smiled. She got angrier. Troy had never called her about Jeremiah's birth. She wondered if his wife gave him her message. She laid him on his back in his bassinet and rummaged through the envelope of things she'd taken from his Daddy's house. On an incomplete Capital One application he'd written his social security number. Kelly hadn't realized that the application was stuck to the cell phone bills last page until now. She typed in his email address and forwarded the pictures of Jeremiah to Troy. In the subject box she typed. GAME OVER, MEET JEREMIAH.

Then she picked up the phone, dialed Directory Assistance and allowed them to connect her call.

"Thank you for calling Alameda County Child Support Services. If you know your parties extension please dial it now. To hear this message in English...."

Gabby was glowing and excited. She'd been doing a lot of babysitting and loving it. Quetti was now on an every other weekend schedule and occasionally she kept her brother while Michelle ran a quick errand. Ashley, TJ and Ronika were over often to play with Quetti. Gabby loved them, but her heart told her she was having a boy. Whenever she went

He Looked Like A Man, Until He Barked

to the store she was always drawn to the boy section. Carla was having a boy any day so it would be nice if she had one too. Then they could grow up together.

Gabby dressed Quetti and combed her hair. They were going to meet Brian at the office for lunch. Tomorrow they were taking family pictures so to have a set of pictures before their family expanded. Gabby loved that Quetti was receptive to her and that she and Michelle had a good rapport. It made things so much easier. Michelle had so much class. She respected Gabby at every turn. Even when Gabby gave Quetti instructions she upheld them. It was the best case scenario of a bad situation.

Brian was hanging up with Troy when Gabby and Quetti walked in. He had a smile that made Gabby smile. Over lunch he shared that Troy had finally surrendered to loving Deanna. Troy had finally decided to respect his marriage. Brian went on and on; Gabby couldn't get a word in edgewise. Her prayer was that it wasn't too late. She knew that Deanna was tired and had been pulling back. Brian reached over and put his hand on her stomach. The baby kicked. A lady sitting at the table across from them dropped a bill on the table and walked out of the restaurant. She had a sad expression as she passed. Without an announcement Gabby knew that she *knew* Brian.

"That is one of them that said their son was mine." Brian volunteered as he leaned into Gabby for a kiss. She kissed him back, somewhat grateful for his honesty. Quetti decided to make spit bubbles which broke up the monotony.

Patriece

Ken went to Deanna's house for the first time. He was a little uncomfortable about being there, but he'd promised. Deanna opened the door. "We only have a few hours."

"I'm glad you followed your first mind and did most of it already. This might not even take an hour."

40

Troy knocked on the door. It opened and he stepped inside. Asia thrust forward a pitcher of stinging cold crystallized water into his face. The water was so cold it burned. The crystals hit like tiny fist. He thought instantly about Al "Grits" Green being burned with hot grits by his scorned wife.

The expression on his face gave Asia a degree of satisfaction. In less than a moment, Troy rushed her, knocked the pitcher from her hand, slammed her against the wall and drew back his fist...as he realized that he wasn't burned, just wet. Wet with water so cold it burned like fire.

Asia never flinched. She was prepared for the consequences of his reaction. Her demeanor frightened him; made him think before he punched her in the face. With his hand suspended he yelled at her. "What is your problem?!"

Asia moved from in front of him to pick up the pitcher. She wanted to secure a weapon, for she knew she wasn't done with making him angry. "What the hell do you think is wrong with me! Yo' black ass is married with two babies, possibly three! You have lied to me from the first day I met you. But, you won't lie to me a minute longer! I'm done! Get out of my house."

Troy stood there with the water dripping from him. He had no idea why he was suddenly freezing. He didn't even notice that Asia had a fan blowing straight into his face. She hoped he would catch pneumonia. Troy began "Asia what are you talking about?"

Patriece

"Do you really think I'm that stupid! You want me to tell you what I know so you can twist and turn it to fit your needs! I'm done playing the fool Troy. See what you don't realize is—I know EVERYTHING! I was *playing* the fool. I'm not strung out on your love! I DON'T Need you!" With a hushed tone, she added "and I don't *waannT* you either." Asia didn't cry. She didn't even want to. Her hurt had turned into hatred as natural as "B" follows "A". She stood there waiting for his response. His mouth was hanging open for what seemed like hours, but it was less than five seconds before Troy spoke. He didn't know what to say, but he knew he had to say something.

His heart was glad that he was free to love Deanna. He was glad that he could be her husband, that he could explore vulnerability. His pride, on the other hand, was wounded. It whispered to his ego *'She leaving you alone. Ha! Ha! Ha!'* For greed's sake Troy defended himself with lies. "Asia I love you. I want to be with you. I really do." He reached out to her. Asia slammed the empty water pitcher into his head and drew it back to repeat striking him as Troy rushed her and forced her into the clean living room. Everything was in order. Asia had cleaned up in her plight to quiet her mind, which was spinning with confusion and vengeful ideas. Troy pushed Asia on to the sofa and held her while lying atop her. Neither stressed over his wetness. Suddenly her tears sprang forward. It did her heart good that he appeared to be fighting for her, but her heart was wiser now and appearances from Troy were no longer enough. She needed to feel his love. It couldn't be shown with a shower of material things.

It couldn't be rubbed with his hand or spoken through his mouth. Asia needed her pulse to race, her head to agree and her soul to yearn for Troy. That was not happening. She knew without any doubt that Troy was not the man for her nor would he ever be. Her pain was the only tangible connection she had with the man that she loved so dearly.

He safely loosened his grip. He felt a measure of guilt, but his ego combined with his competitive nature wouldn't allow him to respect it. He leaned into Asia and kissed her eyelids. He then pressed his forehead against her forehead and cried with her. His tears were genuine. He wanted to let her go, but his ego wouldn't let him. He knew that he meant her no good and this pain would only get worst if he didn't let her go, but he couldn't do it.

They lay together in tears—pain and their end.

Finally Asia moved, "Troy you lied to me. You are still with Ashley's mother. You live with her... and that new baby is yours too." She pushed him off of her completely and sat up next to him. Her anger was percolating, like fresh brewed coffee in anticipation of the lie she believed was forthcoming from him.

"What are you talking about?...I'm not with her, that ain't my baby."

Troy couldn't block the slap that stung his face. Asia slapped him to both their surprise. Troy knew his motives were ill intended so, he didn't respond to the slap. He knew he deserved it.

"You are pathetic! I saw you Troy!! I saw you with these eyes." Asia pointed to her eyes, her face was wet with tears, but her tone was strong again. "Troy I went to look at a house in Elysian Fields and I stumbled upon your car. The one that we dropped off at the airport was mysteriously parked at a home in Elysian Fields." She was matter-of-fact and leaving no room for him to wiggle out of the truth.

Beads of sweet began to coagulate on his brow.

"I went back to that home, and I saw that same lady that was driving your car, you know the one with car trouble and the big belly. Her car must still be broken." She paused for effect. Troy just looked stupid. "A few days later I called Atlanta, you weren't there. You had checked out a few days earlier." Her voice cracked on the sentence; the pain was too heavy to hold. "I knew then that you were a liar and you had lied to me for almost 2 and a half years. At home, I cried and I cried and I cried." Asia regained her composure and began again. "Then I went back to that house, Troy." Her lips quivered as she spoke his name. He looked her in the eyes in spite of himself. "I saw you sitting on the couch yesterday. I dialed your number and you told me you were still in Atlanta. You rushed me off of the phone when the little baby toddled into the living room with you. You said you were being paged by the powers that be of your job and you had to go. You pretended to still be in Atlanta. I couldn't take it so I hung up. I came home and I cleaned up and I searched my soul. You don't love me. You never have. You don't even want me. You are a greedy, selfish, heartless man. I want you out of my house and my life for good. Leave me alone."

Troy didn't dare reach out to her with his hand, but he reached out with his words. "Asia. I'm sorry. I never meant

He Looked Like A Man, Until He Barked

to hurt you." He spoke louder and faster to stop Asia from interrupting him. "WAIT! Let me just say this please. Asia, you are right. I thought you were beautiful and I just wanted to sleep with you. My plan was to get in, hit it and move on, but you are not only beautiful, you are a good woman. You were so accommodating, attentive and affectionate. You were so carefree and trusting. I was attracted to your goodness, since I ain't shit. It was like the magnet between good and evil. And like evil, I just wanted to be in your presence. I know that I was wrong, and I'm sorry."

Asia looked around the apartment and she noticed how much beauty was around her. She had some really nice pieces. The vases and art and frames and tables were all in good taste. Tony loved oak wood and the color green and ceramics and without the clutter she could see him, feel him and embrace him. Yesterday as she cleaned and organized things, into the night, she felt him (Tony) comfort her. Troy was not the one. She knew it. The more she looked at her life with Tony, she knew that she had no life with Troy. It hurt like hell, but it was the truth. Everything stopped. Asia paused and let her tears flow. She walked to her sofa and sat down, then she looked Troy in his eyes, while he stood over her. "Troy. It's over. It hurts like hell, but it's over. My grandmother told me when I was young that 'men don't leave. Freedom comes from women who find the courage to let go'. As much as I love you Troy, I....let go. Please leave."

Troy's clothes stuck to his body and for the first time in his life he felt remorse for his behavior. He wanted to say something to Asia. He wanted to hold her until she felt better or stay with her to stop the pain all together, but he knew she was right. It had to end somewhere. The door was open for closure all he had to do was walk through.

Part of Asia wanted him to beg her, plead to stay with her again. She wanted her feelings to be wrong. She wanted him to profess his love for her and mean it. The only difference is she wanted, to be true, before she needed to hear it, even if it was a lie. Before she allowed herself to function as a fool. With that thought, Asia stood and stepped around Troy. She opened the door. Troy began to walk out of the apartment. Asia stopped him and handed him two bags of clothes and personal belongings. His eyes apologized, but his heart felt freedom. He decided to love Deanna.

Asia glanced at her feet as she closed the door. She stood in the puddle of water. A giggle turned into roaring laughter. *Troy thought he was burned! (She thought about his expression as that cold water and ice sickles hit his butt).*

41

Sheila lay in bed thinking of James. Her biblical teachings were gnawing on her heart. She tried to label her love for James as loyalty, habit or pity, but it was clearly unconditional love. Her mind had been on him all evening. Her heart and her common sense had begun to war about the entertainment of the idea of embracing him. She wanted to see him again. She wanted to nurse him back to health and sanity. She wanted to hold him and take his burden from him. She wanted to lullaby him into courage. Just rock him until he was confident to face this world without cocaine. In their previous conversations she'd learned that her statuesque husband with the bass-filled voice was fearful of people, responsibility and rejection. His fear was so great that he avoided it by using drugs. At first drugs was his tool of acceptance, people liked him when he transformed into the life of the party. Surely, he wasn't expected to be responsible considering his lack of discipline when it came to cocaine. Finally, he didn't strive for much because his addiction disassociated him from opportunity. Sheila had compassion for him and she understood him. She had fears too. She feared loving him.

When James knocked on the door he surprised himself. He hadn't been able to get Sheila off of his mind since he'd been there six days ago. He had promised himself that he'd stay away for at least a week.

"Hey, I was just thinking about you." Sheila's truth spewed from her mouth like larva from a volcano. Her joy was real.

James smiled. Normally he'd think he was "in there" again. He'd exploit her kindness and regret it later. Today he was grateful for her kindness. He was sure he reeked and looked a mess. She treated him like he wore the latest fashions and slept in a bed last night.

"Hey, yourself." He smiled. His teeth were putrid and missing.

"Come on in." She swung the door open. James stepped in.

"I'm sorry to drop in on you like this."

"No problem, want some lunch?"

"Yes. Please."

"You can shower if you like. No offense, that didn't come out right." Sheila blushed.

"It's okay. I'm glad you offered. I'd love to."

"Good. I picked you up a few things when I was out this week."

"Thank you."

Sheila felt a gush of moisture discharge into her underwear. James' stare weakened her. He looked at her with eyes of adoration. He was proud and he was sincere. "You're welcome."

The moment was awkward. Sheila was thinking she was crazy for responding to this homeless crack-head like that. If James were anyone else she would have shunned him.

He Looked Like A Man, Until He Barked

"I'll run you a bath." She walked down the hall feeling James' eyes roam her body as if he were groping her with his hands. After securing the door, she rolled some tissue and cleaned herself. Then she put on a panty liner and cursed herself for loving that man. The man, whom she was embarrassed to have married, bore his children and now desire. She started the bath water. James was still sitting at the kitchen table when she returned. The awkwardness came into the kitchen with her.

"Oh, your clothes." She turned around and went into her room and got the bag of clothes. "Here."

James opened the bag. The clothes were nice. Jeans and this time she bought socks and a pair of tennis shoes. "Wow, babe thank you. You've always been so good to me."

"It's okay."

"I really fucked this up huh?"

Sheila ignored him. She walked into the kitchen and started fumbling around with the dishes.

James eased into the bathroom.

In their separate spaces they thought of each other.

For the first time in James' life he *decided* he was done with drugs. He accepted that Sheila would probably help him, but she certainly wouldn't have him as her husband again. Help was enough.

Sheila cried at the sink briefly. She was disappointed at her heart. She was angry with her body for responding to his presence. Sheila had been intimate with more than her share of men. She made love with men that forced undergrowth from a fresh perm. So she knew that what she was feeling for

Patriece

James wasn't a physical attraction. It was his charm, his manliness, his broken-ness, his childishness, but most of all his kindness. She smiled to herself thinking of how much fun they'd shared. The time he dug in her mother's nose while she was fussing. The time he was chased by a dog and managed to stay on the hood of a Volkswagen bug in dress shoes. The time he grabbed her hand in the store and started running for no reason, then two aisles over whispered that he'd farted and was trying to get away from the smell, as they watched another couple enter the aisle and look at each other accusingly. She was still smiling when he appeared in his new clothes (that fit) looking more like himself than before. Her mouth opened. "James, I know you are sleeping on the streets still. I can't let you do that. You're the girls' father. I'm still single so it wouldn't be a problem if you slept here. I don't want the girls to see you like this so, you'd have to come after they were in bed, but you can sleep in the den. You'd have to be out of here around 6 am, before they got up too. I don't know how helpful that is, but you'd get a meal and a bath and a warm place at night if you want it."

"Of course I want it. Thank you." James held the bass in his voice, but it sounded softer somehow. He blinked back tears. He smiled weakly and he looked at her with embarrassing lust. His erection was evident and caused both of them to look away. Sheila made coffee, hazelnut. James had smelled hazelnut often in the two years he spent sleeping on the street, but hadn't tasted it. Sheila offered him a cup.

"I've been wanting to taste this coffee for years." He sipped his coffee. "It's as good as it smells." He smiled.

He Looked Like A Man, Until He Barked

They talked and watched movies for two and a half-hours. It was if they were never separated let alone divorced.

"Well, I gotta go get the kids. Lil' Tony too. Asia's in recovery from heartache. The guy she has been dating for just over two years looked like a man, until he barked."

"He's married?"

"Yeah. And he was perfect for her."

"That's a strong adjective. I strived for that and it kept me loaded. Now I just want to be loved. When I was out in the streets I'd be hitting the pipe and crying inside. I didn't want to live like that. I wanted to be a man, a husband and father. I wanted to be respected by my family—I just never felt I was enough, had enough, did enough or was good enough. Even now I'm overwhelmed with you. You're so beautiful, kind and strong too. You are fearless and I'm not, but I'm the man." James looked into his empty cup.

"James you can be scared. You just have to move inside of your fear. I've told you that before."

"I know. I couldn't though. Mostly because I stopped wanting too. I got comfortable with the addiction. Blacking out, numbing out and not being expected to do my part was easiest. Sheila it's hard to face failure all day everyday."

"It gets easier. I used to be scared, but I had to find courage because my mother made me do challenging things. As a result I made it."

"I know. No one made me. If I didn't want to, I didn't do it and there were no repercussions. My mother was glad I was around, since she had no man. I doubled as her husband. She ironed for me and everything; it's no wonder I developed insecurities. I was not prepared to do anything." James' tone was apologetic. "Sheila, I'm sorry. I've decided to give up the drugs. I'm ready to face the wreckage of my past. I'm scared, but I want to do it. I've never wanted to do it before, I lied and said I wanted to, to get back in the house but I've never been interested in recovering. Today I am." He smiled. His smile communicated that he was doing it for himself. Sheila had nothing to do with his decision.

Sheila smiled. "Good for you. You can do it. Wanting to recover is a great motivation on the days you get weary."

"I'm going to do it." James sounded strong.

"It's time to get the kids. You wanna ride?"

James could only nod. He realized that Sheila was putting herself out for him and it had nothing to do with what he'd said and he was glad that he was telling the truth.

The girls were glad to see James. He had dinner with them and then he left for a few hours. At 10:30 pm he tapped on the door and Sheila opened it. James slept in the den on the floor and Sheila slept in her room. Both of them slept like babies knowing the other was nearby.

42

Deanna gave Ken a tight squeeze and pecked his cheek with a kiss. She loved him.

Ken smiled. He hoped things went as planned.

"Don't worry about coming in tonight. We'll manage without you." Ken offered.

"Thank you. We'll see how it goes. Here's the paperwork. See you at about 8:30ish. Don't forget, when the door opens after I leave."

"Okay."

"Okay, I'll call you in a few hours."

"Bye." Ken left.

Deanna sat on the sofa for a minute. There was no sadness in her heart. She was at peace and felt good about her decision.

Troy entered the house and smelled the garlic shrimp. He smiled to himself. Deanna had prepared his favorite dish. His heart filled with love. He thanked God for Deanna for the very first time. His appreciation was foreign and genuine. This was Troy's beginning. He had no past. Deanna was his first true love. He committed to Deanna.

His guilt about hurting others was gone. He discarded it on the outside of Asia's door. In his mind he didn't owe anyone any apologies. He hadn't raped anyone. His philosophy afforded him a clear conscious. It's that philosophy that helped him to abandon Kelly and never look back. Troy didn't undress women. He purposely allowed women to be responsible for their own actions. He even preferred to be on the bottom, so it would be clear who was doing what when it came time to end things. His pain from Asia was fleeting already. He loved his wife more than ever. He was glad that he'd crossed over into his manhood. Troy was sincerely happy.

"Hi." Deanna sat in the dining room.

With his heart straining to contain his love for her, he bent down to kiss her. "Hey Babe."

She leaned away. Troy wove his brow together in confusion. "What's wrong Dee?"

"We need to talk. Please sit down."

Troy's first thought was *Kelly and her damn baby!* He sat down next to her and touched her knee. She allowed him that and even smiled.

"What's wrong baby?" Troy braced himself to respond to Kelly's madness. His hands clasped together with paralyzing fear. He prayed for a good lie to explain away whatever Kelly might have done or said.

The use of 'baby' caused Deanna to take the short route to the topic. She was irritated by his attitude. "Troy it's over. Our marriage has reached its end. I have prepared the papers. My attorney has looked them over; everything is in your favor, so if you agree to these terms, and I see no reason why you wouldn't." Troy was sitting there with this look of shock. Deanna continued. "You'll be a free man in a matter of six months or so. In light of your busy schedule I've asked for joint custody of the kids with your taking responsibility for them every other weekend and holiday. You'll notice that I didn't ask for spousal support. This isn't because I'm undeserving, but I'm not willing to fight for it. I know that would have been the one area that would prolong things and as you needed your freedom yesterday, I thought we would proceed without any further delay."

Troy sat there wide eyed with disbelief. His chest was in unbearable pain. Last night they had made passionate love. Deanna had reminded him of their beginning. Her love for him appeared refreshed and anew. Now this. Troy began to feel the pain of deceit and rejection in the worst way. He felt tears rising from his gut to his eyes. He knew first hand what Asia was feeling earlier. He swallowed hard trying to push his pain down. He wanted to be as calm as her. He decided to respond with the same assured tones and not yell. "Dee, Baby what is this about?"

"The dissolution of our marriage." She replied with the same assuredness.

"We ain't getting no divorce. Last night we made love!" (He heard his voice rising, but he couldn't stop himself as he got louder and louder.) "Last night you loved me like a king! Today you dump me like trash! What kind of sick game are you playing?!"

"No game. I didn't treat you like a king last night! I treated you like a king most nights for eight long years. Whenever you were home, your bath was always drawn, and your clothes laundered, your house was clean and your dinner prepared. There were tokens of love surrounding you at every turn. Messages, pages, e-mails, greeting cards...you were too busy swooning the next woman to notice me or my goodness." She was louder than when she started, but composed and strong.

Troy started to believe that this was really happening. He saw a glimpse of hope as he took inventory of the house. Nothing was missing or out of place. He had an opportunity to redeem his marriage. He prayed that there was time, that there was hope. It dawned on him that Deanna was everything he needed. She was no longer his *something to do* she was his wife and a good one too. He realized how many times he'd stepped out on her. Reality combined with fear that he finally lost her blurted out his raw pain "You so smart did you divide the furniture in your little divorce paperwork?"

"As a matter-of-fact I did. You get to keep it. Every pot, every pan, every sheet and blanket, the towels, toothpaste and the detergent. The refrigerator is stocked, keep it all. See, while you were out, I completely furnished my own place. I have no need for any of this. The kid's things and all of my clothes were moved today. Everything in here is yours. I have cleaned the entire house. There are meals prepared for one week in the freezer. Throw them out if you don't want them." With that she stood, handed him the papers and a pen. "Please just sign the papers. It's been over for a long time and we both know it. I've accepted it, you will too."

"I ain't signing nothing."

"I'm sorry you feel that way. I'll have to go another route. I was hoping we could do this civil, but I have to be at work in 30 minutes so I must run." She picked up her jacket and started towards the door.

He Looked Like A Man, Until He Barked

"Work?!" Troy didn't know she had a job.

"I've graduated culinary school in your absence as well. I am a Chef and a vested partner in Cream of The Crop Soul Food Restaurant. My new address is on the refrigerator. The phone number for the girls is there too. They have their own number call them anytime. Please pick them up from Carla's next Saturday morning at 9:00 and drop them at Carla's on Monday morning by 9:00 am. I'll get them from Carla's on Monday evening."

"You bitch!"

"Normally, I would respond to that, but I realize you're going through a tough time right now, so I'll give you a pass." She walked out of the door.

As predicted he ran behind her, just as he opened the door a man stepped in front of him. "Troy Arlington?"

"WHAT?!"

"You've just been served." The man walked away.

Deanna's heels could still be heard as she walked to her car.

Troy stood there paralyzed by defeat.

Deanna didn't go to work. She went to Carla's to pick up the girls. Carla was sitting on the sofa with Gabby watching TV Land when she got there. All of the girls were playing throughout the house. Quetti was over for a play date with Roni and Ashley; little Tj was trying to keep up.

"Hey y'all. It's done."

"What?" Gabby was confused.

"I left Troy today."

"You did what?" Gabby asked. "You implemented the plan?"

"Yes. Completely. Last month I found a townhouse in San Lorenzo for rent. I bought my furniture and had it delivered there. Well, I'm waiting on my livingroom tables, but everything else is already there. It's so pretty. I've been decorating it in my spare time. Ken and I moved all of our clothes and most of the girls' toys today. I paid for the divorce 2 month ago. Ken had one of the busboys serve him tonight after I left. I left everything like I said and I have my own place. I feel great!!" Deanna twirled and let out a yelp of joy.

Gabby's stomach formed a little knot on the right side and then it disappeared. Her face lit up with excitement as Deanna and Carla noticed. She'd felt the baby move before, but no one else could see it. Now the baby's movement was visible to the public. They all laughed with joy that Gabby was having a baby. Carla stood up to touch the baby and pee ran down her leg. She looked at them like she didn't understand what was happening. While everyone was still looking at each other another gush flowed from her. It registered in all of their minds simultaneously they sang "Your/my water broke." Gabby said, "Y'all go ahead I'll stay with the kids. At that moment reality and fear hit her; she was next. She was excited and scared, more scared than anything. Carla moved toward the bathroom. Deanna got all the stuff together. They arrived at the hospital about 36 minutes later. Her contractions were getting stronger, but she was taking them with stride.

He Looked Like A Man, Until He Barked

Ron arrived at the hospital shortly after they got there. When Deanna left to call Gabby Ron was able to talk openly to Carla.

"Babe, I'm sorry about the other night. I don't know what came over me."

"Ron don't worry about it. Deanna left Troy today. She just couldn't take it anymore. I pray that I'm patient enough to be here when your miracle happens. I think you're banking on my love for God to stay in this marriage. Well, God allows divorce too. I'm hanging on because I want to. I love you, note that I'm getting tired." She grimaced with pain. Deanna came back before he could respond. He had to sit with her statement.

A nurse entered. "Do you feel like you want to push?"

Carla nodded. Her legs started to vibrate with pain. She couldn't speak anymore.

The nurse returned with a doctor and a minute later a Pediatrician came in. They were introducing themselves and talking about what was going on when Carla clearly pushed. The doctor sat on his stool and guided Lil" Ron into the world. Deanna cried. She could relate to being born, being free at last. Carla smiled and Ron cried too. He loved his son whom looked identical to his daughter who looked nothing like him. Carla prayed that the world be kind to her son just like she had prayed for Ronika.

On the ride home Deanna thought about her new life. She picked up her kids and went to her condo. The girls loved it. They asked about Daddy and Deanna told them that they would see him on Saturday. The best part of his behavior is that he was not around or home enough to be greatly missed. That night Deanna lay in her bed and talked to Ken on the telephone. They talked about nothing and everything at the same time. She couldn't wait to get to work tomorrow to see him. He was anxious to see her as a single woman. The thought caused him to have and erection. He relieved himself before going to bed and loving Deanna some more.

Gabby laid Quetti in their bed and called Brian. He told her he'd be home shortly. He was at Troy's. She told him that Carla had had the baby, a boy—8lbs. 9ozs. and 21 inches. Then she told him she knew about Deanna's leaving, she loved him and would see him at home later. Gabby went to bed grateful for Brian's change, her stepdaughter and her son (or so she thought). She had been sleeping without any assistance for close to a year.

When Brian got home at 2:00 am, he went to bed in his own gratitude. His wife and their kids were sleeping, one up under her and one inside of her. His heart was heavy for Troy.

Troy cried in the confines of his home alone. He ached for Deanna. He missed her so much. He loved her. He really loved her. Too bad it was too late.

He Looked Like A Man, Until He Barked

Kelly sat at home in misery. Her dream was incomplete. She needed a plan to remove Troy from his home into hers. In her heart she believed that if she could get him away from the little girls they could be a family. In a perfect world he would divorce his wife, marry her and they would live happily ever after. She would allow him to financially support his daughters, but they would never be welcome in *their* home. She would have a daughter to replace them when Jeremiah was two years old. This plan seemed so logical as she sat in the kitchen eating fried chicken, mashed potatoes and corn on the cob from Popeye's Chicken.

43

Ron and Brian had started hanging out quite a bit. Ron had noticed that Brian had changed for the better. He and Gabby had become inseparable. They exuded happiness.

Ron was attracted to Brian's happiness. He loved Carla just as much as Brian loved Gabby. He confessed to Brian that he had a problem with drugs. Brian shared that his shortcoming was other women and that he still finds himself looking at them, but he has been able to refocus his attention on Gabby because above all else he knew that Gabby was the full package. He asked Ron if he'd ever come close to happiness before Carla. Ron answered no. Then he asked him if he felt safe? Ron answered yes. Brian told him, 'then its worth whatever you have to do to keep her, you don't get that from all women. Trust me, I've searched and my Gabby is one of a kind'.

Ron honestly stated that he was trying, but the alcohol calls him and if he don't answer it leaves a message. He was trying to justify his relapses. He chuckled. Brian did not. That was the beginning of their friendship and Ron's sobriety. Brian called and checked on him from time to time after that. They played basketball when their schedules permitted. Brian called Ron on his B-S and Ron respected him for that. Ron learned how to have a good time without alcohol. He stopped hanging in bars and started doing family things with his and Brian's families.

It helped that Ron loved Carla to pieces unashamedly. Brian struggled to support Troy in his plight to get Dee back. He decided the best thing to do was to listen and not get caught up in what was going on with Troy and Deanna.

The sun was beaming and it was a perfect day for an impromptu BBQ. Carla and Gabby to sat under the patio umbrella drinking lemonade while watching the girls play and the guys BBQ. The baby was on the table in his carrier. He had been napping and was expected to wake up soon. Ron was at the grill and Brian was talking to him about JaMarcus Russell and what he's bringing to the Oakland Raiders. Ron wasn't arguing, but he voiced that he was pissed about Tui not getting his fair shot.

When the baby cried out Gabby picked him up. Her anxiety rose as she held him. He made her excited about the arrival of her own baby. While holding him she felt like she was having a girl for the first time. Usually she felt that it would be a boy. Gabby always called him a boy and Brian called him 'baby'. Brian was so excited he didn't care what the baby's sex was, he was grateful to be having a baby with his wife. He loved Quetti—she was his heart. It was a different feeling though, to imagine him and his beloved wife meshed into one. It really made him feel good.

Troy called to say he was on his way with the girls. His weekend was up and it was time to drop them off. Carla's home was still the temporary neutral meeting spot. Deanna didn't want Troy at her place until the court mandated that he had to be there. Troy co-operated for peace's sake. He wanted to get back in her good graces. Carla told the guys that he was on his way and she and Gabby continued talking. Gabby was in pain, but she was bearing it. Next weekend there was going to be a shower at her house and they were all going to help decorate the nursery. Her mother—Esther, Michelle, Carla, Deanna and the girls. It was going to be fun. Today she, Deanna and Carla were deciding on the color of the room. Gabby couldn't decide on a color because her heart told her "boy" but she was giving validation to the gut feeling that she got from Baby Ron, who they all called "Boogie" because he wiggled all the time and he loved music. When Gabby held him he cuddled with her and she recalled her mother saying that opposites attract so he was responding to the baby girl she was carrying. She had three months of pregnancy to deal with. It looked like she was due any minute. Brian thought she was exceptionally big.

Troy stopped by at noon to drop off his girls. He joined them for a minute. He yearned more for what they had as he watched them fuss over the girls, while their wives prepared their plates. He admired Gabby's waddle as he realized that he wasn't home for most of Deanna's pregnancies. There was some pain in his eyes when Carla asked him if he wanted to eat. He was so choked up he couldn't verbally respond. He shook his head no. Boogie smiled at him and he realized he had to go. He'd gotten pictures of Jeremiah from Kelly a few days ago and he loved him instantly. It was like looking in a photo album and seeing himself. Part of him wished he could be apart of his life, but as sure as Jeremiah shared his DNA part of him was Kelly and Troy wanted no part of Kelly. He avoided her like criminals avoid police. That

He Looked Like A Man, Until He Barked

meant poor Jeremiah was orphaned. Troy had received a court date for child support mediation. He was prepared to support him, but he wanted nothing to do with him.

"Say hi to Uncle Troy so Daddy can eat." Carla handed the baby to Troy. Boogie wiggled and smiled as Troy accepted him. No one knew that Troy was miserable sitting amidst their' joy. He noticed that Ron was fattening up and his eyes were clear. From a medical position he knew that he was in the final phase of detoxification, but he stood a good chance of recovery if he continued to practice abstinence. Boogie wiggled so Troy had to reach and grasp for him. Everyone laughed at Troy's fumble and save. Boogie had gotten them all that way.

"Mommy!" TJ ran over to Deanna who had let herself in. She picked her up as Quetti, Ashley and Roni hugged her legs. "Well, ladies I'm happy to see all of you too." Deanna bent and kissed each forehead before they released her legs. Then she put TJ down and took a seat on the deck next to Troy. "Hi."

"Hello. How are you?" Troy responded.

"Good. Tired. You?"

"Stupid, remorseful and regretful."

"Oh. I hope you feel better. Can I hold Boogie?" She reached for the baby.

"Sure." He passed Boogie to Deanna. She started cooing with him.

Everyone pretended like they hadn't heard his response. Troy was shameless. He wanted his family back. He wanted what he saw. He wanted to be a member of this community again! Deanna continued to ignore him. Finally he stood up. He kissed the girls, bid his farewell and left.

In his car he dialed Asia.

"Hey, how you doing?"

"I'm good how are you?"

"Missing you. Can I stop by? No strings, just a friend saying hi."

Asia's heart said no. Her common sense said no. Her body said no, but her mouth said "Okay, for a minute."

She hung up feeling foolish. She loved him so. She wished he could be right, but she knew he wouldn't. She knew he didn't love her and she knew he never would. It was clear to her that he loved Deanna. He'd hurt her to keep from hurting Deanna there was no suppressing that. In spite of what he said Deanna was his true love. Asia showered and freshened up. She lied to herself and said it was a habitual response to Troy's call, but the truth is she missed him. She missed him like that. There was a small hope that intimacy would evolve from his visit. She still hurt, she was still mad at him, but that part of her that loved him, loved him in spite of her feelings. When Troy entered the apartment he found it surprisingly clean. Asia was more beautiful than he remembered. Yet as accommodating, as expected she waited on him hand and foot. She allowed him to vent and she looked him in his eyes as he lied to her about missing her. She believed him even. She responded when he leaned in for the kiss. She allowed him to make love to her. She participated and enjoyed herself. Even when he quit on her, she used his body to satisfy herself and then she lay awkwardly next to him. It was no secret that they had used each other for relief. She felt cheated, stupid and a raw vulnerability. He felt relieved and tense about opening the door with her. He didn't want to hurt her, but he didn't want to be with her either. His heart had decided on Deanna, after all of these years. The awkwardness was so thick neither of them could speak or move. They both wanted to run away, there was a layer of shame in the air. Asia was ashamed of herself for compromising her body. She knew there was no future in loving Troy. It was her hearts desire to be free of his abuse but it was also her hearts desire to be with him.

Troy needed to feel loved. Deanna's rejection had depleted his self-esteem. He needed validation. Sex validated his manhood. It made him feel desired which made him feel good. In this case not quite good, but better.

Finally Asia mustered the acceptance that what's done is done. "I've gotta go pick up Tony."

Troy jumped up. He was grateful for the nudge. "Okay. I'll go. I'll call you later."

"I'd like that." Asia lied. She didn't want to hear from Troy anymore. It was clear to her that she was weak for this man and in his presence she lost her sanity. She had no intentions of sleeping with Troy. Now she knew he was married. Now she knew his true character and even that he didn't love her like that. It was stupid for her to sleep with him. Asia knew that Troy would always come to her for sex and by giving in she revealed her weakness for him. After seeing Troy to the door she showered and slipped into one of Big Tony's shirts. She sat on her couch and she cried. She hugged herself and she cried. While rocking back and forth she realized it was just her and God this time. Never could she explain her actions to Sheila.

Little did she know Sheila would understand completely because she was at war with her flesh too.

James being there had been good for them all. Sheila had become more organized. Without fail these days her girls were in bed by 9 o'clock. After that she busied her hands in preparation for tomorrow. She made sure she had nothing to do but chat with James when he arrived. Today she was excited because he'd gotten a letter from Costco. The promise that it was regarding employment had bugged her all day.

Finally James knocked on the door.

"Hey you. How was your day?"

"It was good." James stopped himself from kissing her. He was there to get off the street. He was not her husband.

"You got mail today." Sheila handed James the letter, trying to contain her excitement just in case.

James read the letter half-heartedly. He didn't want to get too excited either. A smile stretched across his face as he realized he'd gotten an interview. "They want to give me a second interview on Tuesday at 9:00 am."

"Second?"

He Looked Like A Man, Until He Barked

"Yeah, the first one was during the application process. You would either get a rejection or a second request in the mail.

"Well congratulations Mr. Kirby." Sheila kissed James, impulsively. James failed to restrain himself. He kissed her like the moment was rare, precious and fading. He kissed her like he needed her. Like he loved her. Sheila became one with James. Her response afforded him enough amnesia to go further as he slid his hands into forbidden areas of her body. She made herself available, removing and opening her garments to assist him.

The toilet flushed and they both snapped back to reality. Pulling apart they leaned onto each other and giggled like teenagers. "One of the girls is up." Sheila whispered. "Go see about her. I need to shower anyway." He responded.

Sheila straightened her clothes and went to the girls' room, then to the den. While waiting for James she wondered how she was going to explain this to Asia. James entered the den, the pallet and Sheila like a refreshing breeze enters a stuffy room. Gentle, soundless and appreciatively. She was happy, in love and vulnerable. The loving was great the fear even greater. Deanna knew she had crossed the line with James. Her heart had betrayed her as usual for this man. She loved James.

James loved her too. He slept in gratitude.

44

Troy sat at home alone. He'd tried to pick up a woman here and there, but no one took the bait. It was as though all women suddenly knew that he was in love with Deanna.

He'd resorted to calling Asia against his personal promise to himself. She allowed him to come over in spite of her promise to herself too. Both he and Asia knew it was over between them and that they were no longer making love, but having sex. They both regretted sleeping together the last time.

Asia loved Troy and a minute part of her wanted things to blossom. The mass of her didn't trust Troy. Troy cared about Asia. He didn't want to hurt her. His calling and coming by was mostly selfishness. He needed to redeem himself around women. Rejection was new to him. It was uncomfortable and at times painful. Asia never rejected him. He used her as a last resort, as to not complicate things. Troy thought about his choices and the consequences he was living with now. He'd hurt Asia, probably ruined her. And in the process lost Deanna. Kelly was his biggest regret.

Kelly had been calling him. Her conversation was always about her son and her money. Troy found himself hating her and Jeremiah. He wished he'd never been born. He was not proud of his feelings but in being honest with himself those were his feelings. He deleted Jeremiah's pictures as soon as he got them. Kelly had started sending them almost daily. She was also mailing them to the house with nasty notes to

He Looked Like A Man, Until He Barked

Deanna. Troy was the one getting them because Deanna had moved out 2 months ago. The notes made Troy dislike Kelly more and commit to never interacting with their baby. He cringed every time he read the words...

—*Your girls will be orphans soon as Troy realizes he has a son...* —*I don't do step-mother, so keep your girls at home...* —*Every man wants a son it's only a matter of time before y'all have to respect that.*

Troy's life had shrunk to work and isolation. He was uncomfortable talking to Brian. He recognized that he needed help, he didn't know how to help himself. What he wanted was to take it back to the day before Deanna left him and cover his tracks better. He had no idea that Kelly's phone call was the motivation for Deanna divorcing him.

There was nothing of interest on television. Troy missed the girls. He dialed them. Ashley answered. She talked for a minute and then gave the phone to TJ who sat it down immediately. Deanna came by saw the phone off the hook and said "Hello?"

"Hi." Troy responded.

"Hey, the girls ran off. Sorry about that. I'll get them."

"It's okay. You got a minute?"

"What?"

"Dee. I realized the day you served me divorce papers that I love you. I really love you. I know what love is now."

"Troy it's too late for all of this, you don't have to lie to me anymore. I'm over you. So over you."

"Dee, don't say that. I'm not lying. I know I've lied immensely in the past, hell our whole marriage, but I was trying to protect myself from the pain that love can put on you."

"That's what I should have been doing." Deanna squeezed in.

"This may sound stupid, but it's the truth. My first love dogged me. I loved that girl so much. I felt that I'd actually die for her. She was with all the boys. She didn't care AT ALL about my love. I wouldn't have hurt her, but she didn't trust me. Then I found out she was pregnant and it was my best friend's baby. I ain't been right since. Well, I ain't been willing to love anyone like that again. 'Til' the other day. After we made love so passionately in spite of all the mess I'd put you through I realized that you loved me like that, so I was safe to love you."

"That's so sad Troy. We all get hurt; it's unavoidable. The way we respond to it is what matters. You did all of that to me. All that lying and womanizing because you got your feelings hurt in the 70's? Well, guess what? So did I. You're not the first man I've tried to love, but you're certainly the last. This time around if a man can't love me inside of his fear and besides his past, I'm not giving him the time of day."

"Dee. It was more than that. I... I ...I was scared. I was scared of getting hurt." Troy's voice was pleading; his vulnerability was evident. He'd let his guard down finally. Deanna's heart went soft, but her love had dissipated. There was nothing she could do for him.

"Troy. Baby, it's okay. You don't have to be scared. You have to be selfish. You have to love people because you love them, with no expectations. It's beautiful when two people can find a way to love without expectations, it's sad that we couldn't. Troy I love you always will; I just don't trust you."

"Deanna, I need you to try. You won't be sorry. I'll *never* hurt you again. I can keep my hands, my eyes and my dick to myself. I swear on everything I love."

That struck a cord with Deanna. "Troy, look. It's over. I'm not dealing with any more of your mess and if I decided to give you an opportunity at this point I'd have to deal with your son AND his ignorant ass Mama. I ain't doing it. Not when you were my husband to begin with. Now I gotta deal with a baby that I didn't have, and all the pain from knowing you laid down with a woman and allowed her to give you enough pleasure to make a whole baby. A baby we all have to accept and deal with for the rest of all of our lives! Do you know that act alone gave me the strength to leave you? After she called me to tell me that you were Jeremiah's father I realized you weren't with either of us at the moment, so there were 3 of us?"

Troy sat on the phone in tears. The reality that Deanna was done hit him in his heart harder than a demolition ball hits a building. He decided not to lie to her anymore. "Yeah."

Deanna was grateful that he didn't try to lie about it because she *knew* there were three women in his life. "You lied about the length of your work assignments so you could juggle us around too. The one with the baby is a gold digger huh? She calls me all the time. She sends stuff to the house and everything. I can tell you right now, she is not to be around my babies under any circumstance. She hates them and has some warped theory about taking you from them. Keep that sick broad away from my kids."

"Okay." Troy was whipped. He knew it was over. There was no hope of ever getting Deanna back. He regretted ever dealing with Kelly. She'd caused him nothing but grief from day one. "Deanna, I'm sorry. I'm really sorry. I love you but I'll leave you alone."

"Thank you." Deanna hung up. She bathed the girls and then sat in the kitchen with Ken talking about the conversation she'd had earlier with Troy. Ken shared that he was scared too. Scared to love her, especially since she'd taken so long to leave Troy. Deanna broke her own rule of waiting until the divorce was final. She leaned over and fondled Ken then allowed him to make the most careful and gentlest love to her. He made her feel his privilege to be with her. Deanna loved him inside of her fear of getting hurt. They decided to come out of the closet in the morning; Ken stayed the night.

Troy hung up the phone and dialed two numbers. The first one was Kelly's.

"DON'T YOU EVAH— CONTACT ME OR MY WIFE AGAIN ABOUT YOUR DAMN SON. I'M RELINQUISHING MY PARENTAL RIGHTS. I'LL SEND YOU THE PAPERWORK SHORTLY! I WILL PAY FOR HIM, BUT THAT'S IT. STAY OUT OF MY LIFE!!!!!!!!!!" Troy was trembling with anger. His voice was so loud Kelly shuddered at the sound of it. She realized that she'd lost him and it was now a hopeless situation. Kelly hung up the phone and went to pick up Jeremiah. He was truly all she had. She picked him up and she kissed him. The pain was so great she couldn't feel it. It was razor sharp and it took a few seconds to register that her baby was lifeless.

"I need an ambulance now, my babies not breathing!" She screamed into the telephone.

Troy wished he had never touched Kelly. He hated her with everything in him. He disliked his son. Not because he was her son, but because his life had ruined his chances with Deanna. He seriously was going to contact his lawyer first thing in the morning and voluntarily removing himself from Jeremiah's life. He refused to allow Kelly to use the baby against him and that would surely prevent her.

The next call he made was to Asia. "Hey. How are you?"

"I'm good. You?" Asia sweated on the other end. She began to pray. *Please God give me the strength to take care of myself. Deliver me from temptation and bless me with a man that will truly love me. Amen.* She had no idea what Troy said, so she responded. "What?"

"I asked if you wanted some company?"

"Oh no. Not today."

"Please. I need a hug. I need a friend."

"I'm sorry Troy. I'm not strong enough to see you right now. I can't be around you."

"Being around me makes you weak?" Troy was looking to esteem himself over the phone since she wasn't willing to see him.

Patriece

"No. Being lonely makes me settle for your lies." Asia was honest. In that moment she felt free from Troy finally.

"Oh. I'll let you go."

"Thank you. Bye-bye."

Troy's phone rang. It was Kelly's number. While he let her call go to voicemail he walked out the house headed for Brian's. He needed help.

45

Asia knew the time had come to share with Sheila that she had slept with Troy a few times and she felt awful; she wanted the pain to go away. She knocked on the door and James answered. He was fattened up, clear eyed and looking like himself. He was dressed in a Costco uniform and appeared to be leaving there for work.

"Hey Sis. How you doing?" James asked Asia.

"Not as good as you. But, I'm fine."

James leaned in and kissed her cheek, gave her a tight quick squeeze and walked out of the door.

Sheila appeared with her head held high. She expected to do battle with Asia about James being there and she wanted to give her the illusion that she had it all under control. She was not going to mention that she was scared to death everytime he walked out of the door. That she didn't really want him driving her *only* car. The reality was that she'd either trust him or she wouldn't. Things were put into perspective in one session with Pastor Knowit. He simply asked her if her faith was in James or in God? She knew she was expecting God to restore her marriage. The fear lifted with her answer. Periodically the fear returns, but she reminds herself that her faith is in God and it subsides.

Asia didn't give her a hard time about James being there, but congratulated her for overcoming her fear concerning him and following her heart. Over coffee Sheila shared that she hadn't totally overcome, that it was a day to day process. She was honest with Asia about her fears. Their conversation about James prefaced Asia's confession of dealing with Troy on a sexual level.

"Sheila, I'm hurting. I don't know why, but I keep sleeping with Troy. Every time he call me and want to stop by I let him. I already know we going to end up in bed, but that doesn't stop me. I know he's in love with his wife; I know he ain't leaving her; I know he don't love me like that. I know if it's me or her, it's her. None of that knowledge helps me keep my panties on." Asia's tears began to fall. Sheila cried with her because she knew that Asia was in battle with loneliness. The fact that James was home helped combat that for her. She knew that Asia would feel this way until she found someone to share her life with.

Asia began again. "I just wanted somebody to love me like Big Tony. I so appreciate his love, especially now. All that time that I was alone I was longing for someone, but holding out because I feared getting hurt. I asked Troy! Sheila I gave him a pass. In no uncertain terms I offered him sex. See my body needed loving more than my spirit. I just needed someone to hold me, to take away my physical itch. Big Tony's love was sustaining me. Why did he do this? This was so unnecessary. I didn't have to love him. He made me love him. I could have got a dose of pleasure and never talked to him again. That's what I wanted. He told me I could trust him. He told me lie after lie after lie." Asia sobbed. "Now he's all in my system and I'm weak for him. I don't even know why. I should be running when I hear his voice, but I talk like an idiot. I keep listening to his mess. He comes by, sleep with me. He gives me a courtesy call a day or two later and then he disappears until he needs to wipe his feet again. Then he shows up, thang in hand."

"Asia." Sheila interrupted. "Stop sleeping with him, it's that simple. You'll feel better. You'll regain your power and self-respect when you close your legs to him. If Troy makes you feel that way and you know it, then that's on you. Troy ain't raping you. He deceived you true, but now you're deciding to sleep with him. Just cause he hinted or asked don't mean you have to comply. You got to draw on your common sense. When he calls you, ask yourself if you want to feel good for a few minutes or a lifetime? You already know he's only got a few minutes. Then tell his butt no, stop letting him visit you. Do you visit him?"

"No. The one time he took me to his house it wasn't even his house. Troy went to great lengths to deceive me. His boy Brian let him use a house he was supposed to be selling and he took me there like it was his. I figured that out in my quiet time too. He lied about the whole Atlanta thing too. He had a friend intercepting his calls and forwarding him messages while he was right here with his family. Sheila Troy was such a dog he even had a Bible in his glove compartment. That Bible allowed me to let my guard down. I assumed he had some integrity. It's one thing to talk a woman out of her loving; it's sick to go to the depths of deception that Troy went. He looked like a man, but he's a mutt." Asia was empowering herself with her words. She was able to see clearly. Her mind was setting on leaving Troy alone.

Sheila informed. "Asia sometimes lovers can't be friends. You might want to leave Troy alone completely. You might want to change your number, move or whatever you have to do."

"I'm not moving! I'll change my number, but I like my apartment. Big Tony lived there. It is where I feel safe." Asia responded.

"Okay. I'm just trying to help. He's going to keep coming and calling until you convince him that it's really over. He needs to accept that you're not going from a lover to a booty call."

Asia was feeling better. She was glad that she'd come over. They talked for an hour or so more when James called. He told Sheila that he was working overtime and not able to go to church with her. He said that he would bring her the car in time for her to get to church. Asia said she'd drive her, she was going to church tonight too. Sheila was glad that he called and nervous that he wouldn't return. She forced herself into a place of peace.

They retreated to church with the kids in tow. While there a man watched Asia. He'd decided that she was perfect for him. He had a limp that could be mistaken for a cool strut. In truth one of his legs was ½ an inch shorter than the other one. He'd practiced walking normal for so long until he created a stride that made his flaw acceptable among his peers. Especially when he was younger. When he was younger his limp added to his immaturity gained him the reputation of a heartbreaker. He was a mutt too in his past life. To date he was a fatherless man with a big heart, a home on the hill and enough integrity to prevent a war. There were other men in the church eyeing Asia too. Their motives were

He Looked Like A Man, Until He Barked

not as pure as Leon's. In their arrogance they didn't consider him as a threat. Tonight Leon decided to befriend Asia. He introduced himself and invited her to coffee after church. She was going to decline when he invited Lil' Tony too. "Hey Lil' Man you want some chocolate don't you?" Lil' Tony said yeah and so did Janay and Jada. He didn't flinch. "Well, let's all go to Starbucks." Asia nodded "Okay." They followed him to Starbucks. Sheila sat preoccupied with worry about whether or not James made it home. Asia and Leon talked about church and their first impression of Pastor Knowit. Afterwards Leon asked Asia if he could call her some times. For some reason she said "Sure." She noticed his limp as he walked them to their car. It was kind of cute. He dressed nice, smelled good, and was handsome. He was brown skinned, with perfect teeth, a gorgeous smile and what black people called good hair. He wore expensive jewelry and good shoes. Asia wasn't interested in him that way, but he was handsome.

Asia and Lil' Tony rode home after dropping Sheila and the girls off. At the corner they honked at James as he headed home. That was the first time Asia realized that Sheila was worried about James' return home. She was glad that he did.

The next day Troy called. Asia deleted his message as soon as she heard his voice. He paused after stating his name as if he was in unbearable pain. She had no idea that he really needed her. He needed someone to hold him and tell him that it was going to be alright. Someone that cared. He needed to feel the safety that she and Sheila looked for in the arms of men.

46

Troy returned home after Brian wasn't home. He hoped they hadn't had the baby. He wanted to be there. He smiled thinking about Brian's happiness. He thought about how Brian had played as hard if not harder than him and he came out on top in spite of himself. Somehow it didn't seem fair. His heart ached for Deanna. He tried to ignore it.

Ignoring Kelly was not as easy. She'd called him eight times in about three minutes. Each time he hit the ignore button on his cell phone. Troy lounged on his sofa eating Chinese food and feeling bad. He wanted to call Asia just to have something to do. Rejection, however, was not on his agenda if today, she decided to reject him for first time. He knew the day was coming when she'd say no. The feeling of crisis had been on his heart all day. It was the kind of day where he was extra careful, deliberately avoiding disaster. The last time he felt that way he'd wrecked his Benz. He loved that car. It had caught him plenty of women. They looked at his car, his career and their panties slid off. The BMW was cool, but the Benz was a magnet for women. Troy's phone rang from the hospital he answered. "Dr. Arlington." Kelly spoke somberly into the phone. "Troy Jeremiah is dead." Then she hung up.

Troy would have thought she'd taken getting his attention too far, accept her voice was frighteningly honest. He called the hospital back. A nurse, Kelly's friend, answered "Punk we been calling you and calling you, it's time for you to step up to the plate. Your son died get *yourself* down here."

Troy held the phone paralyzed with disbelief. His heart churned with the thoughts of rebuking that baby. The hatred he had for him about an hour ago. The pain of his bad disposition and attitude dropped him to his knees. He loved that baby. He loved his little image the first time Kelly emailed his picture. He was even proud. If the circumstances were different he would have embraced him. Suddenly he wanted to be his Daddy.

Kelly sat in the chapel of the hospital in a stupor beyond description. This tragedy could cause her to catch invisible flies. She was truly destined to lose her mind. Her will to live was already gone. The paramedics had worked on Jeremiah a little while to appease her, as they knew she was a nurse. She couldn't accept it without their efforts. The doctor to pronounce his demise hadn't let her see him at the hospital. He'd been taken to the morgue. She tried to call Troy and his ignorance of her calls only made the situation worst. It depleted any energy she had left. They were trying to get her to leave the chapel when Troy walked in. She didn't care anymore. He walked over to her. "Kelly what happened to my son?" He sounded sincere. She didn't answer him. She looked straight ahead. "Kelly, Baby, what happened to Jeremiah? I need to know."

"They said it was SIDS."

He Looked Like A Man, Until He Barked

"Crib death?! Where were you?" Troy knew that she couldn't prevent it if she were holding him in her arms. It was his destiny.

"Home with him. Troy I carried him from room to room. He was never out of my sight. He slept on his back; he slept with me. I didn't sleep most nights for watching him. I don't know how it happened. I was in the room with him." Kelly began to weep. For the first time Kelly and Troy shared a genuine emotion.

Gabby opted out of attending the funeral. She stayed home with the kids. Brian, Deanna, Carla and Ron all went to the funeral. Deanna decided to go at the last minute. The girls asked her why she wasn't going to their brothers' funeral and didn't she love him too? She went for them.

The church was packed considering baby Jeremiah had no friends. His little casket was white, surrounded by flowers. Amongst the flowers was his first photo from the hospital and next to it was a picture that had been taken of him that morning. In both pictures he looked like Troy, the most recent he smiled and his smile was a small replica of Troy's smile. It would have been impossible for Troy to ever deny him as his son. All of that bothered Deanna. She was whirling with emotions as she read the obituary. Baby Jeremiah's statistics included born to Kelly Smithe and Troy Arlington... Deanna couldn't read any further. She closed the obituary and placed it in her Bible. Pastor Knowit ministered on getting your life right, because no one knows the time of death.

Brian was grateful for his own children. Carla was grateful for her children. Ron was grateful for his family, period. During the service the craving that was itching his taste buds was scratched as Pastor Knowit preached about living rightful and being grateful.

At the end of the service Deanna retreated to the restroom to avoid Troy. During service their eyes locked and he looked pitiful. Finally Troy had experienced pain. Pain that he couldn't conceal. He wasn't ashamed in any fashion for loving his son, nor was he denying that he was his father. He openly kissed him at the casket. Deanna's heart broke when he apologized to the baby. It was a private apology, but everyone heard it. It choked every man in the church. Including Pastor Knowit, who openly cried. Troy freed himself from all his ill emotions. He asked baby Jeremiah to forgive him for not being there, for not caring more, for being too selfish to acknowledge him and for planning to abandon him. Tears burst from him as he ended with Daddy so sorry Lil' Man. So sorry. Brian helped him to sit down. Kelly never spoke a word. She cried silently. She starred at the casket the entire service. In spite of her behavior Deanna cried for Kelly. She wouldn't wish loss on anyone especially a maternal relationship.

The bathroom was empty. It was quiet. The door creaking startled Deanna. Kelly walked in with a humble expression. Deanna's stomach knotted with insecurity of the unknowing. Kelly walked within two feet of her. "Deanna, I'm sorry."

Kelly's tears fell. "You told me to be careful of the traps I set. I was trying my best to take Troy from your babies and mine was taken from me." More pain drained from Kelly's eyes.

Deanna's heart told her to hug Kelly. She couldn't bring herself to do it for fear of Kelly responding poorly. "Kelly I'm sorry for your loss. I really am. May God bless your womb again. Don't worry about my feelings. I'm okay. Take care of yourself. "

"Wait. I need your forgiveness." Kelly pleaded.

"Of course." Deanna's decency squashed her feelings and she embraced Kelly. They cried together briefly, mother to mother. Both women knew they would never be friends, yet they were no longer enemies.

Asia walked into the restroom as the two of them walked out. Neither of them knew that she was the other, other woman. She had accompanied Sheila to the service who went to support Sister Esther who was there to support her son-in-laws best friend, who had lost his four and a half month old son to crib death. They had no idea it was Troy.

Freedom, growth and reality had come to many via Jeremiah's passing. Asia knew that Troy's deceit ran deeper than she ever imagined. The stronghold he had on her was broken.

Deanna eased out of the church successfully avoiding Troy. She'd gotten him a sympathy card from her and the girls. In her heart, that was appropriate as their relationship was over.

Troy and Kelly had no exchange before, during or after the service. Their relationship had officially ended.

Patriece

Alone at midnight Troy called Asia. She was on the telephone with Leon and unwilling to click over and take his call. Their relationship had officially ended as well.

47

Gabby was home with a month left before delivery when her water broke. Though she'd been experiencing pain regularly. Without warning her pain became paralyzing. She called upstairs for Brian. Their plans for the day were to go to the movies and by Cream of the Crop for lunch.

The hospital visit confirmed that her water had broken, she was not ready to deliver yet she couldn't go home. They placed her in a birthing room and left her and Brian alone. Brian had never seen a birth before so he was as nervous as she was. He wanted to call people, but he couldn't remember any telephone numbers. By divine order Esther called him.

"Hey Brian, how are you?" Esther asked.

"I'm—we're at the hospital. Gabby's water broke."

"Are you sure? It's not quite time, I'm on my way."

"Okay."

Esther called Deanna. Deanna called Carla. Deanna arrived, the girls came in and Carla and walked out the door. Troy was working so they left all of the girls with Ron and rushed to the hospital. Ron had some fear of keeping all of the kids indefinitely, but he didn't mention it to them. As they left he started thinking about a drink. He often felt that way during times of stress. Carla had no idea when she volunteered his services that stress could trigger his craving for alcohol.

Before the front tires were out of the driveway Boogie was crying. The sound of the girls playing had woke him up. Ron eased from thinking about a drink to wanting a drink.

Esther, Brian's Mom, Deanna and Carla joined Brian in the birthing room. Gabby seemed to be in the normal amount of pain, yet she was having a hard time breathing. They were considering giving her oxygen when the staff doctor came in he asked the nurse to wait on the oxygen. He then went to Gabby and felt her stomach. "Hmmph. This baby is extremely large. Have you been told that before?"

Brian answered "No. Is there a problem?"

"No. We may have to do a cesarean at which time only one of you can accompany the mother." He wasn't Gabby's regular doctor; he was the doctor on staff for the weekend. He had another hunch, but decided against sharing it. This was his 188th delivery. He knew that Gabby's oxygen problem was fear based, so he leaned into her and whispered. "My name is Dr. Stanley and I've done this 187 times. I may have delivered you." Dr. Stanley smiled as he brushed Gabby's forehead as a sign of endearment. Then he told the family. "We're about to have a baby. Mommy's really nervous, so I need you all to encourage her. This is her first baby and she's in a foreign place. Dad, you need to be right up there with Mommy for now. Tell her something sweet. Tell her whatever you told her to get her here." He chuckled, as did everyone else. "We need her breathing stabilized. That will help, just don't get her too excited." Dr. Stanley smiled at Deanna while winking. As soon as Brian told Gabby he loved her and everyone stopped starring at her in anticipa-

He Looked Like A Man, Until He Barked

tion her breathing stabilized normally. Dr. Stanley reappeared. He examined Gabby again. "She's ready." He announced. "Okay Mommy, I need you to push like you're going to have a bowel movement. Bear down like that. Don't be shy, you'll probably have a bowel movement too, it's perfectly fine. The nurse here will be on top of it, your dignity will remain in tact. Now push. Push. Come on, you can do it. Push."

Gabby grunted and pushed then she lay back to regroup. Dr. Stanley continued talking her through it. Then he smiled. "One more push and we will have ourselves a baby." Gabby pushed. The baby came out. It was a boy. Gabby was right. She smiled as her son was handed to a medical staff to clean and give to Brian. Then Dr. Stanley said I need you to push one more time. Everyone was looking at the baby and having a nostalgic moment. "Right this way people. Mommy still needs you. Dad, Mommy still needs you all." Then he winked again. This time Carla and Deanna caught the wink and wondered what that was all about. *He can deliver the placenta on his own.* "Okay Mommy, one more.... Again...last time." The room was filled with wails. The crying was coming from Dr. Stanley's hands. Everyone's head jerked and they realized that Gabby had twins. "This one is a girl. She's a little smaller than her brother and possibly jaundice." He handed her to the nurse. Gabby cried tears of joy. Everyone cried. Brian was overwhelmed. He couldn't believe it. Gabby couldn't believe it.

Deanna noticed the two baby beds and two nurses in the room for the first time. Dr. Stanley knew there were two babies all along. He also knew that they didn't know. He returned Deanna's smile as he delivered the placenta.

Gabby couldn't believe she had two babies. No one ever told her that there were two babies. She'd gone to every appointment. Sometimes the Nurse Practitioner that she saw referred to the babies, but Gabby charged her with bad grammar and dismissed it. She was never formally informed that she was having twins. Gabby was awestruck.

The second hour of Boogie's non-stop crying Ron began to crave a drink real bad. He called his sponsor. There was no answer. He gave the girls some Dimetapp to calm them down. He thought of the alcohol content in cough syrup and visibly shook his head no. He recognized his demon. It was as though he could see the monkey creeping up his back. Ron cried out. "God help me!" All of a sudden he remembered seeing his neighbor at an AA meeting. He grabbed Boogie and rushed next door. He knocked on the door so hard they armed themselves before opening the door. His neighbor recognized that he was in trouble. Without a word from Ron he yelled for his wife to come help him. Without a word from her husband she took the crying Boogie and asked about Ronika.

"All the kids are at my house. I have my two nieces too. My sister-in-law is having her baby. I'm watching the kids while Carla and 'em are at the hospital." Without hearing the full explanation she began marching to Ron's house. She

He Looked Like A Man, Until He Barked

watched the kids, fed them and changed the soaking wet Boogie who smiled at her then pressed his eyes shut.

Ron talked to his neighbor and he made him comfortable opening up to him. He told Ron about his alcoholic tribulations. He shared embarrassing things openly. Ron shared his mess too. He encouraged Ron to keep going to AA meetings. Ron opened up to him about his fears and insecurities. He said one thing to Ron that made his light bulb come on. Ron would never be the same. Now he could say that he was not going to drink again without feeling like a liar. Ron was conscious enough of his disease to be accountable.

After chatting for a while they went to an AA meeting. The meeting was good and Ron shared what was going on with him. After the meeting he received support from other alcoholics. The fear causing the craving left him. At the house Ron relieved and thanked his neighbors.

"The baby was wet is all. The girls were hungry. They're all fine now."

Thirty minutes later Carla called and told him about the twins. Ron was glad and added "Y'all gone have to keep them." Then he released a hearty laugh.

Carla saw John at the hospital vending machine on her way home and he told her he was divorced and wanted to see her again. She declined his offer. He left her with 'Then let me see my baby.' Carla slid into bed that night regretting having burned Roni's paternity paperwork.

Patriece

Ron slid into bed without disclosing that he'd had a hard time with the kids.

Their secrets made the night restless, but they cuddled and appreciated the days more pleasant event of the new additions to the family. Boogie slept in his crib across the room for the entire night.

48

Troy had lost about twenty pounds. He was missing a lot of work. His countenance was a generic happiness. Anyone that was close to him could discern his depression. Brian noticed when he came to see the twins. He barely looked at them. Gabby noticed too. She called Deanna and asked that she and Ken give her a minute before they stop by. Gabby didn't want them to make it worst for Troy.

Brian expressed his concern with Gabby after Troy left. He mentioned that he felt bad that Troy had lost so much and guilty because he'd done the same thing and nothing happened to him. Gabby comforted him with a kiss and a hug. She remembered her mothers' comments when she was younger that arrogance, evil and hatred were poisonous and they will kill you too. Gabby thought that because Brian loved her sincerely in spite of his behavior he was spared the growth that Troy was getting from his current situation. She agreed with her mother, Esther believed that mean spirited people always got the diseases. Not that it didn't happen to good people, but if a person was mean spirited she would immediately charge their illness to their behavior. Esther practiced kindness and she was a stand up straight, move swiftly, and wear stilettos if she want to kind of elder. At sixty-three years old she looked good. She hadn't even grayed. She looked at least twenty years younger than her age. Gabby didn't mention that she shared her mother's philosophy concerning Troy only because she thought that she was the only person to speak her mother's language. What she didn't know is that Deanna, Asia, Brian and Carla shared her belief that Troy's pain was self-inflicted. Brian had experienced a small amount of relief at learning of Jeremiah's passing. Being the product of an abandoned father himself, he knew Jeremiah's future and he ached for him when Troy told him that he was relinquishing his parental rights. Brian thought that was cruel, but he didn't say anything. Often he let Troy be Troy without correction. Sometimes he questioned his friendship practices around Troy. He was a much better friend to Ron.

Ron and Carla stopped by with their two kids and Deanna and Ken dropped by with their two girls. Michelle and her hubby dropped by with their two babies, so they ordered pizza, for the kids and Chinese food themselves and hung out. The guys embraced Ken like he'd been there all the while. Deanna's heart was glad. Her divorce would be final in a few days and she and Ken would be moving in together. She wanted to introduce him to the group before the move took place.

Troy retreated home having fulfilled his obligation to see Brian's twins. It had taken him two months to get by. He was driving home when he started to feel alone, ashamed and guilty. Rather than deal with his feelings he called Asia. *She still loves me.*

Asia was cracking up as Troy rang her phone. She and Leon had taken Lil' Tony to the park and to lunch. Now they

He Looked Like A Man, Until He Barked

were at her apartment talking. Leon was a great conversationalist. Asia's opinion of him changed as he shared about his past. She had mistaken him for a PK or something. He was diligent about his God and committed to his church and his beliefs, but the comfort of his relationship with slang validated his anecdotes. He shared that he had a motorcycle accident at twenty-seven which caused him to have half an inch shaved off of his right leg. He shared how he'd made women have abortions because he knew he didn't want to spend the rest of his life with them or dealing with them.

"Well, how did you get so wrapped up in the church?"

Leon paused. He had a look of discomfort. Asia was sorry she asked. "Oneday I went to see a psychic, just for fun, me and a couple of friends. I was dating a girl at the time that was into that type of stuff. We all got our cards read. When it came to my turn the cards read death. I'll never forget the feeling I got when I got that news. I knocked the cards off the table and walked out. My girlfriend ran behind me and told me it was a stupid thing and not to worry about it. I said okay. But, it was haunting me. I tried to forget about it, but I couldn't. I doubled back to the psychic and this time I stayed to hear it all. It was the same reading with a clause. The psychic said to me "Go to the secret place and live a full life." She couldn't tell me where the secret place was. I called my grandmother; she was the wisest person I knew. She said, 'Baby you know the secret place. I took you there all the time. You know the way. Go there." My grandmother never took me anywhere except church. I had to get my butt to church, but I was a dope dealer. I had dope that I was responsible for. I had a whole street life to shed. I went to my boy and told him what was going on and he totally understood. He gave me straight value for my stuff and I never looked back. Turns out he was from Louisiana and he believed in all that stuff, voodoo, black magic, witchcraft, all of it. I had no job, no self-esteem, nothing really. I ended up at my grandmothers' house and at church everyday. Now, I'm an employed homeowner. I have no kids, but most important I'm alive. Everyone in my social click is locked up, insane or dead now. I'm grateful. I'm grateful to be out of the drama. The distrust, everybody in that world want something and are willing to go to any length to get it. I like this side of the fence where I can have a measure of trust. Enough about me, what brought you to Truth & Light?"

"Heartache, distrust and a longing for what my best friend got from the church. She got the same thing you got, even found the courage to reconnect with her ex."

"Oh yeah. That's beautiful. You like Truth & Light?"

"Yeah, I guess so. I haven't really thought about."

"Just keep going, you'll learn to like it. Your reason for being there will be revealed."

"I'm sure. Why did you reach out to me? I ain't even a member yet." Asia still hadn't picked up on his attraction to her.

"Because I'm at that place in my life where I'm looking to settle down and....I got my heart set on you."

Asia blushed. She wasn't prepared for that response at all. Somehow she just thought he was a nice guy that needed a friend. If she had considered him a prospect she would not have let him bond with Lil' Tony. Things would have been completely different. She thought about his limp. *He has a limp. What will people think?*

"Asia?"

"Yes. I um...I wasn't expecting that. I'm flattered. I hadn't thought of us that way. I thought you were looking for a friend." She repositioned herself in her seat.

"I am. But for life. What were you expecting some Mack-Daddy stuff? I believe in friendship. You?"

"Yeah, sure."

"You okay?"

"Yeah, just..."

"Why so shocked? You're beautiful. You have a wonderful spirit. I told you about my accident because you didn't ask. You pretended not to notice, not that it wasn't important or you weren't curious, but you respected my feelings and my privacy. Most people ask me about my limp as soon as I make them comfortable."

"I wanted to know. I'm glad you shared. I'm not sure that I share your feelings of starting a relationship." She responded nervously.

"Do you enjoy my friendship?"

"Yes."

"Okay. Then we'll keep it right there. If it's meant to be then it'll happen." He leaned over and kissed her forehead. "I'm going to go now. I know you feel awkward. Sorry about that, I was just being honest."

"You can stay. I like you. I like you a lot." Asia had processed that Leon was doable. He was handsome, Lil' Tony liked him. Sheila liked him. He had no kids. He was generous. And most important, he liked her."

"Not used to sincerity huh?"

"No. It's been so long since I saw it, I didn't recognize it."

"Oh, okay. What's up for the evening? You wanna hang out?"

"I'm supposed to be watching movies with my best friend, it's family night. Her and her ex are back together and they invited me and Lil' Tony, because we're over here by ourselves. You're welcome to come with us."

"Sure. I'm an orphan too." Leon smiled. His smile was gorgeous.

Asia smiled too. *This feels right.* The phone rang again. She looked at the caller ID, it was Troy. She didn't answer this time either. Leon wondered but didn't ask. He trusted that in time he'd learn more about her. The fact that she was interested in him negated all derogatory things.

At Sheila's they walked into the living room. James was sitting on the chaise lounge with his shoes off. Sheila was on the couch. "Hey. James this is my friend Leon. Leon this is my brother-in-law James."

"Caddy Brown?"

"It's Leon now. Man you look good. Real good. I'm so glad to see you."

"Yeah man. I made it out. You look good too."

"I made it out too."

"I see. Man, who would've thought we'd be on the same side of the fence?"

"Life is strange." Leon laughed. James stood and the two

He Looked Like A Man, Until He Barked

hugged.

Sheila and Asia smiled. They were glad they knew each other. It made things easier. The girls watched the movie. The men talked throughout the movie. They learned that in spite of their previous relationship of addict and supplier each of them had wished the other a better life. They kept going over the chain of events that crossed and re-crossed their paths. By nights end they were the best of friends. They talked openly about their gratitude of their second chance at life and surviving the game that killed or ruined people they knew.

When Leon dropped Asia off he carried Lil' Tony inside and gave her a hug and smiled. "I'm not going to kiss you because I might not be able to stop. So, I'll wait." He limped away.

Asia barely noticed his limp. She closed the door and smiled. She felt good for the first time since Troy.

Troy didn't want to go home. He decided to stop by Asia's. She was probably home and avoiding his call. He was prepared to eat crow if he had to. Tonight he really needed to be held. Asia loved him enough to relieve his pain. He saw her at Jeremiah's services, she would understand. She would love all of his hurt away.

He watched her get out of a Chrysler 300 Dodge Charger and walk into her apartment with a tall, handsome man with a thug's strut. He drove off.

Thoughts of Jeremiah were chasing him whenever he was alone or still. He needed company to be free from the guilt of how he'd hated that baby. He dialed Deanna.

"Hello?" Ken answered. They were just getting home from Brian's.

"May I speak to Ashley or TJ please."

"They're asleep. Would you like to speak with Dee?"

"Sure."

"Hello?"

"Just wanted to tell the girls good night. I've been thinking about them a lot lately. All of them, Jeremiah too." Troy waited for sympathy. Sympathy didn't come. Deanna was tired and ready to go to bed. Ken was already laying down. She couldn't wait to cuddle with him. A man at home every night was new and exciting. "Troy I have compassion for your loss, but their really isn't anything I can do for you. Maybe you should talk to Kelly. She's feeling the same things you're feeling. Goodnight." Deanna hung up.

Troy's heart was getting heavier and heavier. Desperation forced him to dial Kelly. Her number was disconnected. He decided to drive by there. Someone else answered the door. Apparently Kelly had moved.

Troy dialed Ron. No one answered the phone. Ron and Carla were making love without insecurities, without alcohol and without the lack of satisfaction. They had found what they'd been looking for in each other.

As he drove home he dialed Brian. Brian was his last choice because he was ashamed, jealous of his wife's for-

He Looked Like A Man, Until He Barked

giveness and his new son, Gentry. Brian answered on the first ring. "Hello?"

"Hey 'B', you sleep?"

"Yeah. What's up man?" Brian sat up in the bed. Gentry and Brett's crib had been moved to their room. They cried unless they were together. Carla cried when she was separated from them. Quetti had stayed with them and she cried if she weren't still the baby, so 'B' was accommodating everyone tonight. Quetti was curled up under Gabby. The TV was playing and everyone was asleep.

"Man I'm hurting." Troy tried not to cry. He really tried but the pain oozed out of him. There was no more room to hold back the tears.

"Where are you? I'm on my way over there if its cool?"

"Of course, the door will be unlocked. I don't want to wake the kids. I'll see you in a few."

Troy hung up. Ten minutes later he walked into Brian's home without knocking. 'B' was siting in the family room. He stood when Troy entered the room.

"'B', man I can't sleep. Jeremiah just keeps crying. Everytime I close my eyes that baby starts crying. It's a scream of fear and the closer I get the louder he screams. The more I try to help him the louder he screams. 'B', man he's scared of me. I'm his Daddy and he's scared of me." Troy was sobbing.

Brian's heart broke. He didn't know what to say or do. Troy started again. "Brian I ain't gone hurt him man. I didn't really hate him. I hated his Mama. I hated the situation. I'm so sorry. I can't take it back. I apologized and he didn't even hear me. He didn't even hear me. I can't fix this man! Help me fix it B. Help me fix it." Troy pleaded.

Brian was choked up. He had never seen Troy vulnerable. Gabby entered the room. She didn't say anything. She walked over to Troy and held him. She laid his head on her engorged breast. After he cried for a while she handed him the warm face towel that she'd brought with her.

"Troy the past can not be corrected, the future can—be a better man and your son will forgive you. Troy you've hurt a lot of people. Make amends, start living right and treating people the way you want to be treated. Walk in integrity and though you may get hurt, you'll feel a lot better than you do right now. Jeremiah's at peace. He didn't need to be here. He didn't need to join the circus you and his mother had planned for him. His purpose was to help the both of you appreciate life. Troy change your behavior and you'll feel better."

Gabby excused herself and went to pump her breast. Her milk had come down while she was nurturing Troy. The weight of the milk was getting heavy.

Troy laid his head back on the couch and wiped his face for the third time. He felt better. He was finally hungry and sleepy too.

"You staying here?"

"Naw man. I'm going home."

Troy sat in his car and he accepted that he had lost everything and everyone. He had some work to do.

The bed was empty, the house was quiet and finally the image of Jeremiah crying left him. He was able to sleep through the night. Troy had his coffee and accepted the task of getting his life together. He accepted that Deanna was gone, she had a new man. Therefore, his girls would grow up without him. Sipping coffee and sifting through the mail he opened his divorce decree paperwork with little emotion. Unlike most people he didn't have an urge to celebrate. The first few months alone helped Troy to appreciate that he didn't like being alone. He knew he'd find a woman again. This time he was going to trust her, love her and respect her. Troy wanted what Brian had again. He wanted the peace of mind of being monogamous. He imagined the emotional stability and the joy of having a permanent partner. The idea of commitment became a beautiful vision.

49

James and Leon had become big time buddies. They went to church together. They hung out all the time. The kids had began to call Leon, Uncle Leon. On a few occasions Lil' Tony had referred to Leon as his Dad. Their relationship was genuine. Lil' Tony loved Leon. He loved having a Daddy too. In the past everyone had a Daddy, but him. Asia was happy too, but sometimes it hurt to see Lil' Tony with another man. She shared her feelings with Sheila. Sheila could relate because it hurt her sometimes too, but they had to get over it for Lil' Tony's sake. The best part is that Leon was a great father. The fact that he had no children was helpful to the situation. Asia liked not having drama from an ex.

Everything was perfect. Too perfect. Asia was beginning to wonder about his sexuality because he had never tried anything. They had been openly seeing each other for close to four months and not one kiss, not one feel up her blouse or anything. He never spoke of it. At first she was grateful for his respect, now she was wondering what was really going on with him.

He finally told her he loved her. She was flattered. She loved him too. The moment was beautiful even without the kiss. His stare was so intensely sincere she blushed. Leon had never loved a woman the way he loved Asia. She had his heart. He wanted to spend the rest of his life, his day, everyday, every minute in her presence.

He Looked Like A Man, Until He Barked

Leon and Asia went to dinner after their exchange of 'I love you' and 'I love you too'. They talked like lovers. They held hands like lovers. They starred into each other's eyes. Leon appreciated the moment. Asia was preoccupied with whether or not this was going to lead to sex. She wanted to experience Leon. She wanted to get as close as possible and she knew that was the ultimate connection. She really loved Leon. He was a perfect mate. He was the one she'd prayed for. He was the closest she'd ever get to Tony. He loved her like Tony.

When they arrived at the apartment she got a phone call on her cell phone. It was Lil' Tony. He was calling from Auntie Sheila's house. He was ready to come home if they were done eating dinner. He didn't want to stay. Leon told her to go on inside and he'd go pick him up and bring him home. Asia smiled and got out of the car.

She walked inside and appreciated Big Tony's nagging about the house. Leon didn't know that side of her. She'd managed to keep the house clean. It wasn't as hard as she thought. She was practicing putting things back where she got them from and completing task. That apparently was the trick.

Asia got on the phone. "Hey girl, he wants to come home. He's so excited to have Leon in his life I think he wants to make sure y'all still friends."

Sheila laughed. "He's sleepy though so you can put his butt straight to bed."

Asia smiled. Her phone clicked. "Hold on Sheila, my other line is ringing."

"Hello?"

"Hey Baby, just wanted to say I missed you the moment you got out the car. I'll be right back. Are you retiring or can I look at you a while longer?"

"You can look at me."

"Okay."

"Okay, bye."

Asia clicked back over, anxious to share with Sheila what she'd just heard. She didn't realize that she'd actually connected the calls. Leon could now hear everything she was saying to Sheila. As he fumbled to hang up he heard.

"Sometimes I wonder if he's D.L. 'cause he ain't never even kissed me. He ain't never even tried to do nothing. The conversation is cool, but I want more."

"I don't think he's D.L. maybe he's got some other defiency...impotence or something. I hope it's something y'all can work around."

"Me too. I like him, so—"

The phone clicked. Asia snatched the phone away from her ear. "Did you hear that?"

"No."

"I think I heard a click. Hang up let me call you back. Call me on the house phone."

"Okay."

Asia looked at the phone and she couldn't tell whether she had connected the calls or not. She prayed that Leon hadn't heard her. She wasn't sure how he would respond to that. Twenty-five minutes later they hung up as Leon walked in with Lil' Tony. When he walked in with the baby he smiled like everything was fine. There was love in his smile. He took him upstairs and put him to bed. Asia was sitting on the couch when he returned. As he approached the couch his countenance changed. He pulled Asia up almost with a jerk and grabbed her wrist and slammed her hand into his groin. "This is for you. I am not on the D.L. I am *trying* to respect YOU. I've slept with plenty of women in my past, but not one man has EVER had the Leon experience." He dropped her hand from his body and he said to her "Grow up. Next time you have a question for me, give it to me. You're too old to be discussing your feelings with a third party. Talk to me. I'm approachable. Practice some self-respect. Everything I do concerning you is out of respect. The reason I don't go into your room is because I've learned that to walk in a bedroom is the same as walking on Holy ground. That is a place of a sacred ceremony. No one should be in such a blessed setting without the proper respect." He gently pulled her head into his chest, hugged her and kissed the top of her head. When I sleep with you Asia you will be my wife and I will be apart of you. I will have the right to dwell in your room and/or womb. Until then, I will respect you." Leon pledged.

"I'm sorry." Asia dropped a tear. She was embarrassed.

"It's ok. You've not had a blessed union before. Neither have I. I understand. I'll call you in the morning." Leon kissed her cheek this time and left.

Asia laid in bed all night struggling with not sharing her exchange with Leon with Sheila and remembering how his body felt in her hand. She remained embarrassed with a hint of gratitude for his manliness.

Patriece

At three o'clock in the morning her phone rang. "Hello?"

"Hi baby. I'm really sorry for earlier. I had no right to come at you like that. I was hurt when I heard your theory. I wanted you to know that I battle with myself the whole time I'm in your presence. Sometimes I just want to pounce you, even in a public place. I love you Asia. I have never sustained from sleeping with a woman before. I'm trying this approach with you because I'm seeking forever with you. I believe doing the right thing to the best of my ability will get me a different result. I've done it wrong before. You've done it wrong. Let's *try* to do it right. Baby, do you know why I don't have any kids?"

Asia answered "No".

"'Cause if you got pregnant by me you had an abortion or a miscarriage you decided. I was so ignorant I thought I was taking good care of myself by treating women like that. Only one woman refused to have an abortion. I'm ashamed to say that, I beat her until she changed her mind. She had one of them 'late term' abortions, where you're nearing five months of pregnancy. She told me that she was terminating because she didn't want to accidentally give birth to Satan. Whatever the reason I was glad it was over. Shortly after that my life changed and I spent about five years alone. I couldn't get a date. Word got around that I was crazy. Now some people think I'm a preacher, I've changed so much."

Asia was holding the phone in tears. "You scared me."

"Don't be scared. I'm a different man now. I would leave you before I hurt you. I love you girl. I can't say that I've ever really loved anyone. But, I love you."

He Looked Like A Man, Until He Barked

"I love you too. I'm glad you changed."
"Me too."

Sheila couldn't concentrate on what was going on with Asia. Her world was in an emotional chaos. She knew that loving James felt good. It had always felt good. The part she didn't like was it also felt stupid. This man had mistreated her, abandoned their family, sold food off the table of her babies and now he was back in her bed; and this is after their divorce. Regardless how good her heart felt, Sheila looked like a complete fool. She was on pens and needles, constantly dismissing her anxiety about his whereabouts, his return, his return time, his payday—will he make it home with his check?, his fidelity…everything. Sometimes while they were enjoying a moment of peace, after the kids were in bed, Sheila could barely appreciate the time together for worrying about what's going on inside of his head. Often she thought of re-lapse. Probably more than he did.

James sensed that Sheila was tense about his fate. He knew that she had fear around trust that would not ever heal, but they could form a scab. He'd learned that a scab covered a sore and protected it while the healing took place. He wished that Sheila would at least develop a scab. The fear in her eyes wasn't successfully concealed though he knew that she'd tried her best to conceal it. He noticed that whenever he moved, even around the house, she watched him. Tonight he'd cracked the door for some fresh air and she'd stumbled on her sentence. That was it for James.

Patriece

Since the kids were in bed he went to her. Sheila sat in the livingroom, agonizing over her distrust. James approached fifty-five pounds heavier than when he first knocked on the door. He was fashionably correct. He was groomed. He was handsome again. His skin and eyes were clear. His teeth had been replaced as he spoke with a full set of upper dentures. "Come here Baby." James sat next to Sheila. He swaddled her in his arms. "Baby. It's going to be okay. I'm going to be okay. I'm where I want to be. I love you and *now* I love me. This time I'm home to stay. You'll pray me out of here before I leave again. I see how stressed you are with worry about relapse. I know you've heard it all. I've lied time after time about coming right back etc. That's the reason I don't say that anymore. Now I simply bring my butt right back." He squeezed her tighter.

Sheila began to cry. "James I'm so nervous." She confessed.

"You have every right to be. I did some real scandalous things to your trust. I was functioning in my addiction. I was only worried about my next high. You didn't matter, I didn't matter, nothing mattered but maintaining the high that kept me from feeling the pain." James was crying too, but no sound was being made.

"I don't know how to relax. I trust you I just can't forget all that we've been through."

"You don't have to forget, you have to forgive. If you find a way to forgive me completely, you will be able to allow me back into your heart. Sheila I don't just want to sleep in your bed. I want to be apart of your life. I want to know what

He Looked Like A Man, Until He Barked

you're thinking. What you're feeling and I want to feel it with you. I want to see every smile that stretches across your face. I want to be with you." James had positioned Sheila to look into his eyes. "We'll work on your forgiveness together. I did a whole bunch to make you distrust me. I'm going to do twice as much to make you trust me again."

"I want to. Baby, I really do."

"It's okay. Just hold your head up. I'm going to make you proud. I know you feel a little foolish, hell maybe even a lot of foolish, but in the end you'll be envied. In spite of my addiction and what I took from you before, my love is ever so true. What I plan to give you now will make anybody that's second-guessing your sanity hit the floor on their knees asking God for a man like me. I love you, baby. I will die for you. That's real." James smiled that smile that was so hard for Sheila to resist. She smiled with him. As she fondled him, he stopped her. "Uh-uh, this is a different kind of moment. Just enjoy it." He held her. They sat in an embrace of sincerity until dawn, reminiscing and loving each other fully dressed.

50

The hospital buzz was that Kelly met a guy and moved out of state. Finally a man that was available and wanted her too. He wasn't a doctor. He wasn't even among her top desired incomes. He held a clerical position with the local government in Texas, which is where they were currently living. Troy didn't know how to reach her so making amends to her was going to be hard. He decided to write her a letter and mail it to her old address. She possibly had a forwarding address. Troy wrote the letter apologizing for misleading and mistreating her. He apologized for abandoning her with Jeremiah also. He went so far as to say that losing Jeremiah helped him to put things into prospective as well as learn the value of life. He felt better after writing the letter. At the post office the clerk rolled her eyes when she took his letter. Troy realized that she too was a victim of his past.

"I know you remember me. I'm sorry things turned out the way they did between us. I never meant you any harm or any good. What happened had nothing to do with you. It was all about me and my selfishness. I'm sorry that I hurt your feelings. I hope life is treating you better."

"It is. I don't know if men know that how you treat us affects our development. If I were a weaker woman I would have lost my self-esteem after what you did to me. Thank you for apologizing and most importantly for taking responsibility for your part." The lady was sincere, not scorned, not damaged. She knew that she hadn't done anything to Troy. She had picked up her heart and went on about her business.

It took Troy nine months to start to feel better. Often he thought of Jeremiah. The length of his little life and wondered what he would have done with his life had he lived. Troy didn't realize it, but Jeremiah had done great works with his 5 months of life. Because of his life his mother realized that money and prestige have nothing to do with love. She accepted a man that made less money than her, but loved her more than any of her wealthier partners ever could have. His father learned the true value of life wasn't how many women you could spend time with, but one special person to share your entire life with. Asia learned to trust her heart and relax into goodness. She knew all along that Troy wasn't good for her just as she knew that Leon was perfect. Deanna learned that if you sit in your tears you'll drown, but if you move you have a chance at survival. Brian learned that his children, his wife his family were his gift from God; he knew he was in position to lose (not have) them all. His behavior was as poor as Troy's. Jeremiah's life had touched the lives it was born to touch. His mission was accomplished.

Troy stopped by Cream of the Crop to pick up Ashley and TJ. It was his weekend. He planned to take them to a movie. In the morning they were going to the Paramount Theater to see the Doodle Bops. He was as excited as they were. When he walked into the restaurant he saw Deanna first. She was wearing a red top, some blue jeans with her hair was pulled back, her make-up was flawless. "Hey Troy how you doing?" She asked in a bubbly tone.

Patriece

"I'm good. How are you?" Troy asked. He knew that this was the weekend of their moving to a new house with Ken. Ken came from the back with TJ on his shoulders and holding Ashley's hand. They had muffins in their little hands.

"You have to eat the banana first ladies." Ken said as he handed them a banana that had been cut in half. Each girl took a bite of the banana. "Good morning Troy."

"Good morning."

"Y'all have a good weekend, okay. I love you."

"Love you too." "Love you too." The girls kissed Ken's cheeks as he placed them at a table in front of warm chocolate. Then he retreated to the rear of the building.

"Would you like some coffee Troy? The girls wanted to eat here since all of our dishes were already packed away. Thanks for taking them two weekends in a row. This will help us get settled quicker."

"No problem. I miss'em. Yeah, I'll take some coffee."

Deanna walked away to get the coffee. She heard Ken on the phone confirming the work schedule and making sure that there would be coverage at the restaurant. This was the first time they both were going to be gone at the same time. She smiled.

Troy sat at the table with his daughters free from jealousy, regret, or self-disappointment. He had made all of his amends with the exception of Deanna. It was so difficult to apologize to her. He'd done so many things that he knew were wrong. The urge to fix things swelled within his spirit. He couldn't contain it. He needed to be free completely. "Dee, can I talk to you for a moment?"

He Looked Like A Man, Until He Barked

"Yeah, what's up?"

Troy pulled her away from the girls. He took her hands and he held them. There was no pain when he saw that she was wearing an engagement ring. He smiled to himself. "Deanna I'm sorry for everything. I treated you bad. I was cruel and insensitive. It was unnecessary and uncalled for. I apologize for abusing your love the way I did. I hope you can forgive me and love Ken without reflecting back on my madness. You have a new opportunity. Look at it with fresh eyes. Love as hard as you can. Your love is good." Troy was sincere.

"Thank you. That means more than you know." Deanna allowed Troy to hug her. She needed the closure too. She let go of her pain, her hatred and her phoniness. The façade that she wore around him, like she wasn't phased by his abuse. She was affected, only now she was healed too. It was over. The part of her that loved Troy loved him again, but the love was different. The love was plutonic.

Ken walked in while the two were embraced. His flesh tensed up, then without reason he relaxed and allowed them their much needed closure. When the embrace ended Ken was sitting at the table with the girls. He was eating an apple and a muffin. Asia and Troy returned to the table. Ken winked at Asia. "Babe, we can go now. The crew will open up. Let's go get the truck."

"Okay let's do it."

They walked out together. Ken held TJ's hand and Ashley held Troy's. Deanna locked the door. The air was crisp. The odor of clean was present. Everyone felt complete. Deanna thought of Sister Esther *what the devil meant for evil God turned into a blessing.*

51

Carla and Ron's marriage was shaky. She'd found a brillo pad in the top of the hall closet. Brillo pad was part of the paraphenelia used by crack addicts. Ron tried to explain that he'd hid stuff all over the house when he was using. She nagged and nagged him about that brillo pad until he went for a ride. He found himself sitting in front of the Sports Page nightclub. He saw a few regular prostitutes still out there, involuntarily he got a hard on. While that was happening, his mouth started watering for a drink. It was literally watering. He parked his car and got out.

"Hey is that Ron? Man what you been up to?"

"Nothing much man. Staying out the way. This madness will kill you."

"Yeah. I know. I just can't get it together."

"Man you need a meeting. An AA meeting. That's where I'm headed. You tired yet?"

"Yeah man, I'm tired. My wife don' left. My kids damn near grown and they embarrassed. I got a granddaughter, she 'bout six months old. My daughter ain't but sixteen. My wife says 'cause I don't love her, she turned to somebody else'. Man whatever. That's too heavy for me."

"Well, I'm headed to a meeting. You welcome to ride."

"Hey you! What's up? You don't love me no mo'?" A prostitute walked over to Ron and wrapped her arms and one leg around him. Her foul odors were transferring to his clothing. "Hell naw! I ain't never loved you!" He pushed her away. Ron realized that he needed to get away from there as soon as possible. He walked around to the driver's side and got back in the car. His buddy opened the passengers door and got in. "Man, I'm ready."

Ron started the car and pulled away from the curb. A block away his phone rang. "Hello."

"Hey man, you alright?" It was Brian. He was getting gas on the corner and saw Ron in the wrong part of town.

"Yeah. I'm headed to a meeting. I was over here by the Sports Page and I was reminded that ain't nothing as bad as where I've come from. One of my boys going with me, he's ready."

"Stay connected man. Stay connected to your program. Call me when you struggling. I'll go with you if you need me to. If your boy really want to go, have him meet you in a safe place. Otherwise give him the info and keep it movin'."

"You right. You right. That was going to be my excuse. I'm heading to the meeting now."

"Alright."

Brian drove off. He liked Ron and hoped that he was doing the right thing. It had been close to three years since he'd gotten clean. He wanted him to make it. Ron was a good dude.

Ron's phone rang again. "Hello?"

"Hi baby."

"Hi. Ron where are you?"

"I'm on my way to a meeting." He didn't tell her that he had struggled.

He Looked Like A Man, Until He Barked

"I'll see you when you get home. I'm sorry. I tossed that stuff out." Carla feared that she'd caused Ron to relapse. She prayed and waited for his return. The kids were in bed. Boogie finally slept all night in his own bed, that was now in the room with Roni.

"Good, next time just toss it. I like my life now. I am happy."

"Me too." Carla meant it. She'd met with the guy from her job and they did a DNA test of Roni and she got the results yesterday and so did he. She had managed to keep her secret.

When Ron returned home he showered before even greeting Carla in case the prostitute's scent was lingering. Then he made love to his wife as if she were one of them. She reciprocated his love while celebrating her own freedom. Each of them wished they could be more honest with each other, but they settled for the closeness that they had. Brian got home and appreciated his family. The twins were walking now and getting into everything. Quetti was still the joy of every one of her parents. Life was good. He knew it and was grateful.

52

Troy was still single. A full year had passed. He had finally gotten a letter back from Kelly. It simply read:

Thank you for the apology. I apologize for abusing you too. I set out to trap you. I was trying to take you from your kids and our beloved was taken from me. I'm finally married and I'm pregnant. Good luck with your life

Kelly.

Troy felt good about the letter. He wished her well. For the first time he started to feel lonely. Everyone seemed to have gotten on with there lives accept him. Deanna was married and expecting a son any day now. Brian was enjoying his family. Ron was clean and sober and enjoying his family. Troy was without a family. He shook it off and went to run his errands.

As he walked into the Post Office Jocelyn walked out. She smiled. He smiled. She loved Troy still.

"Hi Josh, how you doing?"

"Good. You?"

"I'm okay."

"You seem down."

"A little bit."

"You wanna talk about it?"

Troy hesitated. "Sure. Let me drop this mail in the box."

They stood in the parking lot of the Post Office for about eleven minutes as they caught up. They laughed and

He Looked Like A Man, Until He Barked

laughed. Finally Troy asked her if she wanted to get into something?

She agreed and the two made plans to go to dinner. At dinner Troy shared that he had lost a son. He was divorced. How losing Jeremiah had impacted his life. The relationship that he has now with his daughters. How all of his relationships had changed. He talked about his fear of being hurt if he showed his true feelings. Josh listened well, advised well and also shared, no holds barred. She managed to trust Troy, again. He was clearly different. Troy felt good. Being honest did his heart good.

At the counter they paid the tab. Troy turned too fast and bumped into the lady behind him. "Excuse me. I'm sorry."

"It's okay." Asia responded.

"Hi Asia. How are you?" Troy asked.

"I'm good. Thank you. You?"

"I'm okay. How's the baby boy?"

"He's good too."

Leon stood by awkwardly as did Jocelyn and Sheila, James and the kids.

"Troy this is my fiancé Leon. Leon this is Troy."

"I remember you." Lil' Tony chimed in.

"Hey man." Troy picked him up and hugged him as he shook Leon's hand. "Nice to meet you man. He put Lil' Tony down introduced Jocelyn and greeted everyone. They were all genuine.

Asia and group quickly forgot Troy as they enjoyed their night out and celebrated her pregnancy.

53

Life had changed for Troy. He'd begun dating Jocelyn. She found a way to trust him. They had moved in together against her unspoken wishes. She really wanted to be married before she moved in, but she didn't mention it to Troy. Her fear was that she'd push him away. She'd never been married before and she loved the idea of marriage. Her heart longed for her own family, but she didn't want to risk losing Troy, as she assumed he had some scarring around marriage. Their relationship was otherwise healthy. She was so careful not to rock the boat that she was content in their relationship. She wasn't happy. Troy was the best thing to ever happen to her, but her silence prevented her from being completely happy. What she didn't know is that Troy was approachable. He was open-minded. He wanted to know; was interested even.

Troy still looked at other women. He just didn't pursue them anymore. Sometimes it was hard. Sometimes it was easy. The habit of keeping his attention at home was beginning to dictate his life and he loved it. The humility that he'd earned from losing Jeremiah afforded him great gifts. He'd used his manipulation skills in a positive way, persuading people with money to invest in the research of SIDS as well as other charitable things that added to the quality of life of children. He began accompanying Jocelyn to church. He actually held conversations with his girls. He was at their school functions and sometimes took time to hang out with them because they were his and no other reason. Troy's life

He Looked Like A Man, Until He Barked

was finally fulfilled. Things had changed between him and Brian. They were still friends; they didn't hang out as much because their lives were different. Troy was no longer part of "the click". Occasionally he was invited to hang out. Sometimes he invited Brian and family to his home.

Troy had taken a permanent position at the hospital. He no longer traveled. He made himself available to return home every evening. He realized that Jocelyn needed his companionship. She had a big family. She was number four of six. They hung out with her family too. She only had one brother. His wife had a baby less than a month ago. Jocelyn was there almost daily looking at that baby. She wanted a baby, but she didn't know how Troy felt about it, so she swallowed her birth control pills with breakfast religiously. Often she wanted to mention her desire for a baby to Troy, but again she considered that he may not want more children, so she struggled to push her dream aside. Troy didn't necessary want a baby. Yet, he wasn't opposed to having a baby.

One of Troy's responsibilities of his new position included welcoming the new interns. This week new interns arrived. When the interns entered the building Troy smiled. There was one that was handsome and charming. It was a matter of two weeks before all the females working at the hospital were falling out at his feet. He was dating them. He was dogging them.

It took about six months for the bottom to start to fall out of his situation. One day Troy watched him walk into the parking lot and take a plate of food from a lady in a black

Honda Accord, kiss her goodbye, then remove his wedding band and drop it back into his pocket.

Troy's stomach did a nervous somersault at the familiar behavior. He wanted to approach the Dr., but didn't. Rumor around the hospital was that Dr. Young was married.

Troy watched him work the women like a Floor Trader of the NY Stock Exchange. He ran from woman to woman trying to get the best return. For the first time Troy looked into the mirror of his youth. He was disgusted with the young doctor's behavior, which meant he was disgusted with himself also. Troy was much more ruthless than the young doctor was. He flaunted his infidelity. He slept with any ablebodied woman. The young doctor was selective. Troy determined that he was a hip and butt type of man. Some of the senior physicians started a betting pool. They were betting on his car being vandalized or his wife coming to the hospital causing a dramatic scene. For fun Troy tossed $10 in the pot.

A few weeks later a lady was arrested in the parking lot of the hospital for spray painting his car. She painted the words....HE LOOKED LIKE A MAN, UNTIL HE BARKED down both sides of his brand new 5 series BMW. He arrived at the scene along with everyone else. She screamed, "You lay you pay!"

A week later Troy got the opportunity to speak to him. They were in the cafeteria and he had a newly hired C.N.A. under his spell. He strolled over to Troy's table and sat down.

"Good morning, Dr. Arlington."

He Looked Like A Man, Until He Barked

"Good morning, Dr. Young. You got a minute?"

"Sure."

"Let me share some wisdom with you." Troy shared his story with Dr. Young. During the conversation Dr. Young would give a smirk or a smile of recognition as Troy shared his old mindset concerning women and his manhood. He shared about the Bible in the glove compartment to put the snooper at ease. He shared about the hook-up at the Atlanta Hotel that paged him when he was in or out of their facility. He shared about the flowers, chocolates and heating pads. Troy convinced the young doctor that he was qualified to have this conversation with him. Then he shared the less glamorous side of it. He shared about the hell that Kelly put him through, losing Deanna, losing his kids, (he didn't mention Jeremiah's passing), losing his home, etc. Troy petitioned him to change his behavior or live with regret that will attach itself to him like a limb.

"Thank you. I appreciate the advice." Dr. Young seemed sincere. He knew that Troy was right. He knew that his own wife was getting tired. He knew that she was entertaining the idea of divorcing him. In spite of his madness Dr. Young wanted to be there to see his children grow up. He loved his wife too. He really loved her.

"Anytime, young man." Troy handed him his business card. "Call if you ever need to talk."

Dr. Young handed his card to Troy and walked away. Troy placed it into his lab coat pocket and sighed. *Regret that attaches itself like a limb.* The card read Dr. Jeremiah Young.

Patriece

Troy entered the last hour of his shift. He was grateful to be going home. Jocelyn had planned a Thanksgiving celebration at her mother's home. His mother was going to join him there. Troy smiled at the thought. His life had been so much better since Jocelyn. She'd taught him how to move on with his life, forgive himself, be a better person and was working diligently on his faith. Troy found walking into the church a difficult thing, as he was unfamiliar with God and all that. His mind wasn't closed; it just wasn't opened to the idea of spending half a day listening to philosophy.

The code rang throughout the ER. Troy kicked into his professional mode. He hoped he'd make dinner as he rushed to the entering patient. Jocelyn had worked so hard. As he approached the gurney the eyes of the paramedics were moist. He looked for the patient, no patient, finally he saw the little baby. Little Gentry laid on the gurney gasping for air. Troy became a believer at that exact moment. He began working on Gentry with all his might and his heart prayed. After reviving the baby, Troy diagnosed him as asthmatic. He walked into the waiting room and it was filled with everyone he loved. Deanna, Ken, Carla, Ron, Sister Esther, Sheila, James, Asia, Leon, Michelle and of course Brian and Gabby. Troy didn't say a word. He joined hands with them and began to pray. He prayed the most heartfelt prayer of thanksgiving for the restoration of Gentry that it impressed his assisting physician Dr. Young whose hands had found their way into the circle of prayer. Dr. Young would never be the same. None of them would.

He Looked Like A Man, Until He Barked

At thanksgiving dinner Troy's mother beamed with pride as he rose to his full height from a bent knee. She was proud of both he and Jocelyn.

Jocelyn accepted his proposal of marriage, but after she found the courage to ask if she could have a baby.

"Will you be my baby's daddy?"

"Yes."

"Yes, I'll be your wife." She smiled into his smile. Then she cried and looked straight at her nephew.

As they received congratulations and Jocelyn's ring was inspected, Troy quietly stepped into his manhood. His mother sighed with relief; she knew that her baby had finally learned what only life can teach you.

About the Author

Patriece lives in San Leandro, California. Her first novel *When Somebody Loves You Back* broke record sales for a first time author. In July 2006, she broke the author signing record at Barnes & Noble Booksellers, Emeryville, CA. She sold more books than veteran authors. She has several titles waiting to hit the bookshelves. She is blessed with the ability to string words together in a phenomenally entertaining way. Patriece's writing is unashamedly honest with characters so realistic you can actually see their faces. Join her fan base now, you won't regret it!

To Order

He Looked Like a Man Until He Barked
or
When Somebody Loves You Back

Send $21.31* Check or Money Order to:

Pressin On Publications
P.O. Box 2304
Oakland, CA 94614

Visit us on the web at:
www.PressinOnPublications.com
www.myspace.com/justpatriece

*Amount includes $5 for Shipping and Handling and California Sales Tax